DEATH IN THE POLKA DOT SHOES

— A Novel —

by

MARLIN FITZWATER

CCB Publishing
British Columbia, Canada

Death in the Polka Dot Shoes: A Novel

Copyright ©2011 by Marlin Fitzwater
ISBN-13   978-1-926918-68-6
First Edition

Library and Archives Canada Cataloguing in Publication

Fitzwater, Marlin, 1942-
Death in the polka dot shoes : a novel / written by Marlin Fitzwater. – 1st ed.
ISBN 978-1-926918-68-6
Also available in electronic format.
I. Title.
PS3606.I89D42 2011   813'.6   C2011-904637-7

Cover Art by Judy Ward

Cover Design by Mari Abercrombie and Isaac Fer

Publisher: CCB Publishing
             British Columbia, Canada
             www.ccbpublishing.com

Dedication

*For All Those Men And Women Who
Make Their Living On The Water.*

"Listen for the oyster music."

--Shady Side, Maryland waterman

Chapter One

His shoes were never found. My brother apparently was leaning over the side of his thirty-six foot fishing boat about two miles off the coast of Cape Hatteras, sweating from having to work the giant blue fin tuna for nearly an hour, almost sick from the ache in his arms, yet about to land the biggest catch of his life. With a gaff hook in his left hand, ready to tear into the side of the two hundred pound fish, he twisted his right wrist into the last few feet of leader line for one final hoist of the fish into the boat. But facing the certainty of death, the tuna gathered itself for one final whack at freedom. Its gills began to heave and its marble eye focused on Jimmy's cap, which read "Cedar Winds Boat Works." In that instant, Jimmy must have known the violence to come because he started to shift his weight lower in the boat, but he never got to his knees. There was a mighty jerk, and a flash of green and blue scales above a white tee shirt, then nothing. The tuna went straight to the bottom with Jimmy in tow.

The charter captain later testified at the inquest that he was sitting high on the tower, watching the big fish weave its way through the water to the boat, with the heavy filament line flashing where the sun picked up its break with the surface. It was headed straight for the boat, he said, when he glanced down at his depth finder, reading a hundred and thirty feet. When he looked back for the tuna, Jimmy was gone. Simply vanished into the stillness of the day.

The captain said he circled the site for hours and nothing surfaced. He called the Coast Guard and they searched for the rest of the day, but found nothing. No clothing. No fishing gear. Nothing.

Jimmy had been on a bus man's holiday from his regular life as a waterman on the Chesapeake Bay, running an old bay-built crab boat out of Parkers, Maryland, at least on those days when crabs were plentiful and selling for eighty to a hundred dollars per bushel. On other days, he scrubbed up the boat and took city slickers from Washington, D.C. on half day outings for striped bass or bluefish. Fishing had been our family's life for five generations, going back to the great Virginia oyster wars of 1878. Back then, our great-grandfather would end the crabbing season in October, refit the boat with a culling board, pull his hand tongs out of the barn, and spend the winter oystering. Even at the young age of 31, Jimmy had given up the oysters. Too much strain on the shoulders. Instead, he crabbed in the morning, took tourists fishing in the afternoon, and made enough money to give up oystering completely. Next season, he planned to give up crabbing as well, especially if he could convince me to help him buy a new boat. And I probably would have helped, just because I knew how much he loved being a waterman.

Jimmy and I spent our youth on the crab boats of the Bay, helping our father run his trotlines or harvest his crab pots. We liked leaning over the gunnels of our dad's deadrise, the *Martha Claire*, hooking the float lines as the hydraulic winch pulled the crab pots from the bottom of the bay. We eagerly grabbed the pot as it surfaced and pulled it into the boat. The "pot" is a square wire mesh cage that lets crabs check in but they can't check out. They are trapped. As teenagers, we Shannon boys were solid and our shoulders offered the power of a diesel winch. A full crab pot can weigh forty pounds or more and Dad ran nearly three hundred of them. Jimmy and I would flip the screen of the pot open, tip it and shake it until all of the sideways scavengers could scramble onto the deck and into bushel baskets. I used to imagine that

2

every bushel basket was a hundred dollar bill, and that helped ease the shoulder ache as the stack of baskets grew over my head. Then I would shove an alewife or handful of razor clams into the bait box and slide the pot over the side. With the same motion Jimmy would reach for the throttle and power the boat on to the next pot. We loved it when Dad let us drive the boat and help with the catch.

It was a simple repetitive exercise that mirrored assembly lines the world over, except that it was on the water, in the midst of a lonely yet beautiful theatre where you paid the price of admission with every pot lifted. And the old men of the Bay whose bodies were scraped and twisted by the sharp edges of crabbing, could never turn their backs on the delight, regardless of the cost. It was their stage, their sense of freedom and independence, their manhood and their pride.

I never quite inherited those qualities, but my brother did. He absorbed all the family instincts for the water, rowing into the fog on a dreary day, just so he could meet the challenge of a safe return. Our mother would stand on the family dock, watching for Jimmy to come back out of the fog with both oars slowly moving the water, while his head and shoulders were stretched over the side as if he was smelling or listening to the water. His eyes scanned low, under the fog, following the surface and searching for birds, or boats, or landmarks or whatever it was that always brought him safely home. He scared our mother to death, and she told him stories of ships lost in the fog to discourage his interest. But instead of being afraid, he loved the stories and begged for more, until mom finally gave up. She knew he was a waterman.

When I left for college, my family walked me to the car. They stood in the yard like soldiers, with their arms around each other, as if I might never return. Yet all my life my mother had urged me to stay off the water. Even my father, who loved the Bay, lectured me on the magnetic pull of easy cash from a day of crabbing, and urged me not to yield to it. He had given up on Jimmy. But he never stopped urging me to seek another life, away from the water.

Today, when I get really sick of the law library and the pompous clamoring of my partners at Simpson, Feldstein and James, I look back at those wonderful days on the water, colored by the distance of time and the glory of youth. I forget how much I wanted off the water, out of the Town of Parkers, and into a white collar world of fancy cars and exotic travel. I look back at a culture that honored truth, loyalty and the absorbing drama of a sharp bow on a silent bay. Then I remember the cuts on my hands from the crabs, and the heavy rubber gloves that were caked with salt, brine and mud and hung like barbells from my fingers. They never kept out the cold, the water, or the crab's bony pinchers. I had worked for years to escape that occupational fate. So why would my brother's death now draw me back to the water? Why would it start me thinking about the glories of a simpler life and a different culture?

My brother's body didn't come up. The old watermen around Parkers said the tuna no doubt figured out his predicament, and wrapped the line around some bottom debris until it broke, leaving my brother tethered to a fate I didn't want to contemplate. Jimmy's death left me shattered. I could not shake the idea of young life ended, fatherhood extinguished, all the dreams of a wife and daughter vanished. I also felt great guilt for all the inequities of life that my brother faced, and for my treatment of him. He was two years younger, and not nearly so competitive. I would force him to play basketball with me, and then beat him in every game of one on one. I would ridicule him for not wanting to play baseball with me, even though I would always hit the ball over his head and make him run for it. We would argue, get angry, and he would run from me. When I think today about the com-

4

petitions of youth, and how much I owe him for the normal inequities of youth, my guilt is overwhelming. And sometimes in the days since his death, I mourn so violently that I lose my breath and have to stand up to breathe. Then I walk to the refrigerator, lean against the door with my arm under my forehead, and cry out with pain and anguish for my lost brother, and for myself. I intended to make it up to him. But now I can't. He is simply gone forever.

We had a memorial service at Christ Church, a quaint little wood frame structure built in the 1800s of heavy timbers from nearby trees. The sanctuary looked like the hold of an ancient schooner. It was built on the crest of a hill, surrounded by tall pines, with a sloping graveyard on three sides so steep that you wondered how the dead could possibly get any rest. As a boy, I dreamed that the bodies behind Christ Church were all buried with their heels dug in to keep from sliding down the hill. Surely not a peaceful recline. The stone markers were mostly from the seventeen and eighteen hundreds, often with short biographical references, or poems, about the deceased. Many carried the title of "Captain" as a tribute to their life's work. If you owned your own boat, no matter the size or condition, and it worked the waters of the Bay for livelihood, then you were a Captain for life. Most of the crab boat captains had a crew of one, usually a son, sometimes an old partner who had shared the catch and all their troubles for decades. There were a few "big boat" captains behind the church, men who had guided the tall merchant ships for long months at sea, out of Baltimore or Annapolis. I noticed their headstones often looked like the Washington Monument, with small cast iron fences around the graves. Some of those fences had been standing, by the way, for 200 years, as compared to my townhouse fence in Washington that was knocked down about three times a month. The measurements of life are different in Parkers, Maryland, and the monuments are respected.

I bought a burial plot and small headstone for my brother that was still being chiseled with the appropriate dates. As I wandered among the markers after the service, I noticed dozens of flat stones with the simple etching: waterman. Some with flat bottom work boats drawn below the name. The watermen always had been on the lowest wrung of the economic scale, even below farmers, who at least could rise to the top by accumulating enough land. It appreciated. There simply was nothing about crabbing that would appreciate in value. In the area around Parkers, by the year 2009, the farmers had become owners of horse farms or at least landlords and real estate speculators, while the watermen were still struggling to find markets for their ever dwindling catch. Although a crabber who had graduated to using his boat for charter fishing, with some skillful internet marketing, could do pretty well. But the crabbers' fiercely independent trade, involving the lone captain who secured his catch and delivered it directly to market at a local pier, was the occupation most pure and true to its origin, and a source of great pride to the watermen families. I was proud of my dad and my brother.

At Christ Church the watermen of Parkers all stood together and lamented the passing of their friend, Jimmy Shannon, taken by the sea as so many of their brothers and fathers had been. They saw no humor or irony in the tuna's action, only the terribly fine line between life and death that is drawn every day on the water. For them, Jimmy's death could just as easily have resulted from storm, or cold, or a fall from the rigging of a skipjack. I was appalled when the Old Bay Circular, Parkers' weekly newspaper, reported my brother's death with the headline, Fish Catches Man. But the watermen seemed to ignore it, as if the frivolity of a newspaper account had little value or consequence anyway.

There were a few new faces at the service, friends of my brother who had just discovered the chop of the Bay in their varnished sail-boats, or had discovered the little two bedroom bungalows with the beautiful sunsets, houses that could be torn down in an afternoon and rebuilt as glass palaces. The marinas around Parkers were filling with sailboats, crowding out dock space for the crab boats. Watermen saw sailboats as vehicles for pleasure, not for work. And in nearby Anna-polis in 2008 the city council evicted the last working crab boat from the city dock. The economy of the Bay was changing, and the popula-tion of Parkers was beginning to shift as well. I was in the eddy, not quite knowing what the future would hold in these swirling economic currents. Standing under the covering pines with the green shuttered church and the English boxwood along every walking path made me yearn again for the simplicity of my youth. It was so quiet at Christ Church, with an occasional gnatcatcher swooping through the trees, that I almost missed the young woman standing with the watermen, moving somewhat awkwardly with the group as they ambled around the church. I didn't pay much attention, but I think she was laughing, perhaps at a joke between them about my brother. I made a mental note to ask about her later.

Then I spotted three of my old friends from high school and a lump caught in my throat. My mind went to long afternoons of basketball on the town court, and shared conversations about life that are possible only in youth. I started to cry and the tears would not stop. I yanked a long white handkerchief from my pocket and covered my face. I wanted to speak to my dear friends, missed through the years, and now virtually unknown to me. I didn't even know where they lived, nearby I suppose, or they wouldn't have been at the funeral. And they proba-bly came just to see me. But whenever I lowered my handkerchief I started to cry again. It was their youth. I looked in their faces and saw myself as a boy, and realized that I was crying for our lost youth.

These were boys who respected my father, and knew my brother, and now they stood alone under the pines like trees without forests. I couldn't face them, so I walked away, hoping for the distraction of others, another group of mourners who could change my focus. I looked around for smiling faces.

My family's friends and neighbors had great senses of humor, laughing at the sea and its unruly manner, mimicking their friends, exaggerating each other's weaknesses and foibles, and sometimes a joke would lead to a fight. Humor and fighting were linked somehow in ways I never understood, but instinctively knew not to challenge. Perhaps because strength was the final measure of a waterman, fighting was common. Men in their fifties, who had been at sea for decades, could measure every catch by the strain in their arms, and they knew that in the end, it would be the weight of the oyster tongs, or a full pot of crabs, or a stumble while climbing into their boat, that would mark the end of their career. Similarly, the watermen could be incredibly sentimental, helping each other's families, sitting up with sick friends, or repairing each other's boats, because they also understood the capriciousness of their lives, and every soul had its own value. They needed each other.

The story is told in Parkers of "Gunnels" Newton, a first mate who never quite grew out of the position, and at age 52 was still signing on every morning with a new crab boat or oyster tonger, wherever he was needed. He liked to work the oysters because he liked to eat them. He was a relatively small man, with wiry frame, but a huge belly filled every night with beer and oysters. Locally, he was known as the champion oyster eater in Jenkins County. Soon, Gunnels was entering oyster eating contests all around the Bay.

The watermen of Parkers, meeting in solemn conclave one Sunday morning at the Bayfront bar, which was always full by eight o'clock in

8

the morning, especially on Sunday, voted to take up a collection to send Gunnels to the Guinness Book of World Records oyster eating contest in London, England. Gunnels had a special technique in which he shucked oysters as fast as he could, then put them in a bottle of milk, threw back his head and let the whole concoction flow silently down his throat. By this method he could consume pounds of oysters in minutes. He won the Guinness contest, of course, coming home with enough prize money to keep him wet for months. But the strain of ready cash was too much for his heart. One Saturday afternoon, after the final round of the St. Michael's oyster eating contest, he was bent over the gunnels of his work boat dispensing with the excesses of his competition, when he died.

The boys at the Bayfront, realizing that Gunnels had no family or money, arranged to have him cremated. In a ceremony still honored in Parkers, they lined up their work boats, headed out to the Bay, and dumped Gunnels' ashes right in the middle of the Holland Point oyster bed. The final irony of his life was that in the end, the oysters got to eat him.

Gunnels is still honored at the Bayfront with a picture of him beside a stack of oyster shells. The picture comes down occasionally, when Mabel Fergus, who owns the place, becomes "tired of looking at his ugly face," as she puts it. But after a few months, it always reappears in a different corner of the dining room.

This story flashed through my mind because I knew I had seen that girl with the watermen before, and I think it was at the Bayfront. She was very attractive and I wondered if she knew my bother, or just came to be with the boys. Either explanation was possible. I knew most of the crabbers because they were either just behind me in school, or were men my father had worked with. There seemed to be a missing group, my class at South County High, but I knew no reason for it. Other than there were a couple of really bad crabbing years in the early 1980s, and most fathers simply discouraged their sons from staying on the water. In my case, I didn't want to. I had a longing for fast cars, pretty girls, finely starched shirts, linen table cloths and long airplane trips to unknown places. Those dreams required getting out of Parkers.

The memorial service ended, and my brother's friends were standing around outside, smoking or talking. They started drifting back toward the church for a basement reception, which I was not looking forward to attending. That's where the old women in floral print dresses and heavy shoes want to bestow a big kiss and a hug on the bereaved relatives, in this case, me. They seem to think a bosomy hug somehow eases the pain, when in fact it squashes the cigars in my breast pocket and leaves strange smells around my neck. I could do without that.

I had smoked cigarettes in college in order to look cool, and once in the law firm, where the pressure to produce was palpable, my habit had grown to nearly three packs a day. I had ignored all the warnings, the television ads, the government studies, and the statistics on lung cancer. Growing up, everyone I knew smoked. Most of the watermen smoked, from long days of hard repetitive work on the water. So it seemed natural that I would pick up the habit. But one day my lungs started to ache, and worse, breathing actually made a noise. I could hear a low groan with every breath, and it scared me. It was impossible to ignore, or to rationalize away. Breathing should not make a noise. So I started the terrible process of trying to stop, cold turkey, then two cigarettes a day, then one cigar in the evening. The cigar seemed to work, although I knew of course that it was not good for me. Then I convinced myself that one cigar, no inhaling, was alright. And the noise in my lungs stopped. That's how I came to always have a cigar in my pocket, even at my brother's memorial service.

In addition, my favorite place to smoke was in the car. I didn't smoke at home because of the smell and dirty ash trays. But driving was like a personal smoking lounge, with the window cracked for fresh air and no passengers to offend. In this case, I knew it would be a long drive back to Washington from Parkers, and after the memorial service I would need the distraction of a good cigar.

Bucking the tide of people and stumbling down the hill toward me was my father's best friend and retired Field and Bay Magazine photographer, Mansfield Burlington, a strange but very proper duck who chose Parkers for a home some 40 years ago. He was tall, thin, constantly smoked a pipe, often wore a bow tie, and carried himself with a stiffness sometimes mistaken for aloofness. I once saw a picture of Mansfield in some magazine that showed him with his cameras slung around his neck in Venice, Italy while two pigeons tried to land on his head, apparently confusing him with a Michelangelo statue. There was no explanation for why Field and Bay had sent him to Italy. In fact, Mansfield was quite a warm fellow, a great listener and a craftsman. He could touch a piece of wood and turn it soft and brown, yielding the most beautiful flow of varnished grain imaginable. He could build things.

"Neddie," he called, "I'm so sorry about your bother. Almost went out on his boat once. How are you?"

"Fine Burl," I said, surprised at first that I even remembered the more familiar nickname, but then remembering that everyone called him Burl. Mansfield was far too formal for daily use, and it sounded so English. In fact, Mansfield Burlington was born in Minnesota, and was Scandinavian. After photographing the world for nearly twenty years, he had a minor fame of his own. Young photographers familiar with his pioneering use of color and a tenacious sense of purpose in

11

getting the right picture, still dropped by his house for pointers. People said he liked the water so much because he descended from Viking warriors. Locals held him in reverence because he had the touch with wood, an almost mystical connection in which he could run his finger lovingly along a strip of walnut and it would become a table. When he started building a skipjack in his barn, people would drop by on Sunday afternoons just to see the progress, like viewing a sculptor in his studio.

"Burl," I repeated, "did you ever finish that skipjack?"

"Yes," he said with a pleased smile, "rolled her out of the barn at the turn of the century. She's docked beside the Tonsund. Come see her." The Tonsund was a forty-foot sail boat named for Mansfield's Sherpa who had guided him safely up some Tibetan mountain more than thirty years before. Not insignificantly, Mansfield had saved Tonsund's life on the way down by amputating his frozen toes with a pen knife. For a fellow with such formal bearing, Mansfield made the deepest and most lasting friendships.

"Sorry about your brother," Mansfield said. "A good man. Knew the water."

He stopped to light his pipe, stepping back to avoid a falling ash that just missed his tweed coat. It was a knarled old pipe, black around the bowl from countless flames and as natural as the bark of an oak tree. He had fondled the briar, leaving so much oil and sweat on the bowl that it looked almost soft, like fine leather.

"Too bad he got wrapped around that Resort," Mansfield said as the flame from his match died out.

I picked up on that immediately, knowing nothing about any resort. "What Resort?"

"Oh, you haven't heard about the big fight," Mansfield said, almost with excitement. "They're trying to build a hundred acre resort right here on the Jenkins. We call it the hijenks project," Mansfield said. "Going to ruin the crabs. Pollute this whole Bay."

"Are you involved, Burl?" I asked. "Environmentalists up in arms?"

"We're doing what we can," he said. "It's the future of the Bay. No more skipjacks."

Mansfield started building his skipjack when I was in high school, cutting the wood himself from white cedar he had plucked from the forests of Maine and carried to Maryland on the roof of his car. As a boy, I will never forget the sight of a small gray station wagon, with two six-inch square, twenty-foot long pieces of lumber strapped to the top so they hung over the windshield like licorice sticks. He drove all the way from Maine to Maryland with his wife hiding her face in shame beside him. The police stopped him twice but never gave him a ticket. Mansfield was a man's man who had traveled the world, engaging himself in exploits which always seemed to end in a near death experience. And I did indeed intend to stop by his home for a visit, if only to ask if he had heard any strange stories about my brother. Now we had a Resort to discuss.

"Can I come by to see you, Burl?" I asked.

"Sure," he said. "Love to have you. Bring some wind and we'll do a little sailing."

I wanted to get back to Washington before dark, just to be home and sort out my thoughts. I hadn't spent much time at the church with my brother's wife and baby, but we had already shed so many tears together, I just walked away. I wanted to make a quick pass by the Bayfront Inn and take a look at my brother's boat, anchored next to the garden dock. The Bayfront didn't have any rooms, but did have a bar and restaurant beside seventeen slips for crab boats and charter fishing boats.

Somehow, when death stops the world for you, you expect it to stop for everyone. It doesn't. On Sunday afternoon at the Bayfront, a deejay named Footloose played heavy metal music for bikers, girlfriends, and locals who filled the six picnic tables on the dock. I used to move easily in this world. But now, instead of recognizing the biker babe in the black jacket and tattoos as the mother of an old friend, I saw her as slightly threatening, someone I didn't know and shouldn't make eye contact with. The cycles were lined up in front of the building. My God, I exclaimed to myself as I realized the biker babe was Hank's mom, about to get on a maroon Harley Davidson with highly polished chrome and a small bumper sticker that said "Save the Bay." She had to be sixty. And the identical maroon Harley parked next to her must mean that Hank Sr. was still in the building. Hank Jr. was my best friend in high school because he wanted to be an accountant. We had a natural friendship, based on a mutual ambition to get out of Parkers. Actually, he had done well in life, becoming a dot com millionaire of some kind, and probably buying those motorcycles for his parents. As far as I knew, they were still running crab pots out of the West River. But obviously, their lives had assumed a new flair.

I began to fear that the psychological distance between Washington, where I had lived for more than ten years now, and Parkers is much greater than the geography suggests. When you drive to Parkers, the land begins to flatten out as you get closer to the Chesapeake Bay. There aren't any housing developments torn into the side of the road with brick entrance markers, only wood frame homes of varying sizes, sometimes adorned with brick or stone, but always carrying that unmistakable design of the amateur owner architect who has added a room or two. They telescope down in size the closer you get to Parkers, and you realize this is a place nobody goes through. It's not on the way to anywhere. You have to seek it out, or know someone who lives there or at least used to.

The combination gas station and liquor store is the first commercial landmark that welcomes you to town with a handmade sign that says, "ATM Inside." There are a half dozen bank branches tucked away in the corner of roadside buildings constructed for real estate offices and insurance agencies. But the gas station and liquor store comprise the economic center of the community. There is no town center in a traditional sense with community square, grocery store, hardware store, stoplight and main street. There is no main street, unless you call the road along Jenkins Creek the main one, which might be reasonable to assume because the Bayfront Inn and nearby turkey shooting range are along that road. Behind the Inn is a string of houses facing twenty different directions, indicating the randomness of local zoning requirements.

The houses are tied to the Creek by boat slips that can be rented for nearly two hundred a month and represent the retirement nest egg for most of the families in residence. As long as the slips are filled, life is good in Parkers.

But there is a hard edge to Parkers. Many of the small homes along the road have discarded refrigerators and cloth covered recliners in the yard with rusted old cars that hadn't passed an emission inspection test in years. Yards are filled with boats in every stage of repair, with peeling paint, and gray motors hanging precariously from the stern. They are most often parked beside a garage, which has long since lost its door and allows even a drive-by visitor to see the crab traps and lawn mowers stacked inside. The only new element in most of these yards is the hand painted sign for SARP, "Stop All Resorts Please," a protest group of mostly waterfront landowners who want to keep the resorts and any other development out. The SARP message is to keep Parkers in its present state of natural beauty, a somewhat obscure concept to those who use refrigerators as doorstops. Yet they are the first to accept yard signs to save the environment.

The Bayfront was rocking but my mood was too blue for the music so I didn't stop. The *Martha Claire*, my dad's old bay-built crab boat, rolled gently at the pier behind the Inn, responding to the waves from small power boats on Jenkins Creek. Her seventeenth coat of white paint glistened with a red tint from the evening sun, and showed no evidence that my brother would not be returning to her helm on Monday morning. Jimmy had kept her in sparkling condition.

I drove on back to Washington with the top down so I could smell the hay fields between Parkers and the City. I noticed when I left the church there were several frowns aimed at my car. I knew exactly what that was all about; the worst aspect of my small town life: envy. I remember in high school we used to have cliques that were always judging people by their possessions, their wealth, their clothes. As adults, it became a new car, new wife, new fur coat, a job in the city, a new house, or a Saab convertible. The socially preferable mode of transportation in Parkers was a pickup truck, preferably at least ten years old, with dents on every fender. I might have to get one of those.

It was the hard edge I remembered from my youth. My friends were always fighting someone, whether it be individually at a bar, or collectively against the State over a dredging permit. There seemed to be an inferiority complex associated with living in the southern tip of Jenkins County. We were called South Countians in Parkers. And the watermen joked that all the crap in Baltimore and Annapolis would sooner or later be thrown on South County.

In fact, you could get so worked up about the problems of South County, it sometimes seemed a relief to get back to the city where nobody cared. In Parkers we had no chain grocery stores, so we had to drive to Annapolis for food, an inconvenience only the poor recognized as a discriminatory cost of living. Our banks were small branches where the young tellers didn't fully understand how a money market worked, or how to transfer money electronically, and usually recommended passbook savings accounts paying less than three percent interest. There was no local government to respond to any public need, and whether it was police, medical or building permits, we always had to make the trip to Annapolis. Not a great distance, but psychologically it was a million miles. It was also money: every trip to the doctor or the store cost five dollars for gas and incidentals. It wasn't necessarily cheap to live in Parkers.

My townhouse in Washington is just behind the nation's Capitol, recently renovated by a young couple who discovered the original bricks between the row houses. They tore out the ancient plaster and left a beautiful internal façade for the one big room that served all purposes, except sleeping. The bedroom was upstairs. That's why, when the young wife got pregnant, they had to find a bigger house and I was lucky enough to find the perfect bachelor pad. Even at 34, I am still single.

I opened the varnished front door, picked up the paper, and tossed my keys on the granite kitchen counter. It was dark because the only windows were on both ends of the house, and dusk was about to become night. I turned on the television because it provides better background noise than music, poured my first scotch on the rocks for the evening, plopped down in the stuffed armchair, and thought about the day. More specifically, I wondered why my deceased brother wanted me back in the waterman business, and why I might even consider it. There was, of course, the 147 acres of land on the Bay that my parents had left to my brother. In their will, they wrote that I had been given their cash for college, their dreams, and the brains to become a lawyer. Thus the land and the *Martha Claire* would have to take care of my brother. I think Jimmy deeply resented the intellectual implications of that provision, and perhaps that's why he now presented me with this Faustian option. He never showed me any resentment, seemingly happy with his life. But Jimmy's will was nevertheless strange: it offered me half the 147 acres if I would also accept our family workboat and return to the crabbing business for at least five years. The other half of the land was left to his wife and daughter.

What the hell was he up to? You could argue that he knew my frustrations with the law and just wanted to give me the value of a simpler life, for him a better life. Or he just wanted to be fair, rectifying our father's mistaken benevolence. Or you could argue that his final revenge was to force me out of the law and back on the water. He could never understand why I left the water. When I told him I was getting tired of the city, and often yearned for a return to the water, he could never understand why I didn't do it. "Just give up the money, put on your blue jeans, and join me on the boat," he would say. "To hell with the law."

I couldn't figure out his motives, so I poured a second scotch, only for the purposes of mental clarity you understand, and fell back into my chair. I am Irish, as I suppose the name Neddie Shannon makes obvious. But I'm not freckled with light skin and all that. Rather, I have dark skin, dark eye brows and light brown hair that I will never lose because my father and grandfather lived into their eighties with enough hair to start a wig shop. I also enjoy a challenge, a good root for the ole underdog, a fine turn of events, and people who care for other people.

Anyway, I don't have to determine my future tonight. Just before going to sleep, however, I should add that my list of favorite things does not include the law. It's just never been fun. The billing system, where you have to account for every hour spent on a client, has always seemed nuts to me. And I've never had a client who thought it was fair. It detracts from my sense of completion. Start a job and finish it, my dad used to say, and let the market set the price. As I finish this day of sadness and introspection, maybe it's time to reinvent my life, or at least do a little restructuring.

Chapter Two

I hate digital alarm clocks because you can never make them alarm, or it's a.m. when it should be p.m., or it's radio when it should be buzzer, and the settings are too small to read in the dark or when you're snockered. So I just leave those blinking red digits staring at me in the night and trust I'll wake up to read them, remember my appointments for the day and respond accordingly. This morning I thought about my father getting out of bed at three o'clock in the morning to ready his crab boat for six hours on the Bay and I knew my returning to the water was folly. On the other hand, is it a law that you have to start crabbing that early? Why not nine o'clock? I decided to roll over until 8:30 and consider the matter again.

After a couple of cups of instant expresso, I slipped into a pair of kakis, docksider boat shoes, no socks, and a blue denim shirt, the daily outfit of the dot com generation, even if we are lawyers. I was taking the day off after the memorial service, mainly because everyone would expect me to. And I needed some help in thinking this matter through. The answer seemed to be Diane Sexton, a very attractive lawyer in our firm who I had been warned to stay away from. She told me once that she had met my brother in association with one of her clients, somebody with interests on the Chesapeake, and although she wouldn't know a blue crab from a shark, she might have good career advice, at least about the law. She specialized in real estate development.

My Saab swung into a tight parking space in front of Hamilton House on Pennsylvania Avenue, just as Diane stepped through the revolving door. With the top down she recognized me immediately, waved and walked to the car. I couldn't help but notice that although she was wearing a light green summer business suit with brown heels, her jacket was low cut exposing the curve of her cleavage, with no evidence of a blouse or scarf underneath. I imagined her talking off her jacket in my living room, and I wondered if she had imagined me imagining her. I always think women have baser motives than they admit.

"Diane," I shouted, "glad I caught you. Could I buy you coffee?"

"Don't you think I have a client waiting?"

"No," I replied, "you would have been in at six getting ready."

I pushed the door open and she climbed in. One advantage of a low and small sports car is that women have to swing their fanny in first, which she did, and I reminded myself again of the colleague who said Diane was dangerous. But that might be the best antidote to sadness. So I swung out in traffic and headed for the Willard Hotel.

The Willard is the best thing about Washington. As a boy, Dad would bring me to the city to visit the museums and we would drive by the Willard. The museums were the extent of my cultural training because they had ancient wooden boats on display, and were located on the Mall where parking was plentiful. I liked the natural history museum best because of the prehistoric skeletons of elephants that flew, and the like. And I always liked the tired old Willard when it was closed, for about 20 years with pigeons flying through the upper windows and a faded wooden sign on the front that read: Closed for Renovations. A smaller For Sale sign below, suggested that the former was contingent upon the latter. But so many Presidents had lived in, or at least visited, the Willard over the years that the building could never be torn down in this era of historical preservation. Nor could it be renovated at a reasonable price. This project was going to require deep pockets and somebody who would repair the elegance and splendor of the 1930s in a way that would fetch four hundred dollars a night. After a couple of decades, it happened. Somebody bought the hotel and restored its legendary elegance. And now, the marble columns in the grand foyer, the circular mahogany bar, and the plush carpets often drew me to the hotel. It embodies the fine plush world of money and power that I thought the law should engender. And after I discovered that you didn't have to own the firm to visit the Willard, I went about every Saturday night. In fact, you don't really need much money at all. If you have twenty dollars you can spend the evening with two drinks at the Round Robin bar, or the morning with a pot of coffee in the restaurant, and feel very good about yourself. With Diane it was even better.

"Diane," I began after we were seated by the window, "I don't know you too well, but I want to talk about my future. I need a little help."

"Sure Ned," she said. "I'm so sorry about your brother. Is that what this is about?"

"Yes."

"Well, be careful," she said. "Never make decisions in sorrow or in anger."

"Right."

"Let me just lay out the situation," I continued. "Tell me what you think."

She picked up her coffee which had just arrived, raised it to her lips, and took a small sip, noticing the Willard eagle on the side. When she set the cup back on the small, circular table, I blurted it out: "I may leave the firm."

She didn't blink an eye, probably not really caring one way or the other. But she did show the proper concern by asking why.

"The truth is," I said, "I've always wanted to go back to Parkers. I thought it would probably be retirement, to some big mansion on the water."

"Looking for grandeur?" she asked. "Or recognition as the home-town boy who made good?"

"Both, I guess. Parkers isn't much of a town, really. Just a few crab houses with bars and not a one of them has tablecloths."

"Is that your standard of excellence?" she said through a smile.

"Pretty much," I said. "Even as a kid I wanted tablecloths. Clean and white. I think I went to law school to get away from formica."

"I thought you were a fisherman," she asked with a slightly scornful look. "With scales and guts and cutting those slimy fish open on the dock. Now you tell me you want table cloths."

"This may be part of my problem," I said, wanting to get the conversation back to my future. "I miss the water, the independence and orneriness of the people. But there's a Brooks Brother in me that likes the city as well."

"So what's the problem?"

"My brother left me his boat. It's an old wooden thing that my father left him. I have a lot of sentimental memories about it. Dad used it for crabbing for nearly 30 years. My brother was turning it into a charter fishing boat. Taking people out to catch rockfish. I guess the business is changing."

"You want to run a crab boat?" she said incredulously.

"I used to tell my brother that I wanted to get back on the water. I thought it was romantic when I didn't actually have to do it. It sounded great knowing that I had a law firm and enough money to buy any crab boat on the bay. So I dreamed of the smell of the saw grass in the morning, when the herons stand frozen in the marshes, or the egrets line the bulkheads, and the water is as still as porcelain. I miss dropping my hand over the side of the boat and letting the water rush through my fingers."

"Oh brother," she interrupted. Then she looked in my face and saw the yearning that could not be hidden. "Why not just do it. Buy a boat. Or take your brother's. And slip out there on Saturday mornings for a little nostalgia."

"There is a catch to this trotline Diane, that I haven't mentioned," I said. "My brother also left me about 75 acres, much of it on the water, probably worth several million dollars if it's developed right."

"What's a trotline?"

"Sorry for the pun. It's what the crabbers use," I said, "they go out early in the morning, lay out about a thousand feet of trotline -- that's what it's called -- with a piece of bait every few feet. It settles down to the bottom of the bay. The crabs come to the bait for breakfast. The crabber waits a while, then pulls up the trotline, and as each crab comes out of the water, the waterman scoops him with a net and tosses him in a basket. Kids do the same thing when they tie a chicken neck to a string, let the crab take it, then pull him up. Same idea only the trotline makes it a kind of assembly line. Crabs are a hundred and fifty dollars a bushel today so the guy does all right. Pull in ten bushels a day and you live pretty well. Of course, you can't do that every day. Actually, not many days."

"Let's get back to the land and the millions," Diane said. "What's the catch there?"

"I have to work the boat for five years to get the land."

"What!" she exclaimed. "Was your brother a practical joker, or did he hate you? What'd you do to this fellow?"

"No, you don't understand," I said. "I think he thought he was saving me from myself. He thought I belonged on the water. And this was a way to get me back. He probably also thought he would never die, or he could change the whole thing later if I turned out to be a phony baloney ambulance chaser."

"What's 75 acres worth out there?" she asked.

"Probably millions," I said.

"Ned, for ten million I would leave Simpson, Feldstein and James so fast I couldn't remember what the building looked like," Diane said. "Besides, your brother didn't say you couldn't practice law. Hang your shingle in Parkers. Fish in the morning. Lawyer in the afternoon."

"That may be a little much," I offered. But I fell silent, realizing this was a new idea, worthy of consideration, and maybe a solution to lots of things.

"I may even have a first client for you," she said, showing some enthusiasm for the project. "Listen Ned, you don't have a problem. With millions at stake, you only have opportunities."

This is why I liked Diane. Alone among most of the lawyers I know, she was a woman who could see opportunities. Admittedly she had detractors who saw her creativity as unbridled ambition, but I had never known her to chew anybody up or set a course that benefited her more than the client. Seeing around corners was a good quality for a lawyer, and I wasn't the best at it. Mostly, I am a goal oriented, slightly lazy, above average intellect who sets a course and sticks to it, except for Saturday evenings at the Willard when I am likely to stroll off into the unknown with the first lady lobbyist who believes my line about becoming a Congressman some day. That's not a pickup line I use often, but it has worked in some very ambitious circles, and it works amazingly well at the Willard because everyone who goes there expects to become President some day. That's why the Willard is a very strange setting for discussing a new career as a waterman.

I dropped Diane off at the firm, noticing the warmth that comes from having a strong confident professional woman at your side. And the faint smell of pricy bath soap under starched linen was also nice.

My greatest fear of going back to Parkers was that it had changed. I might have lost my sense of reality about the place, with all that education, travelling around the country, seeing Europe for nearly three months after college. Just yesterday, after the memorial service, Parkers seemed raw and slightly dangerous. In high school I never feared going into a bar in Parkers, or visiting a crab house on Saturday night when you knew fights could occur. I knew everyone and their intentions. Now I was an outsider, under suspicion for my ambitions and perhaps my income. The safety of familiarity was gone. But still, I couldn't forget the independence of heading your own boat out on the bay, spending six or seven hours in a cradle of waves, and returning home with the evening sun turning bright red. As I said goodbye to Diane, a single line of poetry floated through my mind: red sky at night, sailors delight. I never knew a waterman who could tell you who wrote that line, but they could all recite it, and most set their lives by it. I was doing it too.

Chapter Three

Martha Claire Shannon's name appeared on the bow of two boats in Jenkins Creek, one a thirty-foot bay-built docked at the Bayfront's pier, and the other a fourteen-foot Boston Whaler that my brother kept on a trailer at this home. One was his profession; one for recreation. He bought the smaller boat and twenty horse motor when his daughter was born, with the distant dream of taking her fishing near the marshes of the Bay, floating aimlessly on a warm summer day and showing her the patterns of life on the water. He knew she would enjoy seeing the long legged blue herons, with their necks stretched tight as a clothesline, skim across the water, then raise their heads and bring down their legs just like a jet airplane preparing to land. Already, at age one, the little girl would cry in the night when she heard the fractious, angry cry of the heron, such an ugly foghorn of a sound to come from such an elegant bird. And Jimmy wanted to show her how the herons came to the marsh at low tide, pranced around in the mud with such satisfaction that they finally drew that long neck down into their feathers, and in a final act of hauteur, raised one leg into their wheel well, and went to sleep, so motionless that they might be mistaken for a Florida yard sculpture. He also wanted to show her how natural enemies like the Osprey, growing in numbers in their big nests on the man-made channel markers, would attack the heron for no apparent reason, forcing them out of the sky in violent battles until the heron could find refuge in the tall marsh grass. None of that would happen now.

My brother had married Martha just two years ago, but they had known each other for several years. She had worked at the Bayfront when he started crabbing on his own. But it took eight years for the spark to catch, and then they wondered how they could have ignored each other for so long. Jimmy always figured it was because his mother was also named Martha, so he avoided her, at least subconsciously. But names seem to have a special niche in the culture of Parkers. Every waterman has a nickname, like Muskogee or Tank or Pirate, that usually comes from some experience on the water. The wives' names are often on their husbands boats, sometimes with middle names never used in other circumstances. And waitresses seem to call everyone Honey, or Sweetie, or Darling.

The anomaly for Jimmy was that his wife and mother had the same first name, but different middle names. However, since he inherited his Dad's boat, and since everyone knows that changing a boat's name is bad luck, he simply kept the *Martha Claire* on the boat and everyone assumed that meant his wife's middle name was Claire. It was complicated, but in the end nothing changed.

Now Martha was alone again, and seeking comfort where she had always found it, the Bayfront on a Sunday morning. The Bayfront Inn exists in every waterfront fishing community between South Carolina and Maine. It's always dark and carries the same worn and splintered façade as the fishing boats. Both the bar and the boats are painted every year, never with all the old paint scraped off, so the surface is thick with coats that build up on door frames and window ledges. And the first day after painting, heavy rubber boots leave sliding marks on the floor, and grease from the diesel engines leaves dark smudges around the door handle. It's only a matter of weeks before the spiders and dust mites have added their special touch of décor. And that's when the watermen feel the most comfortable. The Bayfront wraps her smells of stale beer and eggs around you like a bomber jacket with a fur lining. It's warm and comforting like a dear friend that has known you sick or drunk or foolish and still welcomes your presence.

Martha carried her Irish daughter Mindy in a plastic car seat into the Bayfront bar, set her on a round stool with red cover, wedged the seat in some practiced fashion against the bar, and tied it to a brass rail just under the ledge. It seemed unlikely Mindy would fall from that perch, yet most of the fishermen at the bar left an open seat between themselves and the child, a margin of safety as it were.

Vinnie Tupelo, the first mate on my brother's boat, moved through the outside door to the bar, let his eyes adjust to the dim, and took the open stool beside the sleeping Mindy. Vinnie had been with my brother for six years, and now would have to find another boat unless I picked him up, which I probably would. He had been with the Marine police for 20 years and had arrested every waterman on the Bay at least once for violating one of the many fishing regulations. Vinnie was a very optimistic fellow for a policeman, and he used to brag that in twenty years of issuing tickets for violations, he seldom made arrests or got a conviction. The reason, of course, was that local judges around the Bay would seldom find a waterman guilty of any water-related infraction. The judges figured life on the water was tough enough, and a day of fishing lost to a court appearance was punishment enough. Besides, they were neighbors and friends. It's one of the few breaks watermen get in their dealings with the government. Vinnie came to appreciate that fact, played his role in the drama, and after twenty years he joined the opposition. He became a first mate. Plus he knew that the old days of casual justice were dwindling and law enforcement wasn't so much fun.

"Hi Vin," Martha said, reaching across her daughter to tuck in her blanket so Vinnie wouldn't accidentally pull the whole thing off the stool.

"Hello Miss Martha," Vinnie said in his usual way. "Haven't seen you since the service. Real nice."

"Thanks Vin," she replied. They both took a drink of their tomato beer, the only concession anyone made to breakfast. Martha hadn't been a regular at the bar since she quit working at the Bayfront, but she was the wife of a waterman, and one who kept his boat at the Bayfront, so she was known to everyone. As the bar started to fill up, the boys filed by Martha, expressed their regrets, often with just the word, "Sorry," then took a stool.

Vinnie decided to move the conversation away from sadness by commenting on the Redskins, the Washington football team that was the real reason for the Bayfront's fast gathering crowd. It paid to arrive early on Sunday if you wanted a bar stool for the game at one o'clock. There would be standing room only by game time, which meant tradesmen and watermen three deep around the bar, a sound level equivalent to a diesel engine at daybreak, with people trying to reach between each other to pick up beers or shout orders to Simy, who was tending bar. It was important to be "on stool" by eleven o'clock.

"We may need another new coach," Vinnie said, looking at Simy as she walked to the back of the bar. "The Skins can't gut it up. They choke." No one answered, mainly because the other guys at the bar were reading the sports page of the Sunday Post, and hadn't quite assimilated the prevailing wisdom of the day.

"Vinnie," Martha said, "I never really knew how Jimmy put that fishing trip together. Do you know?"

"No mam," Vinnie said, shaking a pinch of salt into his beer. "I heard his talk about it, but I didn't hear that. He was real excited about going, though." Vinnie was still wearing his baseball cap with

30

the logo for St. Mary's Seafood on the front. Caps were a part of the uniform, mainly because they were always free. As Vinnie says, nobody in his right mind buys a cap anymore. And it gives you a little sun protection. Even so, caps always fall off when you're working the crab pots or the trotline, so it's best not to wear one at all. Hats with brims would be better protection from the reflections off the water, but you can't keep them on at all. Just the speed of the boat will blow them off. But if you walk in the Bayfront restaurant or bar at lunch time, every man in the place has his cap on, and no two will have the same logo. If you ask someone to remove a hat, well, Vinnie never heard of that.

"Vinnie," Martha continued, "who was on that boat with him? I was just told it was the local captain. I keep thinking someone could have grabbed him."

"Now Miss Martha," Vinnie said, "these things happen. There's no sense crying over the water. It goes with the business." Vinnie and the boys didn't like to talk about deaths on the water; it's too capricious. Always happens too fast. Some boy falls in. By the time you turn the boat around, he's gone. Just vanished below the water. It had never happened to Vinnie, but he almost went overboard many times, and he knew the feeling of losing your footing, or dropping a hand net overboard, or having the captain give his engine a quick thrust and the boat lurches out from under you. Happens nearly every trip out, and Vinnie didn't like to think about it.

"I just can't believe it," Martha said quietly. Simy heard the conversation and knew she didn't want in, so she picked up a dish rag and wiped the counter, which meant leaning forward until her already stretched blue jeans were tight as tape across her fanny. Vinnie said nothing, but he watched. Simy scanned the growing crowd for trouble, as she watched every customer for every emotion from crying

31

to fighting, and she set another beer in front of Martha.

I arrived at the Bayfront about eleven, and the bar was full, but the drive from Washington was slow and pleasant, with little traffic and the mid summer air filled with seagulls and the whine of bicycle tires. The Maryland bicycle club surrounded me at the last stop sign outside of Parkers. One of them was very pretty under her helmet, and I wished she would have turned her bare shoulders toward me, but she didn't. She just signaled permission to go in front when the intersection cleared. I wished she had been going to the Bayfront with me.

I was surprised to see my sister-in-law there. It seemed too soon after Jimmy's death for her to be going to bars, even if it was the Bayfront. I closed the door behind me and noticed the poster of seventeen women in bikinis and high heels, with their bare fannies staring right at me. Then I turned to join Martha, silently calculating what I would say to her. She was the one who had called me about Jimmy's death, and we had cried together over the phone, then again when I arrived at their home. That first day we stayed together till late into the night, talking about her future, and Mindy's future. We talked about the will, about the land, and about the insurance policy that would allow her a comfortable life, if she didn't blow it all. She was a little bitter about Jimmy leaving me the boat and half the land, but she and Jimmy had talked about it before, and she understood the boat had been my father's and should go from father to son. I had promised to take care of little Mindy, at least to see to her education, and generally we had worked things out.

Still, it was disconcerting to see her and Mindy at the bar. I thought about the psychologists who advocate the playing of Brahms lullabies around young children, even in the womb, to impart a feeling of warmth and security. I wondered what messages Mindy was soaking up today, surrounded by sentences without verbs and shouts of

"Go Skins." Maybe she would become a linebacker.

I took the only stool open, which was next to Martha, and ordered a beer. Although I had been to Parkers several times in recent years to visit my brother, I hadn't been to the Bayfront in a long time.

"I see they've added a trellis over the front door with fake ivy. Trying to make this place look like a country cottage."

"No," Martha said, "just trying to hide the drunks coming out of the john and still zipping up their pants."

"Is that a problem, here?" I asked.

"Every day," she said.

"Hello Vinnie," I said, leaning forward to see around Martha. "I haven't seen you in a long time. I understand you're taking care of the *Martha Claire*."

"Go out there this morning, turn the key, and she'll purr like a kitten," Vinnie said. "Want to take her out?"

That's what I wanted but was afraid to admit. Driving to Parkers on a Sunday morning seemed like a weekend outing. I wanted to see the boat, but I hadn't really thought about taking her out, which would have involved calling Vinnie, getting the key, and if I had to go alone I might run the whole thing aground. I hadn't been in the Parkers channel for years, where several new marinas had emerged from the banks like marsh grass, and I hadn't run a single screw, thirty-foot, work boat in years. But now it had all come together by accident, so I said, "Yes, let's go."

"After this beer," Vinnie said.

I was looking at Vinnie, so I didn't see where the voice came from, but I heard someone shout, "Hey, you Jimmy's brother?"

The Bayfront Bar was really two long bars facing each other, with taps on both sides, and a barmaid who paced continually from one end to the other. The back end led into a storage room for kegs and cases of beer, and the front end was closed by a swinging door with a sizeable latch on the inside, suggesting that more than one drunk had tried to enter the runway without authorization. I noticed Simy and heard the guys call her by that name, but I had never focused on her before. She had coal black hair streaked with grey, giving it a tint the local car dealer might call "smoked salmon" silver, but it was vibrant, and somewhat unexpected on a woman who appeared to be in her early thirties. Too young for grey hair, even prematurely, but interesting in that she went for the mature look and not for the youth.

I looked across the bar at a large man wearing a red plaid shirt, a hat that said something about plumbing and heating, with loose ends of brown hair sticking below the cap like celery sticks. After a couple of beers on a Sunday morning, he was already loud, but my Parkers instinct said that after a couple more beers, this was the classic belligerent who would be threatening, even with a baby on the premises.

"Yes I am," I said with a smile, hopefully disarming.

"I knew your brother, didn't I Martha," the plumbing man said without waiting for an answer, "and he was a good man; a good waterman who wasn't afraid of hard work. And I'll tell you this, I can't believe he let that tuna get him."

Oh God, I thought. How could he bring this up right in front of Martha?

"Let's talk about this later," I ventured.

"I'll tell you what I think really happened," he said.

I turned toward Martha and she stared straight and hard across the bar, a confused look on her face, unsure of what she heard or how much credence she should give it.

"Neddie," she said quietly, "what's he mean by 'what really happened?' Is there something I don't know?"

"No Martha," I said reassuringly, "he's just blowing off. You know these guys. Every waterman thinks he's infallible."

"I'm leaving," she said, reaching over to untie the car seat, and tuck the blanket around Mindy. "Stop by the house if you get a chance."

"Thanks. I will if we get back with the boat in one piece. If I don't see you, I'll call later," knowing I probably wouldn't stop by the house.

Martha picked up the car seat with one arm and was out the door even before I could follow. It would have been polite to escort her across the street to her car, but she had never had an escort before and I was still paying the bill when she vanished. The plumbing man gave me a shrug, knowing his comment had probably upset her, but he didn't care. These kinds of people somehow mistake rudeness or insults for straight talk and honesty, thereby bestowing themselves with a mantle of satisfaction, even general helpfulness. In fact, they were just rude slobs who wanted attention. I ignored the comment, and turned to Vinnie.

"Vin," I said, "I would like to take the boat out, not to crab, but just to see how she feels, to know the water again."

"Will do, Captain," Vinnie said. "Pay the lady and let's go."

"Captain," I repeated, realizing no one had ever called Neddie Shannon a captain before. It sounded strange, like he might be talking to someone else, or making fun of me, except that watermen never take the title of 'Captain' lightly. It was Vinnie's way of recognizing that the Martha Claire was mine, and a boat is a proud thing, a way of life deserving of the title "Captain." That's why watermen don't like to sell their boats to the "pleasure crafters" from Washington, as they're called, because the weekend owners don't respect the spirits that live in the timbers, the lives that are chronicled in every crank of the engine. When Vinnie called me Captain, he watched my eyes to see if I respected the title, just as he would watch me aboard the Martha Claire to see if I appreciated the chime of the boat and the way she cut through the quiet waters of Jenkins Creek. That's when the waterman is quiet, leaving the pier, when he feels a oneness with the Bay, a man in his role as ecological cog with the fish and the birds and the water. That's when the waterman's focus on the clouds and the weather is so intense that the roaring engine in the middle of the boat is but a whisper in his mind, because he is so much a part of the shimmering world of wind upon the water. I wanted to see if I would feel that power.

"Come on Vinnie," I said, "let's go to work."

The big John Deere diesel roared to life with the first turn of the switch. It belched a small cloud of carbon, coughed a couple of small explosions, then settled into a bottom-of-the-belly roar that smelled like power. These John Deeres would run forever, hour after grinding hour, whether through a heavy storm with the Bay's pounding chop, or across a Maryland tobacco field. It was comforting to know, of course, that Vinnie could pull the box top off the engine and repair about any external part in a matter of minutes. Vinnie eased the *Martha* out of her slip without ever touching the rub rail on the pilings, made the gentle turn into the channel, and said under his breath, "She's all yours Captain."

I took the wheel without saying a word, unbuttoned my cotton shirt so the wind would luft my shirttail, and scanned the creek for the green and red channel markers. "Right on red returning" is the first rule of the road my dad ever taught me, meaning take the red marker on the starboard side of the boat when returning to port, and the reverse is true when leaving. That marks the channel, where the water is deepest. I eased Martha to the right side of the channel and headed for the red marker barely visible in the distance. I had stood in this very boat for hours at my dad's side, yet today it seemed like a new experience as I tried to recall all the lessons my dad had casually bestowed. The first step would be to cut this right and left business. It's port and starboard, I knew.

Vinnie stood with his arms folded under his chin and resting on the sill over the galley doorway, his eyes glued to the water, not in search of trouble, but because that was the magic: the mouth of the creek opening its arms to release us into the bay and the welcoming jacket of morning sun that stretched across the water, ready to warm the bow of the boat. That's the moment when the spirits of the Bay settle into your bones, and for a lifetime, draw you back to the water. I waited some time before easing the throttle forward. Then felt the thrill as the wake lifted and spread out behind us like water over a dam.

"Vinnie," I said, "what was that plumber saying back at the bar?"

"You mean about Jimmy?"

"Yeah."

Vin was reluctant. "There's been some talk Ned. I don't know what it means. A lot of the boys think it's strange about Jimmy. How it happened."

"What do you mean, strange?"

"Well," he began, "we just don't see how he'd get his arm caught in that line."

"But, you know Vinnie," I countered, "I read a couple of years ago where that happened to some guy over at Ocean City. Catching tuna. Reeled him in for hours. Had a gaff on the fish. The big son of a bitch opened his eyes, saw the boat, and lunged for the bottom of the sea, taking the guy with him. It has happened."

"I know it has," Vinnie agreed. "I guess some of the boys just wonder, that's all."

"Well," I said, "I wish they'd keep their ideas to themselves. Now

Martha's all broken up about it."

"I'm real sorry about that," Vinnie said. And I knew he was.

"Listen Vinnie," I said, "if you hear anything else, let me know. But could you pass it to the boys to cool it. We gotta help Martha get back on her feet."

"I'll do it, Ned," he said. "I surely will."

I shoved the throttle forward, noticed the compass at 250 degrees, and figured maybe we could get lunch at Harrisons on Tilghman Island. The open water was easy to navigate. I watched for other boats while Vinnie kept an eye on the crab pot markers. He knew if we tangled the prop in one of the pot lines, he would be the one to go overboard, untangle or cut the line, and spend the rest of the day wet. My main concern was the shipping lane from the ocean up to Baltimore. I didn't want to get in the way of a tanker, probably Liberian, carrying oil or containers and rising about eight stories above the water.

"You know how long it takes a tanker going twenty knots to stop?" Vinnie asked.

"About 10 minutes," I guessed.

"Six miles," Vinnie said, "however long that is."

I didn't see any tankers, just a few fishing boats and some sails gathering in the distance.

I let the sun and wind fall flush on my face, a breeze stronger than expected. Sometimes even when the sky is clear, the wind whips up the waves on the Bay and tosses the boat. The waves crest close in this situation, and it's easy for a wave to catch the bow and throw the boat. Just for a moment, you lose balance and move your left foot to the side for better balance. The wind today was starting to pick up. I couldn't see it, but I could feel it, and remembered the old waterman admonition that a good work boat should be at least 28 feet long, so the boat will reach from the crest of one wave to another. As a boy, I tried to reach two crests at once, but it never seemed to happen that way.

"Vinnie," I said, "why is that boat just circling in the water?"

Vinnie looked dead ahead and squinted, but said nothing. I thought it was interesting, so I turned the *Martha* about five degrees starboard and headed for it. Finally, Vinnie ventured a thought.

"There's a pound net out there somewhere," he said. "Maybe he's circling to see the Loons. Or maybe he's getting ready to empty the net." Loons and seagulls seem to sit on every part of the net, waiting for a free lunch of the fish that happen into the enclosure.

"I didn't suppose they still allow pound nets," I said.

"You mean because they take up so much room, or get in the way of boaters?" he replied.

"Yeh," I said, "just figured their time had come."

"No," Vinnie explained, "but there aren't many pounders still out here. There aren't many small fishermen still out here. They have to get licenses and permits for the nets, and they have to come out every day to load the catch, often before they go crabbing. Then if some damn city slicker in a cigarette boat runs through the nets at night, the waterman gets sued. Not many left."

"I forgot how it works," I said casually, not remembering exactly how the nets collected the fish.

"See those sticks in the water, just to the left of where that boat is circling?" Vinnie asked. "They form a couple of leader nets that funnel the fish into a Hearth enclosure that catches the fish. See those sticks that run about two hundred yards west of the circle? There's a leader net along those sticks. The fish swim into them, panic at the thought of being trapped, then turn to swim along the net until they reach the enclosure. There's a trap door where they go in and can't get out. Then the waterman comes along in his open boat, closes the trap door and scoops them into his boat with a dip net. Not very high tech."

"Still, pretty ingenious."

"There are probably better explanations of the nets," Vinnie said. "But the result is the same. Fish of every kind swim in, can't get out, and the fisherman in an open boat scoops them up. You'll find everything from fish to human body parts in those nets, but they work."

Vinnie hesitated, then added, "They been doing it since Jesus, and probably before."

"No, I just read that some waterman in the 1800s invented the pound net, probably right here on Jenkins Creek."

"Jesus was a waterman and he used nets," Vinnie responded. Vinnie was a little defensive about his religion, and I let it pass.

"I don't see anybody in that boat," I said, moving my eyes from the pound net to the moving boat.

"Maybe that's why it's circling," Vinnie said. "Those new boats have an automatic turn mechanism so if you fall overboard, it circles. Of course, the captain could be in the cabin banging his girlfriend."

I kept on course for the boat, nosing the *Martha Claire* back after every wave pushed us off course.

"Over there," Vinnie shouted. "He's in the water. Probably drunk, or taking a leak."

I couldn't see anybody for the chop, and I momentarily lost track of the boat. Then I found him, a man with his arms flailing, fully dressed and slapping at the water. He was bobbing in the waves, but the boat was circling behind me. I had a moment of anxiety in the thought that I had come to the boat too quickly, without figuring the width of its circle, or where the captain was located. Now the boat was behind me, but the man in the water was in front of me.

Vinnie said calmly, "He's outside the circle of the boat, pick him

40

up first. Get close. I'll toss the line and we'll see if he takes it. Forget the boat."

That's easy for you to say, I thought. The empty boat was rocking wildly. We weren't in any real danger. But sometimes when a wave raised the port side of the *Martha* I could see the man's face in the water, white and unresponsive.

"Why doesn't he look up, or wave?" I shouted. "Is he dead?"

"I hit him with the damn line, and he didn't take it," Vinnie said. "I'm going in."

I realized Vinnie had put on his life jacket while I was talking. He kicked off his tennis shoes, threw his cap on the deck, and jumped into the Bay, not two feet from the victim.

Christ, don't hit him, I thought.

Vinnie was with him instantly, threw back the man's head and turned his body like it was a rubber toy. He took a few seconds to get his legs untangled from the victim, took about three strokes and he was beside the boat. I shut down the engine, mostly because I didn't know what else to do, and I didn't want anybody caught in the propeller. I rushed to the side of the boat and looked down at Vinnie's nearly bald head, with a few strands of hair draped across his head like wet seaweed. Vinnie was nearly cheek to cheek with a small head of coal black hair that showed no sign of life. I fell to my knees, waited for the boat to rock low once more, then grabbed the arm of the motionless man and flung him into the boat.

"Jesus," I shouted, not realizing how small he was, or how the adrenaline had increased my strength.

Vinnie had both hands on the side of the boat and was heaving himself in as I laid the man on the deck and started yelling at him.

"Wake up." But there was no response.

Vinnie quickly turned him on his stomach, hit him on the back,

41

and water seemed to rush from his mouth. He was a little man, with narrow features, and eyes that didn't open, but were set in deep wells. Even for a drowning man, he looked desolate, like he just crawled out of a cave.

Vinnie flipped him again, on his back, and blew into his mouth. That's all it took. The man just started all his systems, like the dashboard of a car that lights up on ignition. His eyes opened. He coughed, again and again. His arms rose as he tried to turn on his side.

"Get her started," Vinnie said, as he tried to help the man get in a comfortable position for coughing and breathing.

"Get the boat," the little man said. It was a weak voice, pleading. "Don't leave the boat."

Criminently, I thought, I almost forgot about the guy's boat. But who cares. The first rule here is save the victim.

"I'm OK," he said, "get the boat."

"Where the hell is the boat?" I muttered, swinging the *Martha Claire* around to find the circling power boat. It was off my stern, circling at a fairly good speed, maybe seven knots. Like a figure skater, repeating the same circle over and over.

Vinnie was sitting on the deck with his new acquaintance, but he looked up enough to suggest, "See if you can get close enough to board her."

"Hell no," I replied, knowing I couldn't do that even if it could be done. She was going too fast.

"How much gas does it have?" Vinnie asked his new friend.

"Fifty hours," he muttered.

"Fifty hours!" I exclaimed. "We could be here for days. Let's call the Coast Guard."

"Wait," Vinnie said. He struggled to untangle himself from the man on the floor. He raised the man's body and leaned him against the engine box. "It will be warm," he said. "Sit here and hold onto the side."

I kept the *Martha* within a few yards of the pleasure boat, but I couldn't hold the circle and I couldn't hold the speed. I would fall behind, and then cut across the circle in the water until I caught up again. The boat had made so many circles that its wake seemed like a permanent scar in the water.

Vinnie went below and came back with a dark green army blanket, my father's. It had been given to Dad by his brother, who fought in the Philippines during World War II. Uncle John had once sent me a hollow coconut from Guam that was finished into a bank, and every year on my birthday he would send a silver dollar to put in the bank. The blanket still had the Army's insignia stenciled on one corner, but there was a sizable hole in the center where some battery acid had leaked on the blanket.

"Is that for the guy?" I asked as Vinnie emerged from the vee birth.

"No," he said, "the boat. Pull *Martha* into the circle wake of that boat. Wait as long as you can, so you know *Martha* is on the same course as the cruiser. I'm going to throw this blanket in the circle and hope the cruiser hits it. Once I throw, get the hell out of there so it doesn't hit us."

I didn't ask the purpose of this blanket maneuver, but it seemed significantly easier than trying to jump into a moving boat.

I found the wake just after the boat went past, threw Martha in neutral, and waited for the cruiser to circle again. It took a couple of minutes to come around. Finally, it was bearing down on us when Vinnie threw the blanket and screamed, "Go. Go. Go." We lurched forward, causing our guest to roll on the floor. But Vinnie never lost balance or line of sight. He saw the cruiser approach the blanket, devour it under its sharp bow, and the blanket disappeared under the hull. And then the cruiser coughed. Like a child with someone's hand over its mouth. Muffled. Then another cough. And the motor died. The cruiser stopped and within an instant was floating in the water as helpless as a styrofoam cup. The blanket had become entangled in the propeller just as Vinnie had calculated, and the big engine stalled.

Vinnie moved in close to the helm and said, "If you can get close, I'll board the boat and we can tow her in." He was looking me right in the eye, I think to see if I was shaken by the whole experience.

"Vinnie," I said, "if I ever drive this boat again, even for one minute, I want you by my side."

"You got it boss," he said, moving to ready his jump.

Chapter Four

Opening my law practice beside a Calico Cat linen store in what passes for the only shopping center in Parkers was not part of my long-term plan. It was actually Effie Humbolt's Calico Cat store, with a subtitle: linen and things. More things than linen, and mostly bolts of cloth that appeared to be Laura Ashley knockoffs, priced for the local sewing circles. I noticed a predominance of rose designs, in colors ranging from pink to green, familiar to every family who uses wallpaper. I hadn't seen much wallpaper since leaving Parkers because the style in Washington had moved to plain walls and ceiling molding, or an occasional stripe. In any case, it gave the Calico a homey feeling that I appreciated, even though my new law office would be spartan modern with plain walls, a wooden desk with Queen Anne legs that I picked up at Rick's Antiques shop out on Route 1, three walnut chairs of mixed origins for the vast clientele expected soon, and a Persian rug of mixed ancestry that gave me the illusion, at least, of some class. All the furnishings totaled less than three hundred dollars and strengthened my sense of frugality.

Every endeavor in life has its fears. The workboat certainly raised physical fears, but the law practice raised economic fears. Clients might never come. Our profession has historically had this high minded idea that lawyers can't advertise for clients. Too unseemly. But it's perfectly fine, even recommended, that we join every low life civic club in North America and grovel before the most corrupt politicians available in the hopes of winning a fee. In my case, two hundred dollars an hour.

I made much more than that at Simpson, Feldstein and James, and I had other amenities I didn't deserve, like a walnut paneled office with leather chairs and pictures of horses jumping over fences in the nearby Virginia hunt country. I had never actually met a horse, but I knew them to be great symbols of wealth and pedigree, often associated with white fences and acreage. In defiance of this legal tradition and with a tip of the hat to local pride, I hung a picture of an oyster boat with two old guys raising hand tongs from the misty waters of the Bay. I liked the freshness of starting my own office.

I didn't have a library, but it seemed unlikely I would need a lot of precedents anyway. I did have a piece of computer software titled: Practical Law Applications. It could have been called a floppy disc for the mellow minded, but it included a sample will with blank spaces to fill in; sample real estate agreements; and instructions for filing civil lawsuits on behalf of any aggrieved party. I figured if I used two out of three I could survive.

I was straightening the furniture when Mansfield Burlington grasped the outside door handle, leaned back on his heels to read the stenciled gold letters, Ned Shannon, Attorney at Law, and entered.

"Hello Burl," I almost shouted.

"What," he said, "no waiting room. No big busted secretary. No cases of empty law books."

"You mean empty cases with no law books."

"You heard me," he said.

"No capital, huh," he said. "I'm here to help. Your first client. I need a new will."

"Come right in, Burl. You're in great luck, because I'm having a first time special on wills, one thousand dollars for the whole process or two hundred dollars an hour."

"How long will it take?"

"About five hours," I replied, "but it could go longer." I saw Burl doing the math in his head and realizing the thousand dollars was a floor in this process, no matter what happened.

"You would be good in the used car business," Burl joked.

I had spent so many years as part of a legal team, advising corporate clients on regulatory laws related to safety and environment, that it made me nervous to define a simple legal service and state my fee. At Simpson, Feldstein and James, all that was done for me. Furthermore, I was getting nearly three hundred dollars an hour there and the firm had devised so many ways to hide the fees that I never had to actually say to anyone, "My fee is…." Rather, it was part of a proposal, presented on paper and explained to the client by one of our administrative partners, who painted our merits with such gusto that people actually couldn't wait to pay us the big money. Indeed, they usually breathed a sigh of relief just knowing that our firm would keep them out of jail, or avoid a fine of even greater dimensions than our fee. Corporations would always rather pay the fee than a fine. It puts them on a much higher road for their public relations team. And over the years we had even made it an honor to pay our fee, a distinction like winning the Purple Heart for being shot in the rear.

"I hear you saved the Blenny Man," Burl said unexpectedly. "Not many people will thank you for that one."

"Who's the Blenny Man?" I asked.

"Word is you and Vinnie plucked that little mouse out of the water, and then towed his boat home like a lost dog."

"We did pick up a guy, but I thought his name was Ray," which was what I thought Vinnie told me.

I remembered that the guy did look like a little mouse, wet and wrapped in a blanket, with black hair draped in every direction. He hadn't said much, except thanks for the coffee. Vinnie gave him a mug on the way back to Parkers Marina. I did remember that when he raised the cup to his lips, his teeth were shaking, and his hands were unsteady when they grasped the handle. On his left hand was a diamond ring that looked out of place, and when he saw me notice it, he pulled his hand back under the blanket, still holding the mug with his right. No doubt new wealth. Even so, I hadn't paid much attention to Ray as we nursed his boat into an empty slip at the end of the pier. Vinnie climbed onto the pier, tied the bow line to one piling and the stern line to another. I helped Ray out of the *Martha* and took back the blanket, all without him saying a word. He looked like a stray animal standing on the dock. We left Ray and his cruiser at the Marina and maneuvered the *Martha Claire* out into the creek channel for the few hundred yard trip to the Bayfront. At least that's the way I remembered it.

"Who is he?" I asked Burl.

Mansfield looked across the office, raised his long frame from the chair and picked up the dictionary, one of three books that I simply couldn't start a business without. The other two were from my first year in law school. Mansfield always looked elegant, even in tan pants and a blue shirt. Sometimes, like today, he wore an ascot, which was so out of place in Parkers that it looked natural. At the Willard Hotel, I would have placed an ascot as among the most pompous of apparel, belonging either to a dandy or a nutcase. But Mansfield pulled it off, the way a fur coat looks all right in church if the lady is elegant in every stitch. Burl was that way, with leather docksider shoes that were richly brown, not scuffed or polished. His brown leather belt was wide, and catalog proper for the ensemble. I made a mental note to dress that way myself, although it seemed unlikely to happen. I just can't seem to shake the inevitability of wrinkles.

Mansfield Burlington picked the dictionary from my desk, flipped through the early pages, and ran his finger to the correct word. He stood erect and read from the dictionary: "Blenny. Any of several small, spiny-finned fishes of the family Blenniidae, having a long, tapering body. Blennius, a kind of fish. Blennos slime, mucus: so called from its slimy coating."

He looked up. "Now tell me that isn't the man you so ceremoniously pulled from the depths of the Bay."

"That's him," I replied. "But is that his reputation? Slimy?"

"I rather like the term, 'spiny-finned,'" Burl said. "Reminds me of a skinny little man I met in Paris. I commissioned a painting he never painted, but he took my money, tried to take my girlfriend, and denied it all till the day he went to jail for forgery."

"Before you launch into another historical tirade on the French, tell me about the Blenny Man," I said.

"Insurance," Burl said. "I think he sells it because he looks so much like death that it frightens people into buying. Also, he has no shame and will push himself into any gathering."

"Burl, I've never heard you so expansive in your disgust for someone," I said. "What did this guy do to you?"

Burl was really warming to the task. "You know when you look through the security hole in your door, and there's a distorted face with fat cheeks looking back at you – that's Ray Herbst. I've known him for years. Everything about him is distorted."

"Well, he doesn't know much about the water," I ventured.

"More than you think," Burl responded. "He probably was taking a leak when he fell off the boat. That could happen to anybody. Blenny has had a hundred boats in his life; he prowls around the marshes of this place and turns up on remote islands for every crab festival there is."

49

"Why are you so down on him?" I asked.

"The resort," Burl said, looking at the floor. "He's fighting it."

"But so are you."

"That makes it worse. He's on my side," Burl said. "But I don't believe him. I'm telling you, Neddie, if the Blenny Man darts in here to say thanks for saving his dark heart, grab your belt cause he's trying to steal your pants."

Mansfield was becoming a bit of a grump in his old age. But I could see why he was one of the most respected men in the county. He helped everyone who asked for it, and he helped in ways that mattered. He doesn't give money to charities, probably because he doesn't have a lot, but he gives himself. He attends all the church dinners, Elks Club bingo nights, and oyster feasts, usually wearing his own apron that's dark blue with red letters on the front that says Field and Bay. He's very proud of his career and his magazine. It's his identity. Along with his ascot, or his bow tie.

"Once we get this "will" business settled, I want to talk about the Hijenks," Burl said. "We've got to stop it."

"Now hold on a minute," I said. "I may have a conflict here and I'm not ready to discuss it."

"What conflict?" he asked.

"I'm a lawyer, among other things," I said. "And I might have a client in this fight."

"Don't you desert me boy," Burl said with a smile. I knew he wasn't really upset. Burl is a democratic soul, and understands everyone has a right to their views. Just the same, I'd rather not antagonize him, not with my first one thousand dollar fee hanging in the balance.

"Burl, here's a simple agreement to sign that says I'll do the will and you'll pay for it. And I've attached a form that will get you started thinking about your will. It will help you make lists of things.

Account for your money and property. List your relatives and friends you want to leave things to, then come back and we'll talk it through."

"Damn, if you're going to make a major production out of this, I sure don't want to be paying the hourly rate."

"Burl, for one thousand dollars, you get everything I know for as long as it takes," I said.

"Neddie, my boy, welcome to Parkers. Again, I'm sorry about your brother."

"Thanks Mansfield," I said, using the formal name. I stood to see him out and he moved toward the door. He took the handle and started to turn it, then looked back at me to add, "You know, your brother was working for the CRI."

"I know Burl, thanks for coming in, and I'll get right on the paperwork for your will."

* * * * *

This was turning out to be a busy day.

Diane Sexton wasn't due in Parkers until two o'clock, well after I would finish lunch with the Calico Cat, Effie Humbolt. By lunch I mean a piece of Dominos pizza, catered by Effie from the pizza shop located in the far end of our building. To call our offices a professional building may have been a stretch. We had an insurance agent, who was independent, meaning he represented a lot of companies when he was sober. Fortunately, there are a lot of insurance companies out there so you can go through quite a few in a lifetime of overindulgence. We also have a second hand clothing store, which does quite well because we have so many available customers. And we have a real estate firm that deals almost exclusively in local property. Its owner is Pippy Plotkin, who is called "Pigskin" because it is alliterative and because Pippy paints his car in maroon and gold colors with Washington Redskin logos on the doors and an Indian in full head-dress on the hood. Pippy makes a lot of money churning beach houses and fishing cottages, then he spends it all attending out of town foot-ball games. I've only met him once, but Effie says he's a pip.

Effie is about forty-five and married to a local appeals court Judge. The courthouse is in Annapolis so I seldom see him, which is fine be-cause then I can dream that Effie loves me. She is a peach, knows everyone who ever lived in Parkers, and comes from one of those "crossover" families who were poor about three generations ago, but through farming and a good Maryland law school, found themselves at the top of the heap with a new house on Jenkins Creek and respectabil-ity as well. Everyone tells me she is the most valuable friend I can make in Parkers and I hope it's true. She's dark complexioned, with defined legs and thin ankles, and shoulders that imply either weightlifting or good ground strokes. In any case, I like talking with her, and immediately accepted the offer of a pizza lunch as soon as Burl was out the door.

"Now listen, Mr. Ned," she said, "we have to get you a bigger of-fice, with a secretary, and a waiting room. You can't have clients just walk in on your meetings."

"Sure I can. First of all, I have this handy dandy answering system that takes all phone calls and records messages. Second, I don't sche-dule overlapping meetings. And third, I can't afford a secretary, and probably don't need one if I'm going to be on the water all morning."

Effie sat in the client chair in front of me, pushed her can of Coke across the desk, and crossed her legs. There was condensation on the can and it left a streak of water across the top. I snatched the can be-fore it could leave any more tracks, and she wiped the water with a Kleenex.

"Are you settled in, Ned?" she asked. "How's this gonna work? Will you have a schedule?"

"Don't know Effie. Depends on the crabs."

"Well, I expect we'll get a lot of people looking for you who end up in the Calico Cat," she said. "And that's all right. Maybe I can sell them a little yarn while they wait."

"I hope so, Effie. You have been so kind," I offered. "And this pizza is pretty good too. Not the Willard, but pretty good."

"Are you a Willard fan?" she asked.

"It's my secret love. If you ever need me on a Saturday night, call the Willard."

"Why you little scoundrel," she mocked. "You've got two lives here and a third one in Washington. I hope you're not dangerous."

"No Miss Effie. Now you've got to go because I have another client coming."

"Two in one day," she commented. "Let the good times roll. Bye Ned." Then she flashed those great legs and left, never looking back.

I always wanted my own office. For a blue collar kid with white collar ambitions, it's like driving a Saab. It's a symbol of freedom and success that doesn't really cost much, but you don't need it or even want it until you've reached that station in life where material luxury dreams are possible. It all comes in stages. I remember in Parkers Elementary School, about the fifth grade I would guess, there were no white collar jobs in our career day. There was a policeman, but we all knew him, or at least his car. And most of us feared him or hated him for arresting our fathers and brothers. To think of him as a role model was preposterous.

There was a fireman. Old Jim was the only name we knew. He sat in front of the station all day in a metal folding chair, leaned back against the building, and slept during those times he wasn't washing the trucks. His ambition was well hidden and it was never clear to me that I should follow in his footsteps. I understood that he put out fires, and possibly saved lives, and his trucks were fascinating to climb on, but still there was something missing. We also had a waterman who brought oysters to career day and showed us how to crack them open and eat them, although many of my classmates had trouble with the sight of fresh oysters sliding out of the shell like egg yokes. My dad caught these things for a living, so I had oysters more often than hamburgers.

We never had a professional man at career day, not even "Pigskin" Pippy Plotkin. We had carpenters and plumbers and clam diggers and one very exciting fellow who dove for oysters. He strapped air tanks on his back and ran an air hose out the window of the school to his rusted pickup truck parked on the grass. His brother, who was only a year or two ahead of me, ran the air pump in the truck and we all got to breathe some of the air from the compressor tank. It was neat. But I did have concerns about the younger brother. Once I had seen him smoking behind school and giving some guy the finger. Not exactly a lifesaving character in my mind.

All of these people worked with their hands, in highly commendable occupations, but they didn't teach me anything about being a professional worker, or how money worked, or about the world of people who spent everyday in tall buildings. What were those people doing? I saw them on television. I saw their new cars and some of the houses being built on Jenkins Creek that implied wealth, but my school didn't offer a clue. It wasn't until high school that I began to sense a larger universe of occupations.

I suspected that Diane Sexton came to this issue from the opposite direction. She grew up in Long Island, New York, someplace I had never visited, and went to college at Vanderbilt in Nashville. Her folks thought a little southern gentility might hone the sharp edges of her life in New York. And it did. She was a perfectly charming blend of smooth manner and raging ambition, like one of those swans with a long elegant neck that will seduce your eyes, then take a chunk out of your leg.

As she finished circling my office, her only response was, "This is it?"

"Diane," I said, "this isn't Simpson, Feldstein and James. It's Ned Shannon. And it's all mine. All me. I do it all, from the phones to the research to the briefs."

"Oh brother, I've seen it all now," she said. "Well, the boys at Simpson send their regards. They think you're crazy."

"I may be Diane, but it feels good, and I'm glad to see you."

"Ned, here's the good news. Chesapeake Resorts International wants to hire you, on retainer for a thousand a month."

"What do they want?" I asked. "Take on the eco-freaks, challenge the Democratic party of Maryland, and clear the land for the building."

"No, they want you to cooperate with the environmentalists. They haven't gotten to the fighting stage yet. That will come. But CRI needs an inside guy. Someone to help them with the permits, to smooth the way with the locals."

"Do you know what you're saying?" I asked. "The permitting process alone will take years, with meetings and fights like you can't believe."

"All the better," she smirked. "That monthly retainer just keeps coming in. And besides, what about those seventy-five acres you own. This experience will show you how to do it. How to develop."

I let the matter stand. She paced and remarked, "You are the luckiest guy I ever met."

"You've been given several million dollars in land," Diane said.

55

"Plan now to do something with it. Help Jimmy's wife Martha develop her land. She probably needs the money now."

"You're right about that," I replied. "I should be helping Martha. She's the one who grabbed my brother by the collar and said, 'let's make something of ourselves.' And she did it the only way it's real, by hard work and good dreams and never losing sight of the goal. She prodded Jimmy to clean that boat up. She put everything on a computer so he knew how many crab pots he had, and where. She figured out how to get three hundred dollars a day for a three hour fishing trip, and sell those city slicker fishermen a crab cake sandwich for another ten dollars and call it a Chesapeake Deli. And then he died. Gave away the boat and half the land and left her with a baby girl besides. For crying out loud, Diane, you're right again."

"Thank you. Now go make some money."

But money just wasn't my motivating factor. Diane was a student of capitalism, and she wasn't motivated by sentimentality. In fact, Diane was laminated with invincibility. There were no soft spots for vulnerability, or sentimentality. In spite of my affection for her, and my respect for her judgment, she had an air of superficiality manufactured by money and pretension. I once had a girlfriend who would call Diane a "fancy" lady. After we quit dating, this girl always asked if I had taken up with a "fancy" lady. She meant any woman with enough money to buy all the parts of an ensemble, understand how they fit together, and wear them. Diane was that woman. I even thought that someday I might lust for her, but I knew she would crawl into bed with earrings, bracelets and sharp elbows. So we had better stick to law.

I gave Diane a quick tour of Parkers that took in the auto body shop, the Post Office, three crab houses that passed for restaurants, and Flossie's grocery store. Flossie's had been a fixture for forty years. It wasn't large by modern standards. The aisles were narrow and never as long as you expected. The store had been enlarged several times over the years, with wings extended in every direction like spokes on a wheel. Sometimes while wheeling your cart, you would hit aisle four, I think, and it would extend the full length of two wings, including all the breakfast cereal, all the canned goods, and a few crackers. The next aisle over might be only a third as long and it would seem like another building. Sometimes Flossie would rearrange the stock and you could walk for miles in search of peanut butter, and no two aisles would be the same length.

We were passing Flossie's when Diane pointed to the side of the road and exclaimed, "My God, look at that."

"Ned," she said, "that woman is smoking a corn cob pipe. And those two scraggy dogs. What is that?"

"That's the pipe lady," I said. "I don't know her name. I used to ask, but no one ever knew. Just "The Pipe Lady." You say that, and everyone in town knows who you're talking about."

The pipe lady pushed a grocery cart along the side of the road every day between Flossie's and her home on Strawberry Point, or so they said. I never actually knew where she lived. Once I decided to follow her home. A little sleuthing. But she moved so slow that I gave up after about a mile. It just wasn't worth it.

The pipe lady had two dogs that followed her, in single file. The black Labrador retriever -- or it could have been some mongrel combination of a lab and several other breeds -- was always right on her heels. Behind the lab was a small shaggy animal with hair that protruded in every direction, covering scars and raw spots where raccoons, possums and muskrats had tried to pick off the little guy at the end of the caravan. Or the little dog had tried to pick them off on some dark night. Rumor around town was that the little dog was a killer, at least of animals its own size, and fearless in defense of the lab and the pipe lady. With those two dogs, the pipe lady was protected on every flank.

Not that she needed it, of course. I never saw anybody with the pipe lady, or even talking to the pipe lady, although she did talk to herself a lot. She wore black trousers, always, and a white starched blouse, always, sometimes under a summer-weight jacket or a threadbare tweed coat in winter. In winter, she wore a black stocking cap and allowed her gray hair to fall out on all sides of the cap. It seemed to me that life might have been easier if she had cut her hair short. Less effort in the morning, at least. Washing it was another matter, although the pipe lady wasn't dirty, that I could tell, unless she had been walking beside the highway for some distance. Then the dust kicked up by cars tended to collect on her white blouse. That was the most remarkable aspect of her ensemble, that starched blouse. It seemed like her one great effort at conformity in the world, an anchor perhaps against totally slipping into the abyss of her reclusive life. Although she wasn't a recluse, in the sense of hiding or staying home. Indeed, she often waved energetically at passing motorists, to the point you wondered if she knew you, or recognized your car, or perhaps needed help. I stopped once, but she kept on walking, and the dogs never even looked my way. There was something otherworldly about all three of them, detached from our life by their own self sufficiency. Perhaps that's why they didn't have personal names, just the pipe lady, the lab and the mutt.

"Ned, this is all quite fascinating," Diane said, "but I can't handle any more mammy yokums today. I better head home. I'll draw up a simple retainer contract and get it to you tomorrow. Also, there's a public meeting on the new resort next week. You better plan to go."

"Diane," I said, "you're a peach. If I get too far into this place, I'm counting on you to pull me out. Drag me back to the Willard and pour scotch down me until I come to my senses."

"Mr. Neddrick Shannon, Esquire, I will do that," and she kissed me on the cheek.

Chapter Five

When the public relations man for Chesapeake Resorts International said his new hotel would bring better highways and streets, a twelve-foot slide flashed on the screen showing a spaghetti pattern of Los Angeles freeways at rush hour. Some young business school graduate no doubt put these slides together, thinking the string of cars inching along six lanes of traffic would be a wonderful backdrop to the words. But to the citizens of Parkers, gathered in the local elementary school to hear the future of their town, it was explosive.

Six hundred people gasped. Air gushed from the gymnasium. And then as one body, as if practiced in some philharmonic hall, every farmer, waterman and wife in the place screamed "NO-O-O-O." And it didn't stop for long minutes. People stomped on the wooden bleachers in the gym. One lady screamed, "My God. My God."

"My God," I said, turning to my brother's wife, "what are the briefers doing? They can't be this stupid."

"Does CRI think we want more cars and roads?" Martha gasped. "They're crazy."

The briefer was turning whiter than the free throw line below his table. He just sat with his four colleagues and said nothing. After several minutes, the audience settled, and he tried to make a joke.

"I guess we took a wrong turn back there," he said sheepishly.

"No Shit!" someone screamed. And then the crowd roared again. The briefers could do nothing but wait until everyone settled down, and hope to start again.

Martha got a babysitter for Mindy so she could accompany me to the first public briefing by the Chesapeake Resorts International, my newest client, concerning their hotel and shopping complex to be built on Jenkins Creek. I invited Martha because my brother had also worked for CRI, but I never heard exactly what he did for them. Maybe Martha could tell me, plus I remembered she had mentioned meeting the corporate brass at some reception. I also thought it would be nice to give her a night out, even if it was work related. That's how I assuage my guilt in these matters.

We arrived at the Parkers Elementary School about seven, and cars already filled half the parking lot. The bleachers in the gym pull out from the walls and one side will hold about 500 people. When we walked in, the corporate public relations people were setting up a slide screen and arranging their papers on the folding table in the middle of home court. I didn't introduce myself, even though I had met most of them the day before in Washington. Rather I wanted to stay in the background, sit high in the bleachers so I could measure public reaction. The CRI boys told me to expect some opposition, primarily from "enviro freaks," as they called them. But they felt most people wanted the resort, the jobs that went with it, and the shopping where none now existed. One of the PR guys, who seemed a bit too cocky in his Levi's with no socks, tasseled loafers, pink polo shirt and blue blazer, said the slideshow would blow them away. He no doubt produced it.

Martha and I sat in the sixth row, near the top of the bleachers. The place was filling up fast, like the last minutes before a basketball game, with neighbor greeting neighbor. And there were a few signs, mostly negative, referring to the HIJENKS project. One of the last remaining tobacco farmers in the county sat right in front of me, wearing Sears overalls with a blue long sleeve work shirt, unraveling at the cuff and a small coffee stain on the pocket. He must have stopped at the convenience store on the way. His missus quietly sat beside him in blue jeans and a leather jacket, slightly more stylish than her husband.

The CRI fellows looked a little nervous as the crowd kept coming in. Some of the people in the stands shouted at them, as if the briefers were foreign invaders. I made a note that CRI needed some local faces at the table, probably mine. Next time. I asked Martha if that's what they hired Jimmy for.

"Yeah," she said. "They wanted a waterman. Jimmy went to one of these over in Tobyville and it went pretty well. But people here are afraid of growth. Truth is, most of the people against the resort are a bunch of rich hypocrites who moved to Parkers, bought the little houses that our daddies built, tore them down to build mansions on the water, and now they want to lock the door. Call themselves environmentalists. What baloney."

"Martha, I didn't know you were so worked up about this."

"Best thing Jimmy ever did," she said. "We need the jobs. I don't want a bunch of new highways and higher taxes either, but I'm tired of the rich folks taking over."

"Want it both ways, huh?"

"Yeah," she said, "we need the food stores, but we don't want to be Orlando." Then came the spaghetti slide of cars and more cars.

When the briefers started again, they were serious to a fault, measuring their words carefully and watching the crowd for any sign of mutiny. But as only the fates of the wicked would have it, they moved into the economic benefits of the shopping center. Just as the words "food centers" reached the audience, the slide appeared of a TACO TAKE OUT, complete with neon sombrero standing about twenty feet above the store. This time the briefers gasped. But it was too late.

The farmer in front of me yelled, "Bullshit."

"No fast food," someone shouted.

"Get out of Parkers," was the next scream, later shortened to just "get out."

The CRI man stood and motioned for attention. "I'm sorry, I'm sorry," he screamed. "These are just representative."

The boos were rising above him until people started to be embarrassed by their own shouting, and then it died down.

"We're going to abandon the slides," the CRI man said, and the crowd screamed its approval. Then the chant started, "No Hijenks, No Hijenks." People were red faced, flushed with anger, and neck veins were dancing around the gym like thermometers of mercury. People were standing and some started to leave, until the briefer begged them to stay.

"We want to hear you," he said, finally understanding the concept of a town meeting. "Everybody can talk. We'll stay here as long as it takes."

My neighbors began to settle down, like sheep after a thunderstorm. Some were strolling around the gym, some talking and grumbling, some picking up their hats and coats in case they decided to exit. It took awhile for the adrenalin to drain away, but the show finally got underway again. .

Martha said she needed a smoke break, which seemed like a good idea to me, even though I don't smoke. Notice that I don't consider one cigar a day as "smoking." I followed her to the lobby, across the highly polished entrance with the trophy cases full of athletic achievements, and out the double doors. Her cigarette was lit almost before the flush of cool air hit my face.

"Can you believe that?" I asked.

Martha just shook her head.

We said nothing for several minutes.

"Martha, tell me what Jimmy did for these people? Who did he deal with?"

We moved over to a concrete ledge just off the entrance to sit. Martha bounced up and squealed softly as her fanny hit the cold surface, not yet wet from the night dew, but close. The lights of the gym and lobby illuminated the entrance, giving us the warm security of knowing several hundred people were just a few feet away. We could hear the dull movement of the crowd as people gathered to finish the briefing.

"Neddie," Martha began, "I don't know everything Jimmy did for CRI. He just went to that one town meeting. I know he met with some guys down at the Bayfront. And he took them out on the boat. That's how they paid him, in boat trips."

"What do you mean? Do you mean they had to have a cover for his salary? Why not just hire him as a consultant?"

"Who knows," Martha said. "Maybe they really liked to fish."

"Who went on these trips?"

"I don't know," she said, "Jimmy just talked about Mike. I guess he was the boss. I looked for him tonight but I only met him once. In the truck when he brought Jimmy home once."

"I'm meeting more of these guys all the time," I said. "I'll ask about Mike."

"Can I get you a cup of coffee?" Martha asked. She lifted herself off the wall and moved toward the light of the lobby. One of the churches had set up a coffee stand and sold styrofoam cups for fifty cents each. Martha's cup was steaming when she returned. I saw her with a cup in one hand and her purse in the other as she came to the door. She turned and swung her fanny into the cross handle, pushing the door open as soon as the latch gave away. Her jeans were more than snug and her starched blouse revealed the outline of ample breasts. I hadn't noticed before, I guess because she was my brother's wife.

I first remember Martha in high school, in my brother's class. Although they didn't date then, she hung around and worked part time at the Bayfront. Even then the Parkers girls had a kind of unofficial uniform, consisting of tight jeans, white sneakers, and a tight sweater. There were variations of all three elements in this ensemble, such as a sweater with a deep vee, or a cardigan sweater over a cotton blouse with two or three top buttons open, or jeans with the legs cut off to make short shorts in the summer.

Martha was attractive, even in the shadows. I remember my brother once saying to me as an unattractive girl walked under a street light: "My, how the dark becomes her." But that was not true of Martha.

"Hold this while I climb back up," she said.

I took the coffee, and a quick sip, while she hopped up and got settled, like a bird on a telephone wire.

"Ned," she said, "it's nice being here with you. I don't know that we've ever been alone like this."

I didn't know what she meant, and said nothing.

"Can I tell you something?" she asked.

I thought about a clever remark, realized what a cliché it would be, and that she wanted to be serious. Her hair fluttered on her forehead as she whistled air across her coffee, then took a small drink.

"Ned," she started, "you aren't the same as us."

"Who's us?"

"The people here in Parkers. I know you grew up here, but you left. You went to a world we never knew. And now you're back because of Jimmy's will. But you've been gone too long. You're not a waterman."

"I'm not trying to become somebody else," I said defensively. "I want to try the life, to mix my law with the water. And I admit it, to comply with the will."

"That's not what I mean," she said. "I mean your dreams and fears are not the same as ours. If you fail at this, you just go back to Washington. If we fail, it's down the ladder to be a plumber's helper. So when we talk about this hot shot resort, we're talking about our life. Maybe it's a better job. Or just as likely, maybe it means higher taxes and we can't afford to live here anymore. Either way, whether you're for it or against it, it's going to change our lives."

"I understand that."

"No you don't. You don't understand that these people, on both sides of the issue, are deadly serious."

"Are you afraid?"

"No," she said. "I have you. But look at your dad's old friend, Burlington. He's an environmentalist. And he's afraid the loss of watershed will kill the Bay, and he's got himself so worked up over it that they're building signs in his garage to paste all over the county. He's afraid of higher property taxes, and too many cars, and rich people like you coming over here and buying his house."

"That doesn't make sense. He doesn't have to sell."

"He will if he can't pay his taxes," Martha said. "That's why he's afraid. He's losing his way of life, and he's better able to adapt than most. More importantly, he doesn't want to adapt."

"What's the point, Martha?"

"I'm just saying that's why these people are so hot, and your CRI boys don't have a clue."

"Whose side are you on again?" I asked.

"I'm for the resort, but I see a future for Mindy and better schools, and condominiums, and maybe a future for myself. So I'm with you Neddie. But not everyone will be."

I stared into the dark, trying to absorb all the meanings in Martha's words, and scanned the cars. Something moved that gave only a flicker of recognition, like a bird in a tree.

"Martha," I asked, "do you see something in the shadows by that blue car? Look near the bumper on the ground."

The school parking lot was nearly half full and the moon traced a path across the roofs of a dozen cars. It was getting near the end of the meeting, and some people were leaving, causing headlights to snake their way back to the street. It was easy to see shadows that were nothing.

We both stared.

"What are you seeing?" she asked.

"Nothing important," I said. "Just movement."

"I see it," she said with just a hint of discovery. "You know what that is? That's the pipe lady's dogs, the lab and the mutt."

"Where's the pipe lady," I asked. "I didn't see her come in."

"I've never seen her without the dogs, or vice versa," Martha said.

"She must be inside. I've never seen her up close. Let's go back in and see if we can spot her. This thing should be over soon."

"Wait," Martha said, "I just saw a flash of light in that pickup... the one in front of the dogs. She must have lit her pipe."

"Why is she sitting out here and whose truck is that?"

"I don't know and don't care," Martha said, concluding her investigation. "Let's go in."

It was almost ten o'clock when we slid into seats on the end of the bleachers. While we were outside, the CRI had set up a small table in front of the crowd with a microphone. A young mother stood behind the table, stoop shouldered so the mike would pick up her voice, and with her hands on the shoulders of her two boys. The boys looked scared and they stood erect. The mother was pleading and it seemed to confuse the audience. She wanted the resort and the shopping center with a passion usually reserved for the opposition.

"We need a real grocery store," she said. "One that's open longer hours so I can go after work. We need better food, meats and produce, so I don't have to drive to Annapolis for everything. Our little store here is ripping us off, with second rate food, unwashed produce and prices higher than anywhere. Why do we pay ten cents a gallon more for milk; six cents a loaf more for bread; twenty cents a pound more for grapes and plums? I'll tell you why. It's because there's no competition here. That's why dry cleaning costs ninety cents a shirt more here than in Annapolis. That's why our little pharmacy doesn't even carry shaving lotion. God knows what kinds of drugs they stock. But I'll tell you this, we pay for being poor. We pay for not having other stores. And for the life of me, I don't know why we're protecting local merchants who are ripping us off." She finished, almost screaming the last sentence, and a few people applauded. But as she turned toward the audience, and guided her boys gently toward their seats, there were tears in her eyes. The crowd noticed and for an instant fell silent, then thirty hands shot up and several shouted, "Next."

"Wait," the CRI briefer said, "it's getting late. Let's cut everybody to thirty seconds. Just make your statement and sit down."

"What?" one man screamed. "You said we could talk."

"You said everybody!" another shouted.

"I'll talk as long as I like."

"You're liars." And the crowd broke into a cheer, repeating, "Liar. Liar. Liar."

The briefers caved again. "Okay. Okay. We'll stay all night if we have to. Who's next?"

I put my head in my hands, stared at the floor, and wondered how this could get any worse. Someone had left a copy of the Old Bay Circular under the bleachers. I bent down, reached through the bleachers, and by placing my chin almost on the shoulder of the man in front of me, I could reach it. I like the Circ, as we call it, because it's so different from the Washington papers. No hard news to speak of, except for the center pages totally dedicated to schedules and events around the bay. I am always amazed by the number of nature walks, art gallery showings, and oyster festivals in any given week. Recreation and public events are not a problem in Maryland.

The paper featured a fishing column every week by somebody named Captain Gil, which I assumed to be fictional. But he told us everything about fishing except the coordinates for the best spots. The unwritten law of the sea forbids any fisherman from giving away his spots. My favorite feature in the Circ is the "News of the Weird," a collection of stories from across America about episodes like the bandit who tried to hold up a McDonald's takeout window, or the bottle that washed up on a Florida beach with somebody's wedding ring inside. The story that caught my eye tonight involved a woman in the Carolinas who found a blue polka dot sneaker on the beach and inside the heel was a magic marker note, "Left Plaid." The woman sent it to Mrs. Barbara Bush, wife of the 41st President of the United States, because Mrs. Bush used to buy several pairs of sneakers, then mix the colors. Mrs. Bush sent a very funny note back, something about when fishes walk; and the lady framed the letter for her grandchildren.

The Circ's cover story that week was about Hank Burroughs, a retired White House photographer who had moved to the Bay some years before, and became a much loved figure of dashing elegance and historic wisdom. He had traveled with Presidents from Truman to Ford and now hung out at the local library. I had never met him, but the article was interesting and I was sure to run into him at some point.

"Put down the paper and let's go," Martha said, squeezing my arm. "My babysitter can't stay any longer."

People were starting to leave in pairs, so it was easy to slip off the bleachers and head to the door. I brought a light jacket, and was starting to put it on, when I saw a familiar figure in the glass. Looking through the lobby, past the trophy cases, and directly at me were the Pipe Lady, the lab and the mutt. Martha had dropped behind me, so I turned to pull her closer and point out the Pipe Lady. But when I turned back they were gone. As we walked to my car, I looked all around, even stopping for a second beside the spirea bushes, but there was nothing to see. They had slipped back into oblivion.

Chapter Six

Vinnie Tupelo emerged from the bedroom of his two bedroom bungalow near the water wearing his long underwear and ready for coffee. Vincent Norton Tupelo had spent most of his life wearing long johns, except on the hottest days. In elementary school he wore them because his father did, and often the whites would show above his socks, prompting ridicule from classmates. The other boys, mostly sons of watermen, also wore long underwear but not with such religious fervor. Vinnie wore them everyday because they made him feel secure, confident in his preparedness for the day, like wearing clean underwear in case he was struck down by a truck and then carted off to the hospital. He was ready.

"Velma," he said to his wife, "I don't know what to do with myself since Ned moved our start time back to eight o'clock. The day is half over by then. I just lay there and roll around."

Velma knew all of this, of course, but she rather liked not having to make breakfast so early. She used to get up at four, make Vinnie some eggs and toast, and go back to bed for a couple of hours. Her beauty shop didn't open till nine. And after thirty years of giving permanents at more than a half dozen local shops during that period, she knew down to the second how long it took to set up for the first customer: three minutes.

"How's the boy getting along?" she asked.

Vinnie pushed his omelet around the plate, examining the mysteries of its content, leftovers from the week. Velma usually made scrambled eggs, but at least once a week she cleaned out the refrigerator with a three-egg omelet, including onions, cherry tomatoes, chunks of beef from a previous stew, and sliced sausage. Vinnie liked this package because it had girth, substantial chunks of meat and plenty of flavors. It also tended to mitigate the blackened surface of the eggs where Velma had waited too long for the flip. He also liked her home fries for the same reason: they were piled high and crispy from overcooking. He sipped the hot coffee, and thought of the full thermos he would carry for a morning on the water, and pondered Velma's question.

"I like Neddie," Vinnie said, "but this isn't real for him. It's just a game. He'll get tired of it some day, sell the boat and that will be it."

"Then why?" she asked.

"Why does he do it?" Vinnie repeated. "Cause he's trying to have it all."

"Well, Vincent, this never seemed like the almighty, ideal, glorious life to me. Is being a crabber having it all?" Velma used Vinnie's formal name when trying for humorous exaggeration.

Vinnie smiled. "Why Velma, do you mean that building beehive hairdos and living paycheck to paycheck in this thirty room mansion is not the ultimate way of life?"

"Vinnie, after thirty years with you, I love just being alive. We have good friends and family, and a good church. But being a waterman is not having it all."

"It might be if you didn't need the money."

"You mean Ned just fishes for fun."

"That's the way I see it," Vinnie said. "He makes his money lawyering, probably stealing inheritances from old ladies, and he steals God's beauty by going out in that boat every morning. That sounds like an easy life to me."

"Vincent, don't be so cynical."

"All watermen are cynical."

"Well, Neddie has been good to us. He didn't have to keep you on. And he's polite, single and handsome," Velma said. "I like having him back, except for losing his brother of course."

"How's Martha?" Vinnie asked. "I haven't seen her since the Bayfront that day. And she didn't look too good that day."

"She was in the shop last week," Velma said, "and I thought she was fine, except I think she's got it in her head that Jimmy was up to no good."

"You mean foolin around with women?" Vinnie asked, screwing up his face in rejection of his own observation.

"Something," Velma said, "I don't know. Maybe it's that resort. Now Neddie is mixed up with those folks too. I think they're fast talkers."

"Neddie can take care of himself," Vinnie said. "But it would have been better if they'd found Jimmy's body. Then Martha would know what happened."

"Put your plates in the sink." Velma didn't have to say that, but it was a goodbye she had offered Vinnie for years, just before going back to bed. It was reassuring to them both because it implied they would be back in the evening to clean up. She didn't have to go back to bed anymore, but she still directed the plates before heading to her shower.

Vinnie walked into the mud room, as he called it, a corner of the front porch he had enclosed some years before. He already had on two pair of wool socks and they slipped easily into the white rubber boots that were waterman traditions, warm, waterproof and skid proof. But they didn't do much for falling arches, and Vinnie's feet hurt from standing in the boat all day. He tucked his jeans inside the boots, cinched his belt one more notch, and reached for the tan canvas jacket hanging on the wall. His rubber waders would be waiting in the boat, and cold, but they would warm up fast from body heat. He liked to leave the house first, say goodbye, and get the station wagon started before Velma was quite ready. Her car, a used Pontiac muscle model they picked out several years ago, was in the garage and a guaranteed start. Velma loved the car. It had a sexy quality as defined by the culture of the 1970s that included oversized tires, a 400 horsepower engine, red and orange flames stenciled along the sides, and some souvenir hanging from the rear view mirror. Velma had a paper mache Hawaiian lei that she and Vinnie got at an Elks Club dance in honor of Don Ho's 60th birthday. It hung from her mirror for several years, and only recently did she begin thinking that she might change it. It was turning yellow and brittle.

Vinnie's car was known throughout the county for being disguised as a moving billboard. Every conservative political slogan and country music phrase ever put on a bumper sticker was part of Vinnie's Chevy station wagon. Some of the stickers were twenty years old, as old as the car, and faded beyond readability. My favorites were Agnew Is Innocent, I Love Hilda Mae Snoops, and No More Kennedys. Agnew was faded; most people didn't recognize former Maryland Governor Donald Schaefer's girlfriend Hilda; and the Kennedy sticker was an all purpose statement against wealth, power, entrenched Democrats and outsiders in general. None of the stickers were particularly clever, but they all had a purpose. Vinnie was a man who stood for things, and his car told you what. His seatbelts were wedged between the seatbacks and encrusted with cracker crumbs, French fries and spilled coffee. The danger of dying in his car from food mold was probably greater than from a car crash.

The car leaned to the rear left corner, for reasons Vinnie never explained. Most people thought it was due to a failed shock absorber. And passengers usually found some way to anchor themselves, perhaps just a finger through the door latch, to keep from sliding across the seat. But Vinnie noticed it had been some time since anyone had volunteered to ride with him. He smiled at the thought of how well his "no maintenance" plan was working.

Vinnie and Velma lived in a typical community of small frame homes, built in the 1940s as summer cottages for the middle class of Washington to escape the high humidity of the city. No heating or air conditioning and not much insulation. The western shore of the Bay, from Annapolis to the Solomons, is crowded with villages called Silent Waters, or Restful Beach, or Clift Haven, or some name signifying the aspirations of their residents. The streets were narrow, and the lots were small, divided by chain link fences often purchased at discount by the community associations to ensure that no one remained unfenced. In recent years, almost all the houses had been winterized and renovated to the point they looked like faded lego blocks, going in all directions with floors that often meant stepping up or down as you moved from room to room. Vinnie bought his house in 1971 for twelve thousand dollars, added a bathroom, oil heat, window air conditioners, and the back porch. The house wasn't on the water, but it was across the street from water, and when Vinnie backed out of his driveway, he could see the sparkling early morning waters where the sun was beginning to burn off the fog. He reached the Bayfront Inn in less than five minutes.

Margaret "Simy" Sims was putting a filter in the big silver coffee-maker behind the bar. The bar and the restaurant were side by side, but separate operations under the same roof. The owner, Mabel Fergus, knew this was not efficient, but it was practical. She didn't want a bunch of drunks pushing into the restaurant for coffee, whether it was to sober up or to fill their thermos jugs for a day on the water. And she didn't want food in the bar, at least partially so Simy wouldn't have to pick up dishes and take food orders. The bar was for drinking.

Simy was making the second batch of coffee of the day, her supply depleted by the first round of crabbers who headed out about six, just after she opened. Vinnie was in the second tier, mostly captains and mates on the fishing boats that would meet their charter parties about eight. The Bayfront fleet was changing. Maybe a dozen crab boats still operated out of Jenkins Creek, at least five of them from berths at the Bayfront. But another half dozen captains had given up the crabbing altogether, and had transformed their boats into "charter fishing" vessels, forsaking crabs for Rockfish. Along the Jenkins and most of the western shore of the Bay the water is shallow, often two or three feet with huge splotches of sandbars that show solid green on the charts. The somewhat narrow shipping channel from the Atlantic to Baltimore may be ninety feet deep or more, but most of the Bay is closer to twenty-five or thirty feet deep. Nevertheless, "deep sea fishing" is the brand name people recognize from fishing fleets along the Carolinas or Florida coasts, so there was a move afoot to build a new sign on the pier that said "Charter Fishing."

Most of the charter captains were charging three hundred dollars a day for a party of six and doing far better than they had as crabbers, with a lot less effort.

Vinnie figured Neddie would move toward charter fishing, if he stayed in the business long enough. Ned was already trying to do two things, crab and law; he might as well add a little Rockfish fishing. But it was too soon to know.

Vinnie moved around the bar, tapping a couple of the boys on the shoulder and saying hello.

"Simy," he said, "coffee black. Have you seen Ned?"

"No Mr. Vinnie," she said, often using the formal prefix for old friends. She took a wide lipped porcelain mug from several stacked on the bar, flipped the black lever, and steaming coffee gushed out, spilling just a bit over the edge. She wiped the excess with a dish rag stuffed in the pocket of her jeans. Simy had been at work a couple of hours but hadn't applied her make-up yet, and her hair was pulled back and pasted to her head with several pins. Her dark green tee shirt said "Spoil Me" on the front, prompting Vinnie to wonder where she got it. He didn't wonder what it meant. He knew that just about every waterman on the Bay had tried to spoil her at one time or another, and for some it was a lifetime project. In fact, one of the most troubling aspects of his association with the Shannons was the knowledge that Jimmy had been interested in Simy himself, although Vinnie wasn't sure much had ever happened. Still, he was careful what he said whenever Martha was around...

Vinnie turned to Captain Petey on the next stool, and asked if he had a full charter.

"I got a hot one today," Petey said, rubbing the mermaid tattoo on his left arm. "A bunch of politicians from the State house. And that guy you saved, the Blenny Man."

"No kidding," Vinnie said, surprised. "He has his own boat. Why is he chartering?"

"Boat's broke," Petey said. "Something about the gas line. And he had these guys lined up for a fishing trip, so I got em."

"Politicians are lousy tippers," Vinnie said. "Plus they want to tell you how to do everything."

"I don't care what they say, as long as they pay," Petey said. "And nobody around here tips anyway. I remember Jimmy took these guys out last year and they gave him fifty dollars. So maybe they're changing."

"Jimmy took out the Blenny Man?" Vinnie asked.

"Yeah, I think it was him," Pete said, screwing up his face as if it hurt to force his brain to recall. "The Blenny Man and four or five others."

"You know that scrawny little guy never said one word to us on the boat, after we had saved his life…and his boat," Vinnie said. "No thank yous. Nothing. Just shivered, told us to save his boat, and walked away."

"That's more than one word."

"Right," Vinnie said. "Still seems strange."

The bar was almost empty as Petey retrieved his jacket from a hook on the wall and started for the door. Simy started cleaning the counter, an easier process after everyone was gone. She picked up the remaining glasses, gave them a wrist rinse in the dishwater, and set them aside for the washer. Even early in the morning, her dish rag was wet from wiping the counter. But she pulled it from her waistband and gave the counter a quick swipe. Simy didn't start many conversations. Usually the customers urged her into them, but Vinnie was alone at the bar and the two television sets perched in opposite corners of the room were off. They were on for soap operas in the afternoon and all sporting events, but not in the morning when hangovers were common.

"Vinnie," Simy said, "how's Velma?"

"Fine," Vinnie said. "She's at the shop. She said she saw you last weekend at the craft fair at Wesley Methodist."

"I went with Mom," she said. "Mom's been going to that craft thing for twenty years. She always buys something. Sunday she got a piece of plywood painted like a dandelion and stuck it right in the middle of her yard. Can you believe that?"

"Your mom's a good woman, you know that?" Vinnie said.

"You know the first thing I do every morning when I get up. I call my mom just to see what she's doing."

"That's nice," Vinnie said. "I thought you still lived with your folks?"

"No, I moved out when my son was born. That's about six years ago," she said, "I live down the street in the old Graves house. Just renting."

Vinnie knew that Simy had a son, but not much else. Velma didn't think she had ever gotten married, but Vinnie didn't know how to ask without prying, so he let it drop. He sat staring at his beer. Simy realized he was out of conversation, so she moved around the bar to get the beer chest ready for chipped ice. That meant emptying two or three inches of water left over from yesterday. Several years ago Mabel Fergus had hit on the idea of iced beer as a gimmick for competing with the other bars in town. And it worked. Something about ice on the bottle was a special treat, especially in the summer when the boys would pour off the boats hot and sweaty, beet red from sun burn, and tired to the bone. They would often ask, "Gimme one of those iced cold beers." So Mabel moved the beer freezer over to the restaurant for steaks and hamburger, bought a five-foot long ice chest, and put it right in the middle of the bar so everyone could see it. Then she bought an icemaker from some industrial supply store in Baltimore, and every morning filled the chest with domestic beers. Simy carried a case of beer from the back room and lined up the bottles in the chest. Then she covered them with ice, heaped it up, and laid several bottles at various angles on top. That was her invention. A little creativity. Something about seeing those bottles laying on top of fresh ice was an open invitation to drink.

Simy went to the back room for a bucket of ice when the phone rang. Mabel kept a private phone in back for the staff, out of sight of patrons, and beyond the use of anyone not on the payroll. The payphone was out front by the door, and Simy was instructed to give anyone with a hard luck story a quarter for the payphone, but never let anyone in the back room. It was me on the phone. I don't think she recognized my voice, but I called her by name, and asked her to tell Vinnie that I, Ned Shannon, wouldn't be coming to the boat. She said, "I'll do it," and hung up.

I figured Vinnie would be worried, but at least he knew I called. And by noon everybody in town would know where I had gone.

Chapter Seven

Ever since the drowning, I have had two recurring dreams about my brother. The first was of his body rolling around in the waves, being gently tossed and turned by every spasm of the ocean until the seaweed and foam finally drew back and left him anchored on the beach. The second was of his unrecognizable body after it had been nibbled, and dibbled, and dabbed by every little fish in the sea. I read that description in a novel once and it froze in my mind like a song from childhood.

The Sheriff of Hatteras, North Carolina had called at daybreak to say that Jimmy's body had washed ashore during the night, and he asked that I come immediately to help make arrangements. Identification might take some time. Somehow I knew that.

I didn't look forward to the days ahead, except for the somewhat quizzical comment by the Sheriff that there were some strange aspects to his discovery. I packed a small bag with some underwear, a shaving kit, socks, one pair of blue jeans, two shirts and a dozen cigars, which I could live on for a couple of weeks if necessary. I tossed a tie and blue blazer in the back seat of the car and headed for Hatteras, a place I had never been, but a name with some intrigue.

Driving, for me, is a mystical experience. I daydream, never watch the signs, spend a good part of every trip lost and turning around or asking directions from convenience stores, and never remember where I've been. But I'm a safe driver, even with a convertible, and will set off for any destination with the certainty that sooner or later I will get there. But often it's later. After about three miles, I realized there was no hurry in getting to Hatteras. Jimmy wasn't going anywhere. And even after I satisfied this identification business, and arranged with the local funeral director to ship his body back to Parkers, there still would be no hurry. Maybe this is what Jimmy intended to do for me in his will, take away the hurry. Life was now a process, not a series of ambitious goals. And there was no boss to please.

On a long stretch of road through Virginia, I remembered Jimmy once telling me that he liked taking the boat out alone because no one was there to say return. And sometimes he didn't. Once he left Mom a note that said, "Back soon," but he didn't return for five days. He took a small sailboat down to Crisfield, an island off the eastern shore of the Bay where the remnants of a waterman culture live in quiet and diminished circumstance. He tied up at the town dock, and was actually angry when Mom called the Coast Guard to report his disappearance. Even after his return, he was silent on the details of his trip, fearing an inquisition about the many disasters that could have befallen a small boat in stormy seas. "I'm home," was about all he said.

When I found the Hatteras Sheriff, he was leaning against the counter in his reception area, talking to a young female deputy in a starched brown uniform whose hair was pulled back and held in place by a headphone. Her eyes caught me coming through the door. When the Sheriff turned, I held out my hand and introduced myself.

"Come in Mr. Shannon," he said. "We've been expecting you."

He nodded to his deputy in a way that put the phones on hold, and led me into his office, a spartan affair with a couple of pictures of fishermen standing beside their tuna on the local dock. He motioned me to a wooden captain's chair, and lowered himself into a slightly larger chair that rocked back.

"I hope my call didn't reach you at a bad time," the Sheriff said.

"I'm very sorry about your brother. We found him down on the beach yesterday by PJ's Bait Shop. I don't know if you can identify him or not, but we'll go over to the medical examiner's in a minute. He's just across the street."

I thought I had a lot of questions, but didn't know where to begin. I decided to start with the present and work back.

"Is his body... can it be shipped home?" I asked.

"Well, we need to do an autopsy," he said. "That will take a couple of days, but I've asked Doc Winters to start today, knowing you'd be coming down. There are a number of hotels out on the highway. I assume you'll want to stick around."

"I'll stay as long as necessary."

"Good," he said. "We do have a lot to go over."

"You said on the phone there were some strange aspects," I said. "What are they?"

My memory of law school training was remarkably short on criminal law and long on torts. But even if I did know the law, I had no idea about dead bodies or drowning, or what people look like after weeks in the ocean. Furthermore, it was an open question just how much I wanted to learn. Even if it was my own brother, I didn't relish the prospect of identifying his body.

The Sheriff kept flipping through some papers on his desk, presumably about my brother, but it looked like he might be trying to decide how much to tell me. So I figured a well directed question might let him know that I expected to get some answers.

"Any foul play?" I asked, not exactly scaring him with ferocity. "You know, some of the watermen back in Parkers think this 'tuna did it' business is a little far fetched. What do you think?"

"Let's not get ahead of ourselves," he said. "First of all, your brother spent a couple of months in the water. Good that it was ocean, because the salt keeps the skin from decomposing. Fresh water, he would have split open like a ripe watermelon. And it wouldn't take long either."

I almost got sick. I told myself to buck up, get some steel in my gut, think of this as a police report, a piece of paper, not a description of a real person. But I wanted to know, and I feared the Sheriff would censor himself if he saw I couldn't take it.

"Was my brother recognizable?" I asked.

"Not to me," the Sheriff said. "But maybe to you. Anyway, identification isn't really the problem."

The Sheriff shuffled the papers some more until he came to three or four photographs that I could see were of a body laying on the sand. I couldn't help myself, and looked away.

"The autopsy isn't done yet, so I shouldn't be going into this. But knowing you're a lawyer, and a brother, I think I have to tell you that it looks like the boy's death might not have been an accident."

"You mean on purpose!" I exclaimed. I reached for my forehead, and planted both feet on the floor. "You mean somebody killed him." That's about as far as I could reason.

The Sheriff clearly was uncomfortable with this part, even though he had done it several times. He didn't like describing the injury. The medical examiner had explained to him once that in order to examine possible brain damage, he cut an incision across the top of the corpse's head, then peeled the face right off the skull. The image was so strong the sheriff could never shake it.

"It looks like your brother has taken a pretty good lick on the back of the head," the Sheriff said. "But we won't know for sure till the M.E. looks at the skull."

My body went limp. I slouched in the chair, without feeling in my legs or arms, simply numb. This had happened once before. I was visiting Aspen, Colorado in the summer and rode one of the chairlifts to the top of Highlands' mountain. I had skied there before, and never had any fear of heights. But in summer, the lift would sometimes swing wildly, and would rise over deep gorges and blind rims on its path to the summit. What looked like a smooth climb upward over peaceful snow in winter now had a menacing quality of varying heights over jagged rocks. The final lift up the mountain disgorged its passengers about thirty feet from the top of the mountain. One could get off the lift at that point, and cover the final distance to the pinnacle on a winding cow path of a walkway that circled the summit to a concrete platform at the very peak. With a handrail around it, the perch allowed tourists the final spectacle of mountaineering, standing at the summit and surveying the world. But I never made it that far.

Perhaps ten feet from the top, I looked down the mountainside, realizing the edge was only inches from my feet, and fear melted every bone in my body like water on a wafer. I just collapsed on the path. I lay on the ground, pressing my face into the dirt and gasping for air, wanting to sink into the mountain and feel the comforting arms of earth hold me in warm embrace. My mind was racing. I couldn't figure out how to get up, or how to get down to the lift. Then my girlfriend was beside me. She bent close and whispered that she would help me down. I rose to my hands and knees, turned slowly on the path, and crawled down to the lift. Normally my sense of manhood would be shattered by this show of wimpish behavior. But the fear was so great that I had no embarrassment, only gratitude. And now it was happening again.

The Sheriff just looked at me, as if he could see the collapse of my physical systems. But he said nothing. Then he started to fill the space with words.

"You see, we can't figure out how he would hit the back of his head if he went overboard tied to a fish. Maybe he hit the rub rail or something as he went over. Anyway Doc Winters will figure it out."

The Sheriff was starting to ease up a bit, realizing I was still struggling with composure.

"Normally, you'd receive a written copy of the autopsy in four to six weeks," he said. "But if you can stick around, I should be able to tell you what happened in a day or two."

Pulling myself together, I asked, "You all had an inquest, didn't you? What did that determine?"

"Well, there you go," he said. "The Captain said there wasn't anyone else on the boat. Normally, he has a first mate to help bait the hooks and all that. But apparently your brother said he was a fisherman and didn't need any help, especially if the Captain would cut the price. So just the two of them went out."

"That doesn't sound right to me," I said. "I just started running my own boat, but I know Captains don't like to go out without a mate. Although sometimes the mate gets drunk and over sleeps, so the Captain doesn't have much choice. And I don't know any Captain who would cut the price either. A day of fishing is a day of fishing."

"Well, that's what the captain testified. Of course, if your brother was killed, then all bets are off. We better try to find that captain... and the first mate that didn't show."

"What do you mean killed?"

"Well," the Sheriff said, "if Doc Winters doesn't find any water in his lungs, he might not have drowned."

I couldn't concentrate. "You mean," I said, "that hit on the head may have killed him?"

"Maybe. But we don't want to rush this. We'll know tomorrow."

"Can I take his clothes and stuff?"

"I think we better wait. We'll need it for the investigation."

"Let's go do the identification," I said. "I think I need to go for a walk and think about all this."

"There is one other thing that seems a little strange," the Sheriff said.

Oh no. I could feel my heart sink again. Now what was I going to learn? Maybe I should have brought Martha with me. No, this would drive her crazy. I started wondering if I should call her, or what to do if she calls me.

"That other thing relates to his shoes," the Sheriff said. "Do you know what kind of shoes he wore?"

"Shoes?" I repeated, a little edgy from the Sheriff's habit of asking me questions I couldn't possibly answer. "I have no idea."

"When we found him, he had one tennis shoe on his left foot," the Sheriff said. "The strange thing, though, it was blue with yellow dots."

"What do you mean," I asked.

"Does that seem normal? He had on cut off blue jeans and a blue denim shirt. Pretty basic stuff."

"That sounds about right," I said, "but blue tennis shoes with polka dots are definitely out of character. On the other hand he's an outgoing guy, and a crazy waterman. He was here on a vacation of sorts, so who knows."

"One other thing," the Sheriff said. "We think it's a woman's shoe. Pretty hard to tell if it fits because of the condition of the body. But it was on his foot, and I'd guess about a size eight."

"I don't know his size, but it's probably not too big. He was average height," I said. My references to Jimmy kept alternating between present tense and past tense as the picture in my mind fluctuated between the brother I knew so well, and the body on the beach. And then the Sheriff produced the shoe.

"I can't take this out of the bag," he said, holding a plastic bag that he pulled from under his desk, "because it may be evidence. The State boys are going to look for evidence, DNA or whatever they can pull out. But does this look familiar to you?"

I nodded no.

"I should have told you this first, but I have to ask you not to tell anyone about this polka dot shoe business," the Sheriff said. "We're withholding it from the press. God only knows what kind of story those boys would make of this. And if somebody gave him this shoe, we don't want to scare them off."

"What do you mean?" I asked.

"This raises an awful lot of questions. We went looking for that Captain yesterday afternoon and it seems he's taken his boat south, or at least it's gone from the marina and nobody seems to know where. Seems nobody really knows much about that Captain either. Not a local boy."

"What are the questions?" I asked.

"Well, I don't want to get into that. But the doc can tell a lot of things in that autopsy." The Sheriff paused as if in afterthought. "You know about diatones. There's jillions of them in the water. They're the skeletal remains of plankton, and they differ depending on the water they're in. Almost like a DNA for water. Doc can take a little water from your brother's lungs, if there is any, and tell us just about where it came from. He might even be able to tell us if the body drowns in one place and was thrown overboard in another. Hard telling what else he can find."

"What else?"

"Down here we get a lot of drowning. Doc can test something called 'pupal cases,' which I guess are bugs, and tell you within four or five days when the person drowned, even if it was two or three years ago."

"That's great Sheriff," I said, "but what now?"

"You go make that identification," he said. "Then we'll get the autopsy. Then you can go home while we conduct an investigation. In the meantime, you be thinking about anything we should know about that shoe, or about why Jimmy Shannon would have been hit over the head."

* * * * *

Doc Winters had been the local doctor for nearly 20 years, but his real love was being the county medical examiner. He made himself an authority on drowning, which was virtually a necessity in a county with hundreds of miles of shoreline. He was very matter of fact, an attitude he had learned from the families of his victims. Emotions in this situation could be wide ranging, and he found it best to be quick and factual.

"Mr. Shannon," he said, "I'll show you your brother. Just his face. It's not pretty, because of the time in water. But I think you can handle it."

He pulled back the sheet, and I recognized the face only by the outlines of his form. I had seen my brother in every contortion imaginable, in bed, in the water, in wrestling squabbles when I squeezed his head so hard his nose was twisted around his mouth. But nothing like this. I just nodded and turned away.

Doc Winters replaced the sheet and turned me to the door. When we got back to the doc's office, I dared to ask about Jimmy's body, the condition and all. I think it was the nibbled and dibbled on my mind. Doc Winters looked me over before answering.

"Mr. Shannon," he said, "normally the bodies never come back.

The fish just eat them up, or at least they eat where there aren't any clothes. The old fishermen here used to talk about bringing back the big tuna lashed to their boat, and when they got back the tuna was 'apple cored.' Kind of like the 'old man and the sea.' That means the sharks ate the body and left nothing but the head and the tail fin. It's different with people. Usually the bodies come back with only their middle uneaten because of their clothes. Your brother was lucky… at least in that regard."

Then he realized how all that must sound, saying only, "I'm sorry."

Doc Winters had a red leather couch in his office that was along the wall near his desk. He motioned for me to have a seat, rubbed his hand through his thin white hair, and massaged his eyes as if the strain of identification had blurred his vision. The couch looked soft and low and I was afraid once I got down, I would have trouble getting up. But it was the only place to sit. I suspected the doc had comforted a lot of people on this couch, and it was relaxing on purpose. So I made myself comfortable while Doc Winters moved behind his desk, slid some papers around what looked like handwritten notes, and glanced over to see if I was ready.

"Mr. Shannon," he said, "we are going to find out what happened to your brother, and the Sheriff is going to find out who did it."

"You mean you already know it was murder?" I exclaimed.

"Here's what we know. Your brother has a big gash on the back of his head. There are marks on his wrist consistent with a fishing line or a wire leader, and that blue shoe with the yellow spots tells me something isn't quite kosher about that fishing trip. But we have a lot of tests to make and we'll find out. First, we want to know if he drowned or if the head trauma did him in. And that shoe got me to thinking, maybe we ought to run some other tests. We might need to check for sexual activity. Maybe it was more than just tuna that got that boy all excited."

"You mean a woman?" I asked dumbly.

"Well, it seems to me that someone else was on that boat."

The doc pushed his chair back and crossed his fingers in his lap. I had nothing more to say. As feared, it was a struggle to raise myself off the couch.

Chapter Eight

Margot Lillian Wildman saw the wake of a ski boat roll silently under her husband's charter boat berthed at the Bayfront. She braced herself on the deck of the *Lil*, gently touching the diesel engine cover in the center of the boat and righting herself almost imperceptibly, never interrupting her conversation with the clients. Her wide brimmed straw hat pulled firmly over short brown hair gave her a breezy look, almost festive, in this row of work boats filled with fishing parties. Most of the men wore blue jeans and knit shirts with company names over the pocket, faded by long days in the sun. And Lillian, wife of the boat's Captain, might have seemed more natural in similarly basic work clothes. But that was not her style. Although her visits to the *Lil* were few, she always arrived like a butterfly, climbing over the transom as if the wind might lift her at any moment to a far away place. Her brightness always lifted my spirits.

A group of five clients with tennis shoes and faded shirts had gathered on the boat. The welcoming hand of a computer engineer from Washington, D.C. studied her as she introduced herself.

"Hello," she said, "I'm Lil, Pete's wife, and he invited me to join you gentlemen today. I hope you don't mind."

"Hell no, we're delighted to have you," the engineer said. "It's a treat."

"This is my Mother's Day present," Lil said. "Opening day of the season. It's a treat for me."

Pete's charter license allowed six clients on board, in addition to the captain and a deck hand. One member of the party had cancelled, and Pete waited until the last day before inviting Lil to join the group. She didn't mind, of course, knowing that they couldn't afford to turn down any paying guests. And it was still a treat because she loved to fish and didn't get many opportunities.

Pete had been on board for at least an hour, preparing the rods and selecting lures for striped bass. He poured Lil a cup of coffee from his thermos, which she took in both hands so it wouldn't spill if the wake from another passing boat hit their bow. She shifted the cup to one hand and introduced herself with the other. The guests were waiting for introductions and her shapely figure did not go unnoticed. But they seemed like a friendly bunch. Lil didn't fit the mold for most watermen wives, who might be expected to appear in jeans and tennis shoes with a tee shirt that said Swamp Circle Saloon on the chest. Rather, she wore pastels. Pink shorts and a pale blue blouse with sandals that she might kick off once they got underway. She looked more ready for a stroll down Pennsylvania Avenue than a day on the Bay.

Pete and Lil were the future of life as watermen. Their new 42-foot workboat was bare bones in terms of amenities, but cost over two hundred thousand dollars. Pete borrowed the money just as a computer company would borrow to bring out its new software package. He had a business plan that told him exactly how many customers would be needed, on how many days, rain or shine, to breakeven. He knew what his costs would be right down to the eels he bought every morning from PJ's bait shop. And if I asked, I bet he could tell me how many pounds of fish it would take to satisfy a month of fishing parties, although poundage doesn't count as much as quantity in the eyes of a "yellow jacket." The boys who fished in their new yellow slickers wanted pictures of fish to show their wives and friends.

The *Lil* was docked next to the *Martha Claire*, and I watched her unload her party every day, at noon for the half-day trip. Pete charged six hundred dollars a day for a party of six, with three hundred to be paid in advance and another three hundred at the end of the day. I knew this was the future, but still, it wasn't crabbing. It wasn't fishing, really. It was entertainment and marketing, but Pete had made the transition so smoothly that most people didn't notice the change. They still crowded the dock at four o'clock each afternoon to view the catch, and watch Pete move his big filet knife so effortlessly through the fish that it seemed like a lady taking off her fur coat. The skin just peeled away and the white meat of the fish sparkled like a patch of snow in the midday sun. The fish were still the main act, and Pete never brought his laptop on the boat.

Pete liked showing his city clients my working crab boat next door. It was like presenting a 1932 Packard at the auto show, giving the twenty first century customers a look at history. I might have resented that if Pete wasn't such a generous and genuine fellow. He stood on his deck with no hat, hair tousled, and wearing a snappy new tee shirt with his logo on the front. It was a large striped bass about to be reeled in by a bikini clad blonde on the stern deck of his boat. Underneath it said: Join the *Lil*, Charter Boat Fishing, PeteWildman.com.

"I see the *Martha Claire* is stoked up and raring to go," Pete said on the morning we first met. I was stacking crab pots on the aft deck, aware of the activity next door, and wondering if the captain would acknowledge my presence. Pete did it with gusto. He walked to the center of his fishing party, which was stowing its jackets for the day and finding positions along the gunnels, and he shouted to me with a voice loud enough to call everyone to attention. HELLO, MARTHA CLAIRE. The show was on.

Pete reached across the sliver of water between our boats and shook hands. "Glad to meet you Ned Shannon," he said. "I knew your brother well, and I look forward to sharing the pier."

Before I could acknowledge, he turned back to his group. "This is Mr. Neddie Shannon," he said to the party. "He's trying to be a real waterman. A crabber. Sadly, he used to be a lawyer, but now he's recovering. This is his twelve step plan. As you can see he's getting his crab pots ready. There's the bait, in that white bucket. And when we get out in the Bay, I'll show you his buoys. Those are the colorful corks bobbing in the water that mark his crab pots. You all can help make sure I don't hit any of them."

The boys laughed gently, feeling the camaraderie between fishermen, although I had said little. Pete was just starting a banter these boys would know for the next several hours, or however long it took to make their catch.

"Don't let me get a crab line in my prop," Pete said to his clients. "Because my beautiful wife refuses to dive in and cut us loose." Their eyes flickered at the prospect of seeing through Lil's wet shirt. And Lil joined the act as naturally as a glance at her watch. "Not a chance, boys," she said. "One of you will have to go over the side."

Lil cut off suggestive humor pretty quickly. She had grown up around watermen and knew that such talk could escalate rapidly into rowdy behavior, or erroneous conclusions about women's attitudes. Low cut blouses, short skirts, and jokes about sex were magnets for a lecherous mentality. Several of Pete's friends had made suggestive comments to Lil about her figure, and she always turned away. She often said to Pete, "Men are so weak." Letting him know that she expected more from him, and that she knew all men are susceptible to temptation.

Pete had a wide smile that seldom vanished. Watermen would tell of once seeing Pete in anger when a client lost control of his reel, creating a bird's nest of monofilament. But he was never heard to yell at Lil, or swear in public, or exhibit bitterness toward the government, all staples of a normal Captain. Pete liked that title, Captain; used it when referring to himself; and always signed his name as Captain Pete.

Since we met, I have watched Captain Pete steer the *Lil* into the slip next to me without ever touching the pilings. His Caterpillar diesel responds to touch like pushing a pen across expensive paper. The boat grunts deep and soft, like a cat in a basket. As Pete spins the wheel, the stern adjusts just a foot or two, and the boat moves backward like a drawer into a cabinet, stopping without ever touching. I remember my brother telling me that boating is not a contact sport. "Never let it touch the dock," he said. I dreamed of the day I could do it, even with Vinnie helping me.

"Pretty smooth Pete," I said.

"Years of practice," he responded.

"You didn't know him years ago," Lil said. "In our old boat, Pete hit the dock every time. He was just learning. The boys used to stand and watch, waiting for the collision. They called him Willy Wildman."

"How did it get to Captain Pete instead of Willy Wildman?" I asked

"That's when they got to know him," Lil said. "Everybody has a nickname, at least for the first few years. I was scared to death the boys would call him chumbucket or mackerel mouth or some other horrible thing. I kind of liked Willy Wildman. But now it's Captain Pete."

"What's your nickname, Lil?" I asked.

"The girls are Miss," she said. "It goes on the boat. Nancy and Jim Kender have been married 36 years, but it's still Miss Nancy. I'm Miss Lil to the other captains."

Pete was arranging his rods and reels on hooks hanging from the inside roof of the cabin. The reels stuck out the back like handles on an arcade game, and fishing line crossed the ceiling like pressed cobwebs. I wondered how people kept from hitting their heads on the rods.

Pete moved with fluid motion around the helm, every instrument within reach, secured for rough weather, and tested for endurance. The *Lil* floated so placidly in its slip, I could hardly imagine the long days in rough seas and high winds that drove the rain right through the button holes of your slicker.

Every waterman has been through storms. But not many have the good fortune of Pete's friends Harve and Catsoup, who according to Pete, were not blessed with intellectual genius. But an even more precious quality seemed to ride in their bow: luck. Pete liked to tell their story as a way to describe the capriciousness of the Bay; how the weather could turn in an instant; how a waterman's experience and physical prowess meant nothing against a rogue wave; and how only one decision really counted in a captain: knowing when to get off the water.

According to Pete, his friends Harve and Catsoup had been together as crabbers and oyster tongers so long that they almost never spoke to each other. They didn't have to. They first met on a hot day in September nearly 30 years ago. Catsoup simply walked over to Harve's boat, the *Minerva*, one day on Jenkins Creek and asked Harve for a job. Harve looked him up and down, dismissed the shirt patches and dirty boots, but noticed the muscles in his arms and his frugality of words. Every captain wants a strong quiet mate, and Harve was no different, although he didn't expect his new mate to stay for thirty years.

"Come aboard," Harve said. "Help me with these pots and you're hired."

The *Minerva* was a wooden deadrise, built in the 1920s and re-paired and painted so often that you could see the outline of every plank. It had not been cleaned as often. The deck was worn and al-most black. A commercial crab potter is allowed to fish three hundred pots per person and up to nine hundred per boat. The *Minerva* was only thirty-foot long and wouldn't hold 300 of the two-foot square pots, even if stacked over Harve's head. But he ran that many pots anyway, and if he took on Catsoup he could run another 300.

The day Catsoup walked up, Harve was sitting on the engine box cleaning pots, a never ending task. His new employee didn't respond directly to the job offer. His response was to sit right down beside a stack of the wire pots and begin pulling dried bits and pieces of ale-wife bait out of the mesh, and straightening wires bent or broke. Two mangy cats were lurking nearby, waiting for scraps among the debris. The stranger took a swipe at one of them and said, "Git. We'll make cat soup of you."

"Catsoup," Harve said to his new mate. "I pay every day when the boat docks. I get paid, you get paid."

"Sure boss," Catsoup said. The name stuck and so did the friend-ship.

Harve told Catsoup to be on the dock next morning at six o'clock, bring his own lunch and the coffee would be provided. No beer. This was a business and Harve had seen too many boats go down with a blurry-eyed crew.

As they eased out of Jenkins Creek the next morning, Harve watched Catsoup closely to see if he knew the ropes. First thing he noticed were traditional white boots, crusted with mud around the bot-tom and smeared with green moss along the edges, as if they had walked a million miles through Bay marshes. He had a canvas jacket over a green cotton sweater, layered over a flannel plaid shirt, all of which could be peeled quickly with the morning sun. His face was weathered, red around the chin, but young. Harve searched Catsoup's eyes and they were clear, set on high cheek bones and devoid of wrinkles. Catsoup had some miles on his boots, but his youthfulness was still evident on the back of his hands. Furthermore, he walked quickly from one position to another, moving from the cleats that held the spring lines, to the stern where he could fend off any contact with the dock, to the hatchway where he could note the path of the bow through the water. Harve was impressed, although he had known other one day wonders that never finished the week. With Catsoup, he would wait and see.

Harve's crab pots were set in a designated area just off Clark's Point, about a half hour run from the Jenkins. The Point was named after General Boswell Clark, a confederate general who commanded Maryland troops on the western shore of the Bay, and who kept a watchful eye for land parcels that he could purchase in better times. Those times came and the name Clark is still found on a half dozen towns and inlets that boast one peculiar geographic circumstance. They all jut out into the Bay and have deep water ports, which must have been high on the General's priority list. On the charts of the area, the Clark properties look like a series of narrow peninsulas jutting out from the shore. Clark's Point survived and prospered primarily because all the other points had washed away over the decades, or their deep water deteriorated to shallow channels, or someone changed the name. This parcel of land had just the right combination of sea grasses to attract the crabs and create spawning areas. Watermen had been setting pots off the eastern edge of Clark's Point for years, and Harve had all 300 of his on a line stretching directly into the morning sun.

Harve guided the *Minerva* and her 1957 Chevy V-8 engine out the mouth of the Jenkins and set a course directly for Clark's Point. The engine had a low roar to it, much as Harve remembered when it used to power his uncle's car. As he reached the eastern end of the Point, just a few dozen yards from the fishing pier, he turned east and headed into the morning sun that was still young and shocking the darkness with an orange band across the water. When the sun hit Harve full in his face, he knew he was on course, exactly one half mile from the head of his line of red and green buoys. He felt good about the day and muttered, "Looks good so far." He might have been talking to Catsoup, but on this first day he had no idea whether the new mate would respond, or talk at all for that matter. Catsoup shook his head, but said nothing.

Harve had pulled nearly thirty pots, with crabs in every one, when the first small cumulous cloud appeared on the starboard side. He didn't notice it in the excitement of the catch. It's not often, in fact almost never, that the first strings of pots are full, and Harve couldn't wait to get them in the boat. So he didn't pay much attention to the storm coming until the waves started whipping the hull and the clouds would occasionally hide the sun like an eye patch in flight.

Catsoup seemed able to carry a fast pace emptying the pots, so Harve edged the engine faster, hoping to get as many crabs as possible in the boat in case the storm intensified. Chances of Harve stopping his work were slim. He had worked in rain so hard it beat entirely through his clothes, and his legs had stabilized in seas so rugged that the boat would not hold a line. Yet wind made him nervous because it sneaked across the water, sometimes hidden in front of a brilliant sun that lied to you about the dangers. Sometimes the wind started as a breeze so gentle that Harve welcomed the coolness on his face, and then it could rear up like a rodeo bronc that meant to throw his boat out of the water, and Harve would cuss and swear and call upon the devil himself to bestill his wrath. But he never lost control of the *Minerva*, and today would be no different.

As the chop of the wave increased, Harve stumbled at the helm, caught himself on the hatch door, remembered his purpose, and reached inside the berth to grab the soiled life jacket. He never wore it, and probably wouldn't even admit to his friends that he had one, but he carried it for these moments. He pulled the jacket out of the hatch, grabbed the helm with his left hand, and righted himself just as the boat took a portside wave that lifted *Minerva* into a three quarter turn on her side. He glanced at Catsoup, who looked worried, but seemed stable as he wedged himself between the side of the boat and the engine box. Harve threw the life jacket at Catsoup's feet to be sure it didn't go overboard but said nothing. Catsoup felt it hit his leg. He looked up and saw where it came from. He slipped it over his head, and quickly tied the one canvas ribbon that held the vest around him. The other ribbon had been torn off years ago, and Catsoup doubted the vest would hold air for a second, let alone save his life in a rascally Bay. But he was a sensible man and he saw that Harve was not going to leave one crab in the water as long as his boat would float.

Catsoup braced himself once more, and wedged his toe under a cross slat near the deck of the boat. He grabbed the next pot that broke the surface, and the engine roared with a spinning, whining shriek as a huge wave lifted the stern and propeller out of the water. For an instant he was level, suspended in mid air, and the boat felt like an oasis. Then it fell. The wave left a sharp trough behind it and *Minerva* fell to the bottom. Harve hit his head on the roof of the cabin, but it kept him from being swept overboard. Catsoup was left in the air. Harve glanced toward him in the midst of confusion and Catsoup was suspended like a cardboard cutout, still holding the pot, looking frozen and unafraid, but at least three feet above the boat. Then he fell. And

Harve was astounded to see him fall flat in the bottom of the boat, the one place where he was unlikely to be hurt. For the first time, Harve exclaimed to himself, "That lucky bastard."

Then he turned back to the helm, hoping the prop was far enough in the water to give him some traction. He yanked the stainless steel steering wheel hard over, needing to turn the boat into the waves. He knew the most dangerous position was to get "side to" a wave. The boat would roll over and either take on enough water to sink, or simply go straight down. He didn't quite make the turn, but a sheet of brackish bay water came over the bow and hit Harve full in the face. It burned, but at least Harve knew he had made enough of a turn to avoid capsizing. Then the wave rolled under him, once again raising the stern. Harve glanced over his shoulder to see if anything was left on deck, some empty pots, a gaff, two wooden oars and an assortment of baskets and buckets. All were gone. And so was Catsoup.

Chapter Nine

Catsoup splashed into the water with a thud, and held. He didn't sink or wrestle the waves. He simply was captured in a cradle of foam and water that cast his face to the sky. It was gray as a plastic airplane, a strange object to be the first thing that popped into his mind. From his youth no doubt. Then he turned his head to look for the *Minerva*, finding instead only flashes of suds like a roiled dishpan. It was a lull like he had never known, so he decided to accept it as a child accepts slumber, but then it ended. He began to feel a mattress of water raise him until he could briefly see Harve in the stern of his boat, wrestling the wheel at the rear helm station and looking frantically at the water. Catsoup knew they would search for him, but he had no control, and was soon whisked away in a distant direction.

Harve called the Coast Guard the second Catsoup flew out of the boat. His eyes scanned the water until they ached. But he didn't see that moment when Catsoup's body was lifted, twisted, and rolled. And he didn't see that moment when Catsoup came down hard on what felt immediately like wood. For a moment the water separated and Catsoup felt the plank under his chest. He grabbed the board with both arms. Then realizing it must be eight or ten feet long, he tried to find the end of the board with his leg, raised his knee over the edge, and clung to the object like so many surfers he had seen on television. He wrapped his body as tight as possible around the board so that even a dip beneath the waves would not wipe him off. He roared up in the air, and down the back side of ugly waves. And then he went black, later remembering nothing. But he rode that board to its inevitable landing on Clark's Point. Right up to the pier, like a power boat delivering its passengers, the long plank hit the steps at the end of the dock, wedged itself in some fashion, and when Catsoup regained consciousness, he was laying on the dock with the storm about to die out around him. He had not recognized anything since being thrown overboard as normal, or natural or planned. Finding himself suddenly on the dock, his body beaten into submission, he simply yielded to the experience, closed his eyes and slept while the storm blew itself out around him.

Harve had struggled with the boat and his emotions, but he couldn't find Catsoup. The Coast Guard patrol boat that pulled along side *Minerva*, called a helicopter to help make the search. They asked Captain Harve if he wanted help, and he said nothing, exhausted by the waves and frightened by the loss of Catsoup. The Coast Guard offered to tow the *Minerva*, but Harve refused. That would be another indignity no waterman wants to endure. Instead, he started for nearest land at Clark's Point. About a hundred yards from the pier, Harve squinted toward the dock and wiped his sleeve across his eyes. He was astounded to see Catsoup's plaid shirt on the dock, and what looked like his body. He began shouting and screaming until the figure on the dock slowly raised his head and began to clear his thinking. Catsoup sat up as the first ray of sun broke though the clouds. Harve climbed from the boat, righted himself on the dock, and watched as Catsoup struggled to his feet. As often happens on the Bay, the wind was dying and the waves were diminishing as the two figures met. They gave a kind of half hug, grabbing each other's shoulders, and Harve said, "Catsoup, you are the luckiest son of a bitch I have ever known. But don't you ever leave my boat again."

They just stood on the pier for several minutes. Finally Harve said, "Let's take the *Minerva* back on down to Parkers and get her ready for tomorrow."

"OK," Catsoup said. And another idiom of the Jenkins Creek watermen was born: "The luck of the Cat." They all wanted it.

Chapter Ten

Pete Wildman's boat was fiberglass, no maintenance they called it, meaning no painting required, no rotting wood to be replaced, and no bright work to be varnished and stained. But it still needed the barnacles scraped off every year and a new coat of bottom paint applied. Pete was proud of his boat, partly because he had done most of the work in building it. The boatworks had supplied the hull, the basic finish work on the cabin and the electronics. Pete respected fiberglass, but he didn't like it. He hated the work of finishing because it meant breathing the fine white dust that fiberglass produces. But he added the rod and reel holders himself, put in a special bench seat that was more comfortable than a captain's chair, and added the fish tanks and assorted cushions. He was a proselytizer for the many savings that fiberglass produced over wood, but it never felt the same.

"Ned," he said one morning as he poured coffee from his thermos, "the future is in charter fishing. The crabs are gone. You ought to convert full time."

Pete pushed his hair back under his cap, as I straightened up from arranging the crab baskets in the stern.

"I'll be glad to help," he continued. "We could clean up the *Martha*, give her another coat of paint, add a few rod holders, and you're in business. The hard part of this game is marketing, and Lil will show you how to do all that. Hell, she'll build you a web page, design you tee shirts, and probably fish with you if you buy her breakfast."

Pete and Lil were fast becoming my best friends in Parkers, partly due to the circumstances of our boats being berthed together, and part-ly just due to their generosity. They were always helping people, and genuinely concerned about other's welfare. They could be intrusive. But they had the knack of backing off quickly if people didn't appre-ciate their interest.

"Pete, let's talk about this later," I said. "Things are so compli-cated right now. Let me get my life in a groove, and then we'll see."

"I understand," Pete said.

It was a yellow sun that flashed across the water this morning, and gave a new color to the fishing boats. But it was bright and full of promise, no doubt contributing to Pete's expansive attitude.

"What have you found about your brother?" he asked.

I was reluctant to discuss this issue with Pete, or anyone for that matter, but he was my best friend on the water and I needed some help. Truth is, I didn't know where to begin. The circumstances of Jimmy's death seemed so far away because it all happened in Hatteras. Yet the roots of the problem had to be here in Parkers, and I didn't know the first thing about investigating crimes. My specialty was torts and liabilities. And I hated the idea of guys sitting around the Bayfront bar spreading rumors about the murder. I also knew that every time I asked a question, it would fly up and down the dock like a scalded seagull. But there didn't seem to be any alternative.

"Pete," I began, "I need to ask you a couple questions. But I really don't want to start a bunch of rumors. Can you help me?"

"Sure, Ned," he said. "What do you need?"

"You've got to protect me on this."

"I will," Pete said. "Don't worry, I won't say a word."

"OK," I said. "Here's my problem. I need to know any reason why Jimmy could have gotten into this trouble. Why would anyone hurt him? Do you know if he had any enemies, any strange activities,

God forbid, any affairs or angry husbands? What was he up to?"

Pete pulled his hat down on his forehead, stared at the deck as if pondering a serious question, then slowly looked up.

"I don't know anything," he said. "No affairs that I know of. Some said Simy, maybe. But that was before he got married."

"Any fights?" I asked.

"Well, let's see," he said. "There are always fights. But none that you'd take all the way to North Carolina. Maybe he got into something down there."

"The autopsy said somebody hit him," I offered.

"What about the tuna?" Pete asked.

Leave it to a waterman to ask about the fish. "What do you mean?"

"What about the fish?" Pete said. "I thought he caught the big one and it took him down."

"The Sheriff down there isn't sure there was a tuna," I said.

I didn't want to tell Pete what the Sheriff really felt. "He said there were some marks on Jimmy's arms that could have come from the leader line, but he suggested that the Captain hit him, threw him overboard about a mile off shore, and that's why the body surfaced."

"Do you mean the Captain killed him on shore, and took him out to sea just to make it look like an accident?" Pete suggested.

This kind of speculation was my fear. Everybody immediately jumps to their own conclusions, their own conspiracies. I couldn't see how to walk the conversation back, so I decided to march it forward, away from the details of the crime.

"The key now seems to be to find that Captain," I said. "The Sheriff is looking. But I haven't heard anything."

Just as Pete was about to ask another question, Lil emerged from the Bayfront to say goodbye. She had joined Pete for an early breakfast, lingered inside while he readied the boat, and now was ready to leave. She saw us talking and gave her infectious wave with a big smile.

She walked to the stern of the *Martha Claire* and asked, "How's business?"

"I'm starting to get the hang of this," I said. "Haven't made much money yet, but I can see how the water claims its victims. Crabbing is addictive."

"I don't mean the crabs," she said. "I mean the law. Are you gonna make it?"

"That's a little forward, isn't it?" I said in mock shock. "Of course I'm gonna make it."

"That's the right approach," Pete chimed in. "Everybody makes it at something. It's just that some ways are slower than others. Some of these boys go from crabs to oysters to rockfish and end up eating most of what they catch. But we all make it."

"Now I assume you're talking about the water and not the law," I said.

"Of course," Pete said.

"Same is true of other businesses," Lil said. "My dad would crab in the summer, carpenter in the fall, do a little plumbing if you needed it, and paint your house if times were tough."

"Yeah," I said out of professional pride. "But law is a little different."

"Not really," Pete said. "It's just another service to put a few bucks on the table. Think of law as just another way to afford fishing. Hell, it doesn't take much money for that."

I shuddered to think how my colleagues at Simpson, Feldstein and James would react to the firm being treated like a plumbing contractor. We had such high and mighty causes in the law firm that even defenders of killers would pose their trials in terms of high moral concepts like protecting the innocent, fairness, or everyone deserves a defense. I certainly believe those principles, and could not have defended so many scoundrels without that moral underpinning. Indeed, I assume my practice in Parkers, although now limited to buying houses, selling boats, and wills, might someday return to a criminal defense. But the reality of my practice today is mighty close to making a little money to go fishing. And remarkably, I feel rather good about it. Perhaps that's why Pete's insight had been so helpful with his charter boat.

Pete Wildman's success is largely due to the internet. He knows computers, developed his own website called *Miss Lil's* Charter Fishing, and writes a weekly column that chronicles the exploits of all his clients. It has the dual objectives of advertising his prowess at fish finding, and feeding the egos of customers he hoped to lure back for repeat performances. The website had almost replaced word of mouth as his best source of customers. Pete had paper place mats printed that featured a drawing of his boat, and a caricature of Lil. It was distributed to every restaurant in Parkers, none of which had tablecloths, and all of which accepted anything free. You couldn't sit down to lunch any place in town without reading that the best fishing in Maryland could be reviewed on www.Lil.com.

Lil also led Pete into a life of philanthropy. She understood instinctively that "giving" didn't require a lot of money, or a foundation, or a press release. It just required a big heart and tons of enthusiasm, which she and Pete certainly had, not to mention the most giving of instruments, a boat.

Lil invited me to go on their annual fundraising crab feast trip as a way to meet the other watermen, and a long list of their friends and clients from charters past. The money was to pay medical bills for Anna Mostelli, eleven-year-old daughter of an oysterman from the nearby village of Shady Side. Lil didn't seem to know much about Anna's disease, or how much the treatments cost, but she knew that no oysterman could ever afford his medical bills, and the Mostelli's needed help. She also knew that every time she asked Gus Mostelli about his daughter, he cried, long silent tears that slid through the cracks in his face like the gallons of bay brine that had gone before. He didn't even wipe them anymore; he just kept talking. It made Lil so happy to be helping that she couldn't wait to schedule another dance at the Elks Club or a blue grass festival at the ballpark. And Pete always offered a fishing trip as grand prize in the silent auction.

We boarded Pete's boat on a Wednesday night, bound for Teddy's Crabhouse on Poplar Island, about an hour's ride across the Bay. Six other Captains had volunteered their boats to the fleet, conveying about one hundred guests at fifty bucks apiece.

The last guests on our boat were Burlington and Marilyn Mansfield. Burl was wearing a seersucker suit of gray and white strips, a blue button down shirt, red tie, and panama hat. He could just as easily have been going to a steeplechase race. He seemed overdressed for eating crabs, a somewhat messy affair involving newspapers on the tables and rolls of paper towels for wiping the bay seasoning from your hands. This did not deter Burl, however, who had nothing to prove to anybody, and probably planned to eat raw oysters instead of crabs.

Marilyn followed closely, dressed in chiffons and silks flowing in the breeze like fireflies in the night. As a couple, they floated where others stumbled. They stepped off the dock, toes touching the edge of the boat as someone's outstretched hand guided them into the party.

"Hello Ned," Marilyn said. "So nice to see you."

"The news about your brother is quite alarming," Burl said. "Any new developments?" Burl was essentially a no nonsense conversationalist. With fifteen or so people on the boat, Burl shook hands all around and returned to where Marilyn and I were discussing the weather. He edged around so he was facing me, and shielded himself from lip readers.

"Nothing new on Jimmy," I said. "Still looking. They're now thinking bar fight. So who knows?"

"I need to talk with you about the CRI," Burl said. "You tell those boys we might go for a scaled back version of the resort. Build it as a replica of Captain Amos Song's house so it's consistent with our architectural history. No bricks. No neon signs. Not more than one hundred guests."

"Burl," I said, throwing up my hands in exaggerated disbelief. "How can they make money? Even at seventy to eighty percent occupancy, that's not enough to pay the mortgage, run the restaurant, and build a pool."

"Why do they need a pool?" Burl asked. "They have the Bay."

"Why do you environmentalists think you can prescribe every window and table in the place?" I said.

"Because the devil is in the details."

"No," I said, "it's because you want control. You want to tell people how to live. You want us all carrying recycling bins on our boats."

"No Ned," he said, "we just don't want your pollution."

"I hear you want to outlaw those little ski boats because they make too much noise," I charged. "What's next?"

"Ned, my boy, you haven't been here long enough," Burl said. "I respect you because of your father. But don't think just because you're a lawyer, you can start running things in Parkers."

I realized it was time to lighten up. I also realized I had better get over to Burl's house some afternoon soon and pour a new foundation for our relationship. I wanted his friendship and I enjoyed the country gentleman nature of his home. Burl had a tobacco barn which anchored sixteen acres of waterfront on the West River, with four hundred feet of bulkhead built by R.T. Smith, the oldest and best pier builder in Jenkins County. R.T. charged a hundred dollars per running foot for a new dock and bulkhead, with pilings topped with copper that glistened brown when installed and turned green with age. Apparently Burl was ignoring the environmentalists who claimed that pretreated pilings killed the fish and led to depletion of the oyster beds as well.

Tobacco barns dotted Southern Maryland, remnants of a vibrant past. The agriculture that had flourished for two hundred years, fed generations, and spawned a reliance on slavery and cheap labor, was passing. In 2002, the State adopted a buyout program that paid farmers not to grow tobacco, and the auction houses closed for good. Some of the older farmers grew small patches of tobacco, just for a little cash and a good memory, but they had to truck it nearly a hundred miles to St. Mary's county to sell. That practice would not survive long.

The tobacco barns were bought by developers, moved to new home sites, and considered ambience for gated communities called Plantation Village or Tara. They were never called Tobacco Way, however, because public attitudes toward smoking were the executioner that eliminated tobacco in the first place. People want to be reminded of the bucolic joys of plantation life without the painful side effects of smoking, cheap labor, and segregation. The innocence of a tobacco barn was the perfect symbol for a twenty first century Levittown featuring five-acre home sites and white fences that set off a riding ring or a three stall horse barn.

Burl's barn at least was not an ornament. A thriving farm had once flourished on the banks of the river before it was broken into irregular parcels of fifteen or twenty acres back in the nineteen thirties. Tobacco barns were open just above the foundation, by perhaps a foot or two, to allow a free flow of air to dry the leaves. Similarly, the side boards were loosely fitted, so large cracks allowed air from all directions. Only the roofs, usually tin, were built to keep out the elements. Even when they became rusted and twisted, they kept the barn dry as a bone. Burl renovated one corner of the structure to serve as a tool shed and carpentry shop. No more moisture. He wouldn't have rusty tools, and kept his wood chisels clean. He even polished his favorites. In the main part of the barn he had built the *Lady Marilyn*, a thirty-four-foot skipjack that now rolled in the soft eddy of waves at his dock.

I was a little surprised that Burl was so worked up about the Resort project, but this didn't seem like the moment to further explore his attitude. Indeed, he had given me a message to deliver to my new client, thus making me a player in the game. If the SARP (Stop All Resorts Please) people had decided to use me as a conduit to Chesapeake Resorts International, so much the better. I probably owed Burl something for my new stature. Maybe I could give him a break on his will, although that couldn't be much. In any case, I was in the loop, and that felt good.

Teddy Harvest was a legendary waterman who ran his crab house and inn as a way station for politicians searching the eastern shore of the Bay for votes, and for corporate giants and movie stars who showed up for the duck hunting season. Pictures of Teddy with all the governors of Maryland, even the ones who went to jail or left in disgrace, adorned the walls. Teddy knew how to take care of his guests, and he had six slips vacant for Captain Pete and his fellow Captains.

I stepped off our boat as it edged toward the dock, grabbed the stern lines thrown by Lil, and tied them to the dock cleats. I was about to help Lady Marilyn off when somebody tapped me on the shoulder. I turned and was more than surprised to see the Blenny Man. My initial fear was that I couldn't remember his name, and it seemed unlikely that he preferred being called Blenny Man.

"Hello Ray," I said. "Let me help these folks onto the dock." I set about the task while Ray Herbst waited. When the last guest was off the boat and walking up the dock toward Teddy's, Ray began again.

"Nice to see you again, Mr. Shannon," he said. "I hope to see you inside." As he turned to follow the others, I noticed he was wearing black dress shoes with his khaki's. Somehow this man never quite fit in. He clearly wanted to, with his Caterpillar cap and dark green knit shirt with red letters that said, "Fishermen Get Caught At The Bayfront." But the black shoes were a giveaway. I kept thinking someone should take his shoeprints, just in case a serious crime was ever committed in South County.

Later I found Ray at the bar, eating raw oysters on the half shell, smothered in ketchup. The oysters were magazine quality, presented on a large plate shaped like an oyster shell, and in enough quantity to suggest he was determined to get his money's worth. The oyster take from the Bay was down this year, but still it seemed unlikely Teddy would run out before the Blenny Man could get his fill.

Blenny had another unusual quirk. Instead of using a fork to lift the oysters, or throwing his head back and sliding them down his throat the way some oyster eaters do, he slurped them into his mouth like an anteater. I watched closely for several minutes in order to time my arrival when his tongue might be approaching a rest stop.

"Ray," I said gingerly, pushing myself onto the stool next to him, "I trust your boat is running smoothly. I don't remember it too well from that afternoon we found you in the water, but it seemed like a nice boat."

"It's a dandy," he said. "Did you notice that day how it kept a perfect circle? Newest thing. Newest thing. Like an automatic pilot."

"Well, I'm glad we were there," I said, trying to turn the conversation. He didn't seem too comfortable with the possibility he might have to explain how he fell overboard.

"I saw you at the public meeting on the new Resort the other night," I said. "But I didn't hear you testify. Do you have an interest?"

Actually, I knew which side he was on, the environmentalists. But I didn't know why. He was a developer, a builder who had locked horns with the environmentalists in the past, and a man who had fought tooth and nail over county permits to tear down a tree. Suddenly, on the biggest land use fight to ever hit Jenkins County, he becomes a tree hugger. I made a note to find out if he had contributed to the cause, and how much.

"I just think this resort is too big for Parkers," he said. "We'll lose our village atmosphere. We'll have to build houses and schools and sewers everywhere."

I think when he said those words, he instantly realized they were arguments for a quality of life that he'd been arguing against for years, and probably seemed strange even to a newcomer like me.

"I know that may seem strange, coming from me," he said, "but it's all a matter of scale. We have to keep things in proportion."

This all seemed a little glib to me, and totally unnecessary to have to listen to at a waterman's charity event. I edged off the seat to leave.

"Wait Ned," he said, adopting the more familiar term. No more Mr. Shannon. "I just want you to know I appreciate your pulling me out of the drink the other day. Also, I'm glad you represent CRI. Maybe we can work together some day."

"Thanks Ray," I said. "I'll see you later." And moved away from the bar, wondering what in the world that conversation was all about. I started it, but whose side was he on in this fight?

The return trip to the Bayfront was mainly a matter of keeping warm. The dark settles into the Bay like an ice cube in a glass of tea, and suddenly the world is cold. The spray from the hull brushed over the gunnels and soaked those standing too close. It sent shivers that never stopped. Pete was heading for the barn and must have jacked up his engine to full cruising speed. It was a rough ride as the *Lil* slammed against some of the waves, not enough to be dangerous but enough to throw the passengers off balance and leave our legs tense and tired.

Tying up at the Bayfront was like the end of most trips, boring and unremarkable. The guests exited rapidly, just wanting to get home and shower the smell of Old Bay crab seasoning from their hands and face. I hung back, mainly to help Pete clean up his boat. He shut her down pretty quickly. Without fish to clean or rods and reel to refit, a quick spray of the deck by the first mate was all it took.

I stopped by the *Martha Claire* for a routine check of the bilge pump, locked the cabin door, and started for my car. Pete and Lil had already left. I noticed that the Bayfront was still open, although Simy was turning out the lights. I figured I could use one quick drink to take the edge off before going to bed.

I pulled the front door open and its hinges squeaked. It had a brass handle with large splotches of brown tarnish, but no brass toe plate across the bottom. The wood had splintered from water exposure and the corners had rounded from being kicked or slammed. The grease from working fingers of plumbers, electricians, boat mechanics and every other tradesman in the county left large stains you could see in the shadows. As I opened the door, the single light bulb overhead danced the shadows so it was hard to tell the dirt from the light. This was significant only because washing your hands in the Bayfront forced you to confront the dingy bathrooms with sinks that carried the fingerprints of earlier patrons, especially at the end of the day. I had washed my hands on the boat so I gingerly pulled the door open.

It was always dark at the bar, but I had never entered when it was empty, leaving the place with a lonely feel, as if I shouldn't be there. Then Simy's voice, tired and a little edgy, called me in.

"Come in, Ned," she said. "I saw you tie up and thought you might stop by."

"Thanks, Simy. We had a good trip to the island. Made a few dollars for the cause. I think people enjoyed it."

"That's good," she said, "Lil and Pete do a lot of good work around here. For new folks, they understand what it's all about. Can I get you a beer before closing?"

"Thanks," I said, edging onto a stool. "Are you about to shut down?"

"Close," she said. Simy continued to drag the dish rag around the counter, not functionally, but in a slow even motion suggesting a long and understanding relationship between her and the wood. She had a history at the bar. Fights and brawls, words screamed in anger, deals made for motors and secondhand boats, spilled beer and broken bottles, even a couple of bullet marks from trajectories through the high windows on the street side of the building. Simy had often stared at those windows when she came to work, wondering how the shooter could have gotten high enough to put a bullet through the window and down as low as the bar. Her conclusion was a truck cab, an eighteen wheeler, passenger side. At least those giant trucks were rare enough that she didn't worry much about it happening again.

"Ned," she said, "we haven't had a chance to talk. How do you like being back?"

"Great," I said. "It takes some getting used to. But I like the people. The pace is so slow here it's like being retired."

"Not if you've always lived here," she said. "Not if your life depends on showing up every day for work."

"Sorry," I said. "I didn't mean to imply anything. I'm just adjusting, that's all."

"Have they found your brother's killer yet?"

"Not yet," I said, realizing the word must be spreading.

"Sorry about Jimmy," she said. "He could be so sweet. I remember when he first started using his boat for charter fishing, and the crabbing of course. My daddy said that was another sign of the end. He said when the boys go from catching fish to kissing ass, we're in trouble."

"Well," I ventured, "I'm still fishing."

"Look at Pete and the *Lil*," she said. "They have a new sonar that tells them where the fish are located. GPS tells them where to go. All he has to do is bait the hooks, and take care of the guests: that's the tough part, ice, beer, tee shirts, hats, seasick medicine and deli sandwiches. God only knows what it takes to pamper those people."

"That's the future," I agreed.

"I don't care," she said. "I just hate to see change."

"Why?" I asked. "You're a beautiful young woman. Change is good for you."

Simy was wearing a black tee shirt, tucked into her jeans, that even late at night exposed her ample breasts and full figure. In fact, now that I thought about it, she must have tucked her shirt since I came in. Sprucing up a little, as my granddad used to say.

"Neddie," she began, "I used to live with my folks over on Jenkins Creek. My daddy would come home with a big batch of crabs and my mom would steam them into the best Sunday afternoon crab feast in this county. And Daddy would bring home oysters, and we had em raw, on the half shell, fried, baked and every other way you can cook em. My brothers and sisters had a wonderful life. Our own little boats tied up at the dock. We'd go out in the evening and drink beer and float in when the sun came down. I even lost my virginity in that boat. My boyfriend laid down in the bottom and I sat on him. And every time a wave came by I would float up and down on that boy. It was the best sex he ever had. And I didn't even know what I was doing. But that's life on the water. Livin and lovin just kind of run together. We didn't plan anything. We just ate, and fished, and swam and made love as it came along."

"What happened to the boy?"

"What boy?"

"The one in the boat."

"Oh, that was Kevin. He became a waterman. Worked for my daddy for a while, and then got killed in a car wreck. He was a nice boy."

"My daddy owned so many businesses around here, nearly every boy in the county worked for him at one time or another. He owned a liquor store and even the grocery store for a while. But they never seemed to work out, and Daddy would drift back to the water. Those crabs were always there, free for the pickin."

"When did your dad retire?" I asked.

"Several years ago," Simy said. "I don't remember when. How can you tell? One day he started collecting social security, so I assumed he was 65, but he's gone now."

Simy seemed within herself, talking about her father as if reflecting on a distant past. She took another drink of beer, and set the bottle down gently. She seemed to soften in the dark, and I started to wonder if she might enjoy an evening at the Willard.

"My daddy was always looking for opportunity," she said. "I remember once he decided to get in the "buy boat" business. It used to be that restaurant and other buyers would take your crab baskets right off your boat, pay cash, and bring them back the next day. Then the refrigerated trucks started showing up. They would meet you at the dock, and pay you better money because they could carry more fish, or oysters, or whatever and deliver them longer distance.

"My daddy looked at that and said to himself, 'Why can't I do both?' So he bought a used refrigerator truck, just a pickup with a cold box on the back, and bingo, he was in business. This was back in the fifties, when nobody had to worry much about licenses and permits and all that stuff. Anyway, he loads up a ton of oysters and heads for a big restaurant on Long Island. As he finishes unloading his oysters, three guys come up behind him and grab his arms. They throw him against the truck and give him a warning.

"This is our territory and don't ever come back." Then they threw him to the ground and walked off. But Daddy was a pretty tough old bird, and he still had a half truck of oysters left. So he pulls himself together, and drives into New York City to deliver the rest of his load to the Fulton Fish Market. That's a big market down on the tip of Manhattan that's been there for years. So he finishes unloading his truck to all these Italian boys and bang, the same three guys grab him from behind. They say, "Didn't we tell you not to do business here?" Then they hit Daddy, and knocked him down, and kicked him. He came home in terrible shape, even with a broken arm. Mama got him all fixed up with liniment and all of her home treatments, then took him to Annapolis to have his arm fixed. The next day Daddy didn't get up till noon. But he put an ad in the paper for that truck, and that was the end of the fish wholesale business. Two days later he was back on the Bay, crabbin."

"Did you go to college, Simy?" I asked. That was a Washington question. Sometimes the old ways crept back and reminded me again that the cultures had changed. At the Willard, I always asked girls about college, jobs and what neighborhood they lived in, hoping to strike a line of conversation. In Parkers, we ask about family or boats. I shouldn't have asked Simy about college, because most waitresses haven't gone to college, and some are embarrassed about it, not because they didn't have the brains or the talent. The problem was money, and the fact that few families made college an important objective. Getting a job or married were the important goals.

"I have been working right here all my life," Simy said. "Sure, I left for a while. I had big jobs in Baltimore, and down in Miami. But I came home. They didn't work out."

"Did you like Florida?" I asked.

"I loved it," she said. "I drank a lot of beer and spent a lot of nights on the beach. But after a few years I realized I hadn't met one boy with long-term intentions, and no job ever lasted more than a few months. High turnover everywhere. No future down there."

"When did you come back?"

"A few years ago," she said. "I got a great job with an insurance company in Washington. But it wasn't much different than Florida really."

"Everything temporary," I suggested.

"No. Everything about sex. I worked for three bosses and they all propositioned me. I said no and I never got promoted. One day I called my mom and said I want to come home. She made one call to Mabel here at the Bayfront and here I am."

I was getting tired and decided to let the conversation drop. It was quiet as I reached for my last drink. Simy said nothing, but she lifted the bar top that allowed her to escape the barmaid's pen, walked be-

122

hind me and sat on the stool to my left. I hadn't noticed that she had left a bottle of beer on the bar, almost directly in front of her present location. She slid the bottle closer, drank, and then wiped the condensation from the bottle. She wiped her face with the bar rag, possibly leaving more stain on her face than she removed. But she had been sweating, and small beads remained on her forehead. I was a little surprised by the feeling of familiarity, of sensuality in the darkness of the bar, but it was there. I tried to look at her closely, sitting just inches from her face, to judge her age and the hard times that must have lodged in her pores. But she was pretty. Her skin was smooth, and I wondered why she looked more attractive up close than from a distance. Most times it's the other way around.

"Promise me you'll be careful," Simy said. She looked directly in my direction, although it took a few seconds to make the eye to eye connection. She moved her hand to my leg and slowly stroked my thigh. I couldn't tell if it was sexual or just out of friendship, and I didn't really know which I wanted it to be.

"I promise," I said.

She stared at me with warmth. "Neddie, you're so sweet. And here's my promise to you," she said. She moved her hand to cover the zipper of my jeans, and rapidly flicked one finger to record the unmistakable offer.

"Goodnight Ned," she said, moving quickly off the stool and back behind the bar.

Chapter Eleven

I was working on a little property dispute involving a small water-front community of cottage dwellers who claimed ownership of a thirty-yard tract on the water. The Community Association also claimed ownership, so now I'm trying to sort out the history of competing claims. Community children would put their crab pots in the water at the end of the tract, and in the past, when most of the homeowners liked each other, there were picnics on the property overlooking the Bay. But since the issue of ownership was raised, the ensuing squabbling and animosity between the Community Association and homeowners bordering the property pretty much ended the picnics.

Unfortunately, my clients were the two families who lived on either side of the easement. They got together one Sunday afternoon and decided that they owned the property, and that it wasn't community property at all. At least not the legal kind. They examined their deeds and discovered that the two of them owned the property, no easement was recorded, and that in fact the community was using the property due to the largess of their deceased relatives, who had invited in the neighbors some fifty years ago. Their first step in reclaiming the land was to notify the community. Their second step was to ask Pippy Plotkin for a real estate appraisal of the value of the property, which they excitedly learned was several hundred thousand dollars. And their third step was to hire me. Not that reversing that process would have changed things. But I would have preferred to have been first.

I was going over their deeds when the Calico Cat, Effie Humboldt, pushed open my office door.

"Effie," I said with some surprise. "Come in. I was just thinking of you."

"Ned," she said, "you come and go so fast, I never get to see you. But I hear about you all over town. The watermen think of you as an apprentice. I think they waiver between fearing you'll be lost in a storm, or leave town over anguish about your brother. They don't get many newcomers in this business and they hope you'll make it."

"Thanks Effie," I said. "They've been very helpful."

"How's the law business?" she asked.

"Not bad," I said. "Parkers may be the luckiest town in America. They haven't needed many lawyers. A few spats between neighbors, but not many lawsuits and very few contracts. People here don't seem to worry much about getting things in writing. They build houses without contracts. They even die without wills. Actually, it could be a gold mine for me."

"Have you had any bad experiences?" she asked.

"No," I said. "I didn't mean that. Just different experiences. I had a guy come in yesterday who had built a new bulkhead on his waterfront property. He hired old Sam Sharpe from over at West River, who's been building piers here for fifty years. Most people say he's the best. Anyway, it seems Sam pulled on to my client's property in his beat up 1973 pickup truck, looked over the job, then walked from one side of the waterfront to the other, turned around and said, 'It's a hundred feet and I'll do it for fifteen thousand dollars.'"

"My client said that sounded fine, and asked Sam if they needed a piece of paper of some kind, a contract. Sam said he never used a contract, so my client observed that fifteen thousand was quite a bit of money and he would like a piece of paper. Old Sam seemed a little baffled, but he smiled and said sure. Then he walked over to his truck, which had papers of every kind stacked on the passenger seat, on the dash and the floorboard. He fished out a small pad of paper and pencil, walked back to my client and wrote the number, fifteen, on the pad, tore off the page and handed it to my client. My client was laughing so hard he didn't even mind when Sam asked for five thousand as a down payment."

"But six months later old Sam came in with his rusty crane and a bull dozer, dug out the old bulkhead, set about twenty pilings in place, and finished the job in every way except replacing several tons of dirt between the new bulkhead and the yard. Then big as you please, he walked over to my client and asked for another five thousand dollars to replace the dirt.

"What could my client do? It might take weeks to get someone else to replace the dirt. And they might not do it right. So he paid. Now he's coming to me to get some of his money back. And, he didn't even keep that little piece of paper with fifteen written on it. That's business in Parkers."

"Have you talked to Sam about it?" she asked.

"Not yet," I said. "My guess is that Sam was so mad about being asked for a contract of some sort, that he just decided to screw the guy. And my guess is he still feels the same way."

"Who's the client?" she asked.

"I can't say," I replied. "But he tore down a cottage and built a big glass house on the property, and I suspect old Sam saw all that and said to himself, this guy can afford it so I'll show him how things work in Parkers. And he did. I doubt we'll ever get a penny back. But new people are coming here, and their lawyers are coming with them."

"You're not like that Ned," she said. "You're a good and fair man."

"Effie, I love you for that. And that's why I have a special request."

"Remember, my husband's a judge, so don't you make any indecent offers," she joked.

"Nothing like that," I said. "I'm told you are a very successful business woman. Your shop is well stocked and beautifully decorated. And I need help."

Effie got a worried look on her face, fearing a request she didn't want to deal with.

"How about managing my office," I said carefully. "Not phone calls or daily stuff. I'll do that. But how about part time, see that bills are sent out, taxes paid, cleaning lady shows up, and files are kept in order?"

"Why Ned Shannon," she said, a smile of appreciation on her face, "thank you. But I have a shop of my own to run. I don't have time to be keeping your books."

"Well, let me try one other track," I said. "I just bought a little piece of property overlooking the Bay down in Osprey Cove."

"Congratulations!" she shouted. "You're a Parkerite."

"Not yet. You see, there's no house on this property. It's only a quarter acre overlooking a little marshland, but I figure I don't need a dock cause I have a slip at the Bayfront. And I don't want a yard to take care of. And I don't have kids who need space. I just need a view, all the way to the edge of the earth. I want to see the curvature of the planet under a pale blue sky."

"You get all that with a quarter acre?" she asked.

"I do if I build a little house on pilings. I want to put it about 15 feet in the air, overlooking the marsh and anybody who walks between me and the mud."

"Can you afford this?"

"I can if we do it right. The land cost ninety-nine thousand dollars. And I can spend another hundred thousand for the house."

"That's not going to do it," she said. "You didn't let that Pippy Plotkin sell you property with the idea that one hundred thousand would build a house on it."

"Well, maybe. But that's what I need you for. How about helping me with the plans? Maybe a little decoration and general oversight."

"Ned Shannon, I don't know beans about building a house. And I don't decorate for bachelors, whether they're lawyers or watermen."

"Here's what I want to do, Effie. I want to build a two bedroom, two bath, French Colonial, with one big room for living and dining, and the bedrooms above it. And here's the coup de grace. I will park my truck under the house, right beside an elevator. How about that, an elevator to the top floor, and French doors on the main floor that will let the Bay breezes blow through every room."

"Ned, you are nuts. It sounds clever, and beautiful, and I can just see the sunsets from the balcony. But this is Parkers, not Paris. Are you crazy? Nobody in Parkers has an elevator."

"Why not me? What woman in Parkers wouldn't want to come home to see my elevator?"

"I will not be a party to debauchery," she said. "But I would love to have an elevator. And I'm happy to see you're settling in. I also caught that remark about parking your truck under the house. Does that mean the Saab is about to be history."

"I think so," I said.

"Well, here's how you do it," Effie said. "You start driving by those empty lots near the liquor store, and the First Methodist Church, and Flossies. Trucks for sale are parked there all the time."

"What about the Ford dealership over on the highway?"

"You're not gonna buy some fancy truck with leather seats and a stereo system. You want a used truck about three years old with a couple of scratches on the side that will carry a few dozen crab pots. You want a working truck that you can park with the rest of the boys down at the Bayfront."

"Is that necessary?" I asked.

"This is as close as we come to image building in Parkers," Effie said. "And you want to pay cash. You know why watermen pay cash; because they have to stay flexible. No mortgages."

"You mean don't buy what you can't afford?"

"No, I mean storms, and broken legs, and red tide, and state regulations, and divorces, and all the other uncertainties of working on the water. Get yourself a good used truck and park that sissy convertible of yours under the house."

"You're starting to sound like my business manager."

"Not a chance," Effie said. "Just a friend."

Chapter Twelve

A slim, silent figure dressed in blue jeans, black and white tennis shoes, and a black tee shirt walked quickly around the back of the Bayfront Inn, keeping in the shadows, heading for the dozen or so charter fishing and crab boats anchored along Jenkins Creek. He walked past the fish cleaning stand on the edge of the pier, put his hand assuredly on one corner of the scaling tank, and turned toward the *Martha Claire*. Plenty of clouds tarpapered the sky and the boat offered no reflection in the night.

The visitor never broke stride, moving directly to the stern of the boat, hopping over the gunnels, and crouching beside the hatch cover that allowed access to the big diesel engine. He raised the hatch and braced it quietly open. He pulled a small flashlight out of one pocket, and a pair of wire cutters from the other. In seconds, he reached past the engine and clipped the electric wire to the automatic float switch, disabling the bilge pump that emptied any water that collected in the bottom of the boat. In another second, the hatch was closed and the intruder hopped off the boat and back on the pier. He reached for the garden hose wrapped in a circle where Ned had left it after cleaning his boat earlier in the day, draped it into the boat, and turned on the spigot. A steady stream of water slid across the deck, as deadly as poison in the blood.

I was still asleep at 5:30 in the morning when my phone started ringing. Calls that early pierce the night like fire alarms. They usually mean problems on the water, or boats that won't start, or other watermen who need a ride. I stretched, knowing the ringing would not stop, cleared my throat, and reached for the phone.

"Ned, this is Mabel Fergus," she said. "Somebody swamped your boat."

She didn't hesitate to see if it was me, or give any details, or prepare me for disaster. In fact, she used the word swamped, which every waterman knows means a deliberate act against your boat. I simply said, "Thanks Mabel, I'll be right there." Explanations wouldn't help. There is no official to call when your boat goes down, especially at the pier. Police can't help. Firemen don't raise boats. No one is threatened. And a hundred of your best friends can't raise a boat. The only person who can help is someone who can be sympathetic. I would call Vinnie from my cell phone. He's no doubt up anyway.

I drove through Parkers in a haze of incomprehension. No one had ever committed a deliberate act of malice against me before, at least not a physical act, and not one I could instantly recognize. In law practice, there were times when a colleague undercut me with a partner, but that was an understandable move to advance someone's career. Perfectly understandable in that world. I was mugged once on the streets behind the Capitol, but even that was less shattering. It was for money, not for the express purpose of hurting me. Swamping my boat was different, a singular act aimed at hurting me in some unspecified, yet meaningful, way. Somebody wanted me out of the crabbing business, or out of Parkers, or out of my law practice, or out of investigating my brother. This latter reason seemed the most likely, yet I wasn't really investigating anything. The police in North Carolina were doing that. I kept asking questions about my brother, but mostly I just wanted to know his last years, what was he doing, how he ran his business. But I had offended somebody, or scared somebody. Hell, maybe it was an old boyfriend of Simy's. Every kiss that has ever been stolen in Parkers has been passed around the bar like cold beer. Who knows what emotions that might stir from somebody thinking I was interested in Simy. And the fact is, of course, that sinking a boat with a garden hose is a childhood trick known by every boy on the Bay.

All of these possibilities raced through my mind, and clouded my vision, leaving Parkers a cold and lonely place, smudging the rouge of warmth that had always coated the place. Even the familiarity was gone. The trash in the ditch, fast food wrappers thrown from truck windows, plastic bags from the grocery, seemed luminous and disgusting, signs of a trash community I had never noticed before. Why was I here? What about this horrible threatening town had ever attracted me? I passed the grocery and it seemed foreign. There was no longer the anticipation of meeting friends, of seeing neighbors, of discovering relationships. The town was just buildings, and pickup trucks, and I almost missed the parking lot for the Bayfront.

Several crabbers were readying their boats for a day on the bay, putting their bait buckets in place, stacking the bushel baskets for the catch, and checking oil, water, and hoses on their engines. Most of these Captains had already checked out the sunken *Martha Claire*, her outlines just visible beneath the water. A couple still stood on the edge of the dock, peering down at the wheel house that emerged from the water, signaling shipwreck in a backdrop of normalcy.

All I could do was join them, and stare.

"I'm sorry, Ned," one of them said. "You better get her up fast. Less time in the water, the less damage."

"Who do I call?" I asked, which seemed like the only useful information I needed.

"Call Johnny Noonan over at the Marina," the Captain said. "He's got a salvage business. Knows how to raise boats. I don't see how somebody could claim salvage rights on your boat right here at the dock, but stranger things have happened. I'd get that crew working for you as soon as possible."

"Then what?"

"Well, once you get her up, then you have to check the engine and the wiring. You can repair the wood, dry her out, and repaint her. But the engine and the electronics; that's the problem."

"Thanks," I said. I seemed so helpless. Actually, that's a common feeling on the water. I remember other situations, when the motor goes out in the middle of crabbing, or when crab pots have been emptied by a yellow jacket or even another waterman, when another boat is bearing down on you, or an island appears that isn't on the charts. There are just so many ways that the Bay can overwhelm you. But I never even considered my boat sinking at the dock.

"Thanks boys." I turned to go in the restaurant, only to be confronted by faces pressed against the window, not looking at the boat, but peering at the owner to see his reaction. Word had spread that Ned Shannon was here to see his boat, and people actually left their scrambled eggs just to see the look on my face, the desperate fear in a waterman's eyes when he sees his livelihood under six feet of water. They misjudged me, of course, because crabbing isn't my life. But it's still a difficult and fearful time. In addition, word had spread quickly that it was a deliberate act. From the moment the first waterman arrived this morning, found my boat, and pulled the garden hose out of the stern, everyone in Parkers knew I had been the victim of a threatening act. And they had a hundred reasons for why this could have happened: stolen crab pots, infringement on another's fishing area, a girlfriend, money or bad debts. It could be anything. And they wanted to see how I would respond. This incident would be passed on by Bayfront customers and Parkers watermen for years. The only unwritten part of the story was me. How would I react? And my response was to visit the oldest and most knowledgeable friend I had in Parkers, Mansfield Burlington.

* * * * *

Burl was working in his barn, standing tall and erect at his woodworking table, with classical music floating softly through every grain in the wood. I stopped for a minute outside the door, watching him make calculations on a piece of scrap paper. He was slow and deliberate, deciding the angle of the wood he was about to cut. To make a mistake would be to waste wood, and lose time. Burl was careful to do neither.

He looked up, and beckoned me in. I closed the door gently, not disturbing the music, and felt the immediate warmth of the place. A small cast iron stove was burning wood and casting off considerable heat on a fall morning. Coupled with the two overhead lights dangling from the ceiling, and the music, the room had a special softness in which the light settled into nooks and crannies of cobwebs and darkness. There were no sharp edges or shadow lines associated with corners or excess lighting. I was aware of organization, every tool aligned in its shelf, or holder, with perhaps fifty screwdrivers at soldierly attention along the wall. A band saw, and a wood press, and a butcher block no doubt retrieved from a yard sale, stood as room dividers as I walked to the work bench.

"Nice to see you Neddie," Burl said, reaching for my hand. There was an incongruity between Burl's starched blue work shirt and his broken fingers, cut and scarred with physical labor, black fingernails from accidental pinches between lumber, and darkened hand lines from the dust and grease of daily work. Burl made nearly everything in the barn, from hoe handles to saw blades, and he had gadgets that were invented for measuring, or drilling, or marking when he was building the skipjack. Yet his voice was elegant and smooth, refined with words from the volumes of his reading.

"I hear you had a little trouble this morning," he added.

"Burl," I said, "thanks for seeing me. I need a little help figuring this thing out. I just can't understand why this thing happened."

I kept calling it a thing, because what do you call a physical attack on your property, and an implied threat against your existence. An assault. A threat. It was sure as hell more than a bump in the night, which is what my mother might have called it. She always took the long view of matters, and predicted that most everything would pass. She would take the position that the sinking of my boat was an act of God, because somebody lost their faith and their goodness, deciding to commit this violence against my boat. Certainly, she would never discuss the motives involved, or an investigation of any kind. We would simply raise the boat, repair the engine and electronics, give it a new coat of paint, and continue catching crabs as if nothing happened. To her, this would be an aberration, never to be repeated. I could never understand this logic, except that it must have come from her abiding belief in John 3, verse 16, a biblical direction that according to my law experience was almost never followed. Indeed, this seemed like a defining moment to me, as the politicians in Washington might say, and I had offended someone mightily. Most likely, someone in Parkers had a hand in my brother's death, and now I might be included in their plans.

"Burl," I asked, "have you heard any animosity toward me? Have I made anybody mad?"

"I don't think so," he said. "You charge too much for wills, but that hardly seems like a boat sinking offense."

"How about your work at the CRI?" he continued. "What are you doing for them these days?"

"Not much really," I said. "I have to go to a cocktail reception in Annapolis next week. Meet the Governor. Pretend I'm a real waterman. Probably don't have to say anything."

"Ned," Burl said, "you are a real waterman. You go out with your pots; all kinds of weather; sell your crabs to the buyer, or anybody who shows up at the dock. That's a waterman. Maybe not an honored waterman. After all, this is your first boat to sink. But you're a waterman, so don't make sport of it."

"Sorry," I said. "Do you think it's a waterman who did this?"

'No, I don't. You're not a threat to watermen. Do you think those few bushels of scrawny crabs you catch are going to empty the bay? You're not fighting over a girl. You don't owe anybody money. That takes care of the great motivators for malice in Parkers. So look elsewhere."

"It must be my brother."

"Maybe, but this place is hard to figure," Burl said. "Just last week a good ole boy waterman from down on Broom's Island killed his ex-girlfriend for going out with another guy. Thing is, the waterman hadn't dated this girl since high school. Hadn't even seen her in a couple of years. In fact, last time he saw her, he beat her up, was arrested, and ordered by the Judge to never go near this girl again. But he was a good ole boy, came from a long line of Parkerites, ran a little crab house on the island to sell his own crabs, and made his daddy proud. Hell, he'd been in trouble with the law over and over, but the judge was his uncle so all he ever got was probation.

"Couple weeks ago, he runs into his high school sweetie at the grocery store, and she's with a new boyfriend from Washington. That night he went to her house with a shotgun and blew her head off. Said he couldn't stand to see his true love with a yellow jacket. Now with that kind of rationale, any damn fool in the county could have swamped your boat."

"What do I do now Burl?" I asked.

Burl looked at his lathe, glanced up at me, then returned to sharpening his saw blade. I guess he wanted to see how I was taking this whole affair, decided I really was in the dark, and started again.

"Well," he said, "here's what I'd do. First, call the police. Somebody else will, if you don't. Fact is, they are probably with the boat right now, or will be by the time you get back to the Bayfront. So let them know you called. They won't find anything, of course. Won't spend a minute looking. They'll figure it's just some kind of fight between two watermen and forget about it. But you need that police report for insurance, and just in case this is some nut who just likes to sink boats.

"Then, my advice is forget about it. Get insurance money if you can. Forget the police. Raise the boat, put it back together, and get back on the water. You got to show your stuff. These old boys around here have been on the water for four or five generations. They've seen every natural disaster known to man, and they've seen boys like you wilt in the midday sun. Don't wilt Neddie. Just get back on the water."

"Burl, you've been a great help. Thanks," I said. "You just gave me the same advice my mother would."

"One other thing, Ned," he said. "Find out what happened to your brother. That's family, and that's different."

Chapter Thirteen

Martha Claire Shannon's nickname, and the only name her high school friends called her, was Marti. I always thought it was a good name because it conveyed her wonderful spirit, a sense of irony and humor that was quick to rise, and a youthfulness portrayed by optimism, even innocence. She never believed the worst in people. If she saw evil, or cynicism, she just ignored it. And her chirpy little girl voice, even in her thirties, enhanced all of these qualities. First time phone callers thought she was Jimmy's daughter. And other women liked her because she never threatened them, and always lifted their spirits with an infectious laugh that was a part of her basic fiber.

That day at the Bayfront bar was the lowest I had ever seen her, preoccupied with her husband's death, fearful of the future, wading into the unknown world of single motherhood. But I had seen her many times since, always up, planning her future and her daughter's. There was something special to learn from her, about honesty and loyalty. And I started looking forward to her visits because she treated me like a real brother, with confidences and secrets that only a family can keep.

It was Sunday morning, and we often went to brunch together, the only time most of Parkers' restaurants served breakfast. Usually she called to suggest a place to go. Today, she just asked to come over, and we would decide later on food. Coming up the sidewalk she carried Mindy under one arm, and a large manila folder under the other. It was a cool fall day, and she wore a dark maroon sweater, with the usual four or five gold bracelets and a simple necklace with a pearl. She had a sense of style that suggested wealth, even with blue jeans, and even without an education. The bracelets were uncommon among working women. They get caught on tablecloths, or clothes, or boats. But Marti would simply take them off in those situations, and put them back on later. They weren't expensive jewelry, mostly purchased from the kiosks at the Annapolis mall, but they said hello. Marti often said her mother advised her to wear clothes that said hello. And she did. I met her at the door, and she looked worried.

"Ned," she said, "I want to talk about something." She moved to the couch, arranged herself cross legged, and held the manila folder tight to her chest.

"A couple weeks ago," she began, "I went to the doctor to see why my legs hurt. Sometimes they would jerk involuntarily. My doctor took some tests, and stuck little needles in me, but nothing turned up, so she recommended an MRI. I guess she thought, 'Let's get a picture of her brain and work down.'"

At this point I'm beginning to feel quite nervous. An MRI on the brain usually meant cancer. I had met a waterman with brain cancer just a few weeks ago. He was a big strong guy, who had retired from the water, but worked tirelessly in the community for church and civic affairs. He was diagnosed with a brain tumor, had an operation on the back of his neck of some kind, and came home to recover. I saw him at the grocery store a few days later and he seemed pretty healthy, a little pale from the hospital, but walking and talking like normal. Two weeks later he was dead. I never knew the details, but it left me fearful as Marti mentioned the MRI.

"I got the pictures back yesterday," she said, shaking the folder to indicate I was about the see them. "And the doctor says I have a meningioma, which is some kind of tumor in the brain. She wants me to go to some kind of brain surgeon immediately to talk about an operation. Will you go with me?"

"Of course, Martha," I said, adopting her formal name, I guess to signal I took this seriously. "I'll be glad to go. Do you have an appointment?"

"Tuesday," she said.

I couldn't think what to say. The questions were there, but I didn't want to say anything insensitive. The thought, Martha is going to die, ran through my mind. Then incomprehension. How could this be happening? She didn't look or act sick. She never complained. There must be an explanation, or at least some confusion.

"What do the pictures show?" I asked, assuming she brought them to be shown.

Martha bent the clamp on the folder, and pulled the negatives free. I held the top one up to the light and could see about ten different views of her brain, but what they meant was blank. Martha moved next to me on the couch, and started to describe the MRI.

"This is the brain part," she said. "And you see this dark area, like a hole of some kind, that's the tumor."

I almost gasped. The tumor ran from her neck to the top of her head. It was the whole center of her head. I kept staring at each picture, hoping somehow that the angle would change, and the picture would change, that it would be smaller from the back, or the side. But it wasn't. I just stared, trying to think how to ask the most devastating question; she looked at me as if judging my reaction. I wondered what bravery looked like in this situation; how would tears look. My God, she must be scared. I'm scared. But she only looked sober, frightened by the unknown. Then she said the only negative thing she ever said about the whole situation.

"I always thought you would go first."

It was the kind of thing a wife might say to her husband, and I suppose I was a surrogate husband. How could this happen? I thought of my brother. Two catastrophic deaths, unexplainable and unfathomable, to a husband and wife in the same year. What had our family done to deserve this?

"The doctor said she thinks it's meningioma, which usually isn't cancerous, but we need to see the neurosurgeon as soon as possible," she said. "That's Tuesday."

I noticed the change to 'we' in her language. It felt comfortable, and I was glad to help share her load, although it raised so many questions. What about Mindy? Regardless of what this was, who would take care of Mindy? What would be my role? I felt ashamed of that concern, ashamed that I would think of myself.

"Let's not try to speculate about what we don't know," I suggested. "Let's go to the computer, learn all we can, and make a list of questions for the doctor."

"OK," she said, and began to slide the negatives back in the folder. She put her arms around my neck and held on, for dear life, as my mother used to say.

* * * * *

The office of Doctor Robert Noon seemed a little spartan for the man who was going to save Martha's life. I guess I expected a modern high rise with large glass windows, modern furniture, and a larger than life feel, as if this indeed was the office of the savior. But Dr. Noon's outer office was small, with a leather couch cramped in one corner, a receptionist behind a six-foot counter, with metal files behind her. The doctor's inner office was a mirror image. The only thing over-sized was Dr. Noon, who stood about six feet three inches tall, with large puffy fingers, and a huge belly that hung over a wide leather belt, and left little doubt that this man either drank or ate a lot, without remorse. My immediate reaction was: how does he hold a scalpel, and how does he get close enough to the operating table to work? But he was friendly. He welcomed us to two captain's chairs in front of his desk, and said he had been called by Martha's regular doctor with a briefing on the MRIs. I had trouble concentrating, in spite of the seriousness of the moment, because I couldn't resist the yellow post-it notes stuck all over the walls, the sides of his desk, the window ledges, and any other spare location. I was surprised he didn't have some stuck to his belly, a sizeable oversight. Most remarkably, even though some of the yellow post-its were only a couple inches square, every one had some kind of scull drawing with a brief note. I couldn't tell how he kept the patients identified, but maybe the little yellow slips were just educational and not supposed to be patient specific. Honestly, most brains look alike. So I forced myself to turn back to the doctor, who had taken the MRI pictures from Martha, and was sticking them on back lights behind his desk. Under this intense light, the tumors lit up like Christmas bulbs in row after row of brains.

Dr. Noon explained that meningiomas are normally hard, encapsulated tumors that grow slowly, and seldom are malignant. That was the good news. Unfortunately, they are also very hard to remove, often entwined with nerves that affect various parts of the body, and can be fatal if severed. Noon said Martha's tumor was extraordinarily large, and probably had been growing very slowly for fifteen or twenty years.

"Is that why I didn't have any symptoms?" Martha asked.

"Probably," he said. "I'm surprised you haven't had balance or hearing problems."

"I have," Martha said, looking at the floor. "I just never said anything."

Noon was direct but sympathetic. "Well," he said, "here's the problem. I think I'm a very good surgeon, but I know I'm not good enough to do this operation. That's the difference between most surgeons, you know. Those who don't know their limitations."

"What if we do nothing?" I asked.

He focused directly on Martha. "It will kill you."

"How much time?" I asked.

"Soon," he said. "Maybe within a couple of months. You see, this tumor has grown so slowly, that it has pushed the brain nerves back into the head without causing them to react. But now there is no more room to push. And as the tumor grows, it could hit the nerve at any time that could kill you, or paralyze you, or make you go blind, or do something else."

"Who can we go to?" Martha asked. She was remarkably stoic; no tears, or screams, or expressions of fear or even exhaustion. She just wanted to know how to get rid of this problem.

Noon looked at the ceiling. "I tell you," he said, "I only know one doctor who could do this. Nablani in Philadelphia."

"Who is he?"

"Meningiomas are all he does," Noon said. "He used to be chief of neurosurgery at a big hospital in New York. But they weren't rich enough to buy all the equipment for brain work, so he left for Philadelphia. They promised him the moon. He's writing a book. And every day he does this kind of surgery."

"What about other great hospitals: Hopkins, Mayo, others?" I asked, thinking it might be good to find someplace closer to home.

"They are all good hospitals," Noon said. "But do they have the doctor who can do this? I don't know."

"Give us the three best hospitals or doctors in America to do this operation," I said, a bit more aggressively than I intended, especially if the answer was in Los Angeles or some other distant location.

"I only know two," he said. "Nablani and the Ward Institute in Austin. They only do meningioma and they teach it to other specialists. You should get some copies of these MRI pictures that you can send to other hospitals."

I couldn't think of any other questions at this point. It was clear that we were on our own. Perhaps Noon could sense that we were starting to feel the loneliness of the search ahead.

"I have phone numbers which I'll give you," he said. "But I should add one thing. All of these hospitals you go to may tell you, 'Don't go to Nablani.'"

"Why?" I asked quickly.

"Because Nablani only cares about the operation. He takes risks the others won't take. He has no bedside manner and you may never see him again after the operation. But I still think he gives you the best chance."

After a long pause, he said, "Good luck. And if you run into questions along the way, call me."

Martha and I walked out of the building in silence, climbed into the car, and simultaneously let out a sigh of exhaustion.

"I'm so sorry," Martha said. "That I had to come to you, Ned. I don't know anybody else that could have handled that conversation. Let's go home."

"And start contacting hospitals," I added.

* * * * *

The first person I called was Vinnie. I needed to tell someone about Martha, just to get the feel of the words. Saying it made it real.

I had experienced this same phenomenon when my brother died. One can understand a car crash, when the twisted metal is there to witness or a long illness when the effects of disease are evident in appearance. At least there is some time for preparation, to think about what is happening. But with murder, or a brain tumor, there is no time and no rationale. So talking it through was necessary, at least for me. And Vinnie seemed like the perfect candidate. He might even have some perspective, or some experience, that would be helpful.

Vinnie wasn't home, but I found him at the boat. It was evening, and red sky left its warm glow on the deck of the *Martha Claire*. She had been delivered back to her slip by the Marina only yesterday, completely retrofitted following the sabotage. She received a new engine, a 345 horsepower diesel, and all new electrical wiring. Her old wooden body looked as good as new, with a white paint job that sparkled in the sun, probably brighter than it ever would again. With the first rubber boots that set foot on her deck, the ageless deterioration process would begin again with crab pots, and buckets, fish guts, and crab claws, and hundreds of other appearances that scrape and scar a boat. It was a rebirth that seemed slightly incongruous in view of the human events of the day. It made me sad that people can't be put back together quite as easily.

Vinnie was arranging and rearranging the fishing rods that hung from the cabin ceiling. The deck was clean and empty of crab pots. I had a couple of white plastic chairs, the kind that most discount stores sell for seven bucks apiece, stacked near the engine.

I climbed into the stern, and separated the chairs for Vinnie and me to talk. Watermen often sit in the back of their boats, just to think and survey their world, sometimes to have a drink of bourbon, or ponder their problems. Vinnie heard me hit the deck and he turned away from the cabin to say hello.

"Hi Ned," he said. "How did things go with the doctor?" I had told Vinnie I was going with Martha, and the broadest outlines of why. He could take the boat out by himself, or try to find a mate, or not go at all. I left it up to him. It turned out he did go crabbing in the morning, caught several bushels, and returned to the Bayfront early afternoon.

It took me about forty minutes to spill the whole story to Vinnie, including descriptions of how I felt about the situation.

"Vinnie," I said, "I feel so close to Martha, certainly like family. She is, of course. But I never felt this close to her when Jimmy was alive. But now I do. I have to take care of her Vinnie, to get her through this. I don't know if she's going to die. I don't know anything really. I suspect we're just starting down a long road together."

"How's she holding up?" Vinnie asked.

"I can't tell. Too early," I said. "It will take her a while. But I'm sure she has already thought about dying, and about the welfare of Mindy. Beyond that, I don't know."

"How can I help?"

"Vinnie, the first issue for me is the boat. Martha doesn't have much time, so we have to start now to find a doctor, a hospital, and a place for Mindy. I would like to just put the boat on hold, shut down the law practice, and deal with this problem. Would you like to run the *Martha Claire* yourself? I'll take ten percent for expenses. You can hire your own mate. Just run it like you own it."

"How long?" he asked.

"That's the hard part. I don't know. But let's figure two months at least."

* * * * *

146

Our first hospital was in Philadelphia, a large teaching hospital with a celebrated neurosurgery department. It was recommended by one of the partners in my old law firm. I discovered that as people found out about Martha's condition, everyone seemed to have a recommendation, perhaps a family experience, perhaps the name of a doctor they had read about or seen on television. We couldn't figure out how to judge these things. In addition, if one doctor was recommended, another doctor would say he's a quack. There seemed to be significant jealousies and competition between doctors and between hospitals. So we made our own rules: we wouldn't consider anyone who didn't have three positive recommendations; work in a teaching hospital which meant they did a lot of operations; and be located near affordable hotels where I could stay, or Martha could recover if rehabilitation was necessary.

The first hospital was modern and seemed quite efficient. We soon came to realize that the quickest way to judge a hospital was by their computer system. The best gave us a personalized plastic card with an identification number. If we visit the hospital a hundred times, all we had to do was show the card. As one nurse said, "You only check in once a lifetime here." The most remarkable aspect of this system is that not every hospital has it. We immediately crossed those off our list.

In Philadelphia, we were assigned a young neurosurgeon who had studied at the Ward Institute and specialized in meningioma. This made Martha feel some comfort.

"I like the feel of this hospital," she said. "And at least the doctor was trained someplace we have heard of, someplace that Dr. Noon has recommended."

The doctor walked directly to us, shook hands, and introduced himself. He took the MRI's from Martha and invited us to follow him into a nearby conference room. He was young with a smooth southern draw, wore horn-rimmed glasses, and was thin enough for his clothes to hang straight with sharply defined creases. I couldn't get over the fact that we were choosing a strange man, in a very short time, in a strange place, who would either save or lose Martha's life. What if the very best surgeon was ugly, or cold, or arrogant or any of a hundred other things causing us to reject him? What if the doctor is warm and wonderful, but a terrible surgeon? We had already heard about several of these. There didn't seem to be any way to ascertain competence, so we decided to consider recommendations, education and compatibility. It all seemed like a crap shoot anyway.

It was beginning to be a ritual for the doctors to stick the MRIs onto a backlight and start their analysis. Remarkably, every doctor was different. The Philadelphia doctor was meticulous, moving from frame to frame, showing the size and location of the tumor. We had learned to wait patiently for the part where remedies were discussed.

"Martha," the doctor said sympathetically, "this is very difficult. This tumor is so large, that I expect the top half could be hardened, with some nerves inside the solidified area. The bottom half may be more liquid because it's newer growth. I don't believe there is any way we can remove the entire tumor… without threatening your life."

We were silent. The doctor stopped, letting it all sink in before starting again.

"We might be able to put a shunt in your head and drain some of the spinal fluid off the brain. That would relieve the pressure and the immediate danger."

He stopped again. But Martha interjected, "How would that solve the problem? Would I just live with a drain in my head?"

"For a while," the doctor said. "But I think we could do a skull-based surgery that might allow us to remove the lower half of the tumor, the soft part. Then if it's growing slowly enough, you could live with the other part remaining in place."

The reality was setting in that no one thought an operation could take this tumor out. But Martha pursued it. "What are the risks?"

Now the doctor stopped. He paced back and forth behind the long conference table, looking at the MRIs from different angles, as if he might notice a crevice that would allow a different conclusion.

"I would say this," he began. "If we assume an operation to remove just the soft part, there might be a twenty percent chance of facial paralysis, some droop in the right side of your face. Probably a fifteen percent chance of hearing loss. And probably a five percent chance of death."

That stopped us cold. I was on the verge of running through a laundry list of physical repercussions, asking for the odds on paralysis of the arms, or legs, or ability to talk. But the odds on death rendered all that moot. To me that meant a greater than five percent chance that anything could happen, and probably all involved wheelchairs and permanent disability. I looked at Martha and she was coming to the same conclusion. I felt the tears coming, welling up behind my eyes, driven by some emotional force in my body beyond control. I didn't know how to turn it off, until I looked at Martha. She was without expression. That's when I realized for the first time that she was far stronger than me.

* * * * *

Within hours after we returned to Parkers, we heard from the Ward Institute. The doctor said they had received our MRIs and had studied them very closely. He wasted no time in going through their analysis and it was reassuring at least to hear their view of the problem was nearly identical to that of Dr. Noon and the Philadelphia hospital: a total operation couldn't be done. But the Institute did offer two operations, a first to remove the bottom half of the tumor, and if that worked without undue damage to the brain and its nerve system, go back in two weeks for a second operation to remove the other half. The doctor wasn't very optimistic for the second operation, but he said it was possible. He gave us the same odds on serious damage and death.

I found this "odds" business very strange. It's one thing to come to terms with death, but quite another to calculate the impact of blindness, or a drooping face, or hearing loss in one ear. In many ways a five percent chance of death is much easier. It's all or nothing. At least it was in my mind. I suppose you could live and beat the five percent odds, but still be blind or deaf. But once you get home, the doctor isn't there to ask about all the possibilities of the numbers. I wondered, for example, the odds of surviving the operation, going blind in one eye, and then the tumor returns in a few weeks to start the whole process again. What would be the odds of that? So I just assumed that death met death, and life met life, good and full and long lasting. But I knew that wasn't true. Nothing is ever that clear cut. And I should discuss it with Martha, but I decided to let her raise the issue. And I wondered how she could ever sleep through the night, with all these consequences running through her head. Strangely she never raised the issue. But the next morning she called to say, quite bluntly, "Let's go see Nablani."

Chapter Fourteen

Dave "Chumbucket" Roberts walked down the pier of the Palm Tree townhouse complex, stopping at slip number eleven where his 36-foot fishing boat had been berthed for over two months. Chum had followed his instructions to the letter, removing the windshield and radar attached to the fly bridge, dropping canvas over the stern so it hid the varnished transom that might be identifiable to a passing yacht or police boat, and removing the outriggers that carried the fishing lines for deep sea fishing. He did all that while moving the boat from North Carolina to Florida, and when he pulled into the slip, the boat looked for all the world like its Captain: unused, unemployed, and disheveled.

Chum's new neighbors at the Palm Tree may have wondered where he came from, but they never doubted Chum's story. He was bringing the boat down from New Jersey to be refurbished by the new owner of unit eleven, probably in the spring. Only one person had even asked who he was: the lady in unit ten who parked her Cadillac in the adjoining driveway. She introduced herself one morning as Chum was walking down to his favorite restaurant on the Intracoastal Waterway, just a few hundred yards from his townhouse.

"Hi," she called to him, as she opened the door of the car. "I'm your neighbor, Betty Ramos, can I give you a ride?"

"I'm Chum," he said, walking around the hood of the car, and offering his hand. "Chum Roberts."

"That your real name?"

"Actually, it's Dave," he said. "Chum is a nickname. It's what they call the dead fish and other bait that fishermen throw out to attract the big fish."

"Are you a dead fish?" she asked.

"No," he said, "but I used to be a first mate. My job was to throw the chum overboard behind the boat as we trolled across the Bay. Somebody called me Chum and it stuck."

"Welcome to New Smyrna, Florida," she said. "You don't bother us, we don't bother you. That's our motto."

"That's not on a bumper sticker, is it?" he asked.

"No," Betty said, a bit sheepishly, "but even the chamber of commerce calls us a laid back community. I work in the school system, and we're glad to have you."

Chum told her thanks and moved on down the sidewalk. He wanted the community to know he was friendly, but he didn't want them to know too much. The thing that scared him the most was the internet. Before computers, a person could find some small town and hide forever with a raft of made up facts and history. No more. One tiny piece of the wrong information, and people would look you up on dot.com web sites of every kind, from phone directories to satellite phones. It was damn hard to hide anymore.

Chum had been picked for this job anonymously, and he didn't know yet quite what had happened. He had just returned home from a daily fishing trip with three Washington business men. He ran his fishing boat out of Pilgrim's Harbor and was making pretty good money when the call came from a voice that began the conversation this way:

"Chum, this is an old acquaintance from your days growing up in Calvert County, Maryland. You won't remember me, but I knew you remotely when you first dropped out of high school and worked as first mate on the *Scatback*. I want to hire you for a fishing trip."

Chum was stunned. He let the phone dangle from his hand as he considered the options: an old friend from South County; maybe a Captain he had recently met in Newport News, but who would have a job to offer?

"Who is this?" he asked.

"I can't tell you Chum," he said, "but listen to my offer."

"Is this legal?" Chum asked. That wasn't necessarily the first question he usually asked. Indeed, Chum had spent enough time in reform school, and in the backseat of police cars, to be too sensitive about the law. Legality always had a rather broad definition for him, ever since the days when he would steal lumber from new home builders and sell it to customers coming out of the hardware store. Chum got caught a lot, but few people pressed charges, usually because it was just one piece of lumber, like a 4x8 piece of plywood or maybe a couple of two by fours. But talking back to teachers, or picking fights in class, had gotten him kicked out of school on several occasions and made him well known to the county police.

The reform school stay resulted from a breaking and entering charge against Chum for living in a neighbor's house while they were on vacation. He didn't do any damage, but it scared the whole neighborhood to have someone just move into a vacant house. It also happened that the incident occurred shortly after the Columbine school shootings in Colorado. And when the newspaper published a list of ten factors to look for in children who might be harboring malicious feelings, it became common knowledge that Chum had exhibited most of them. The most frightening was number eight, "Tries to harm animals." Chum was known for poking the eyes out of frogs, dropping cats from the roof of the garage, killing snakes, and throwing rocks at the family dog.

The community was glad to see Chum finally get a job on one of the local fishing boats, with many people hoping he might fall overboard in a storm. But they were pleasantly surprised to find that Chum loved the water, took to business, and within a couple of years had bought his boss' boat and moved to Newport News. Reports had filtered home that he was still a loner, but dedicated to his boat and not coming home.

Chum continued to hold the phone and ran through his mind all the friends and neighbors he could remember, and considered all the strange voices he could remember, but no bells were ringing.

"Well, I tell you, Mister," Chum said, "I'm pretty busy right now."

"I'll give you $10,000."

Chum was silent again. So was the caller.

Finally, Chum was starting to register the buying power of ten thousand dollars. He didn't worry much about taxes, because fishing is a cash and carry business. Chum's policy was to declare any amounts paid to him with a check, and forget the cash. This would surely be a cash deal, because of the secrecy, and ten thousand would clean and paint the bottom of his boat. He made a note to himself to deposit the cash in five thousand dollar amounts so as not to alert the banks who alert the tax man of anything over ten thousand in cash. He was rather proud of himself for knowing such a business fact.

"What do you want me to do?" he asked the secret caller.

"This isn't much really," the voice said, "but I need a little of your time. I need you to take your boat down to Cape Hatteras and take a friend of mine out tuna fishing."

"How much time?"

"Well Chum," the caller said, "I'd like you to go down about the first of September. I have a slip for your boat. You stay on the boat, and I'll call you when my friend is coming to fish. It should be within

154

two weeks."

"Who's the friend," Chum asked.

"No names, Chum."

"How many people?"

"Just one. Maybe two. Just a day of fishing."

"Let me think about it," Chum said. "Call me tomorrow."

"OK," the caller said, and hung up.

Now that it's all over, Chum plays that conversation around in his head a hundred times, wondering why ten thousand was so important and how he got caught up in this disaster. Now he's a hunted man, and hiding out in a town he never knew existed. His boat is out of work and sits at the dock like a ghostly remnant of the last hurricane.

Chum pushed the ball cap back on his forehead and moved across the street. He liked the morning in Florida, when it was cool and smelled fresh, and he could taste the hot coffee and scrambled eggs at the IC Diner. The IC, for Intra Coastal, opened at six so commuters and fishermen alike could get an early start. It was cheap, and food seemed to be the main extravagance eating into his ten thousand of new money.

* * * * *

Chum's only new friend in Smyrna was a house painter named Horace Yoakum, who arrived every morning at the IC Diner to get a scrambled egg sandwich and a thermos of coffee. He ate the sandwich in his car on the way to whatever house he was painting that day, and sometimes the drive could be lengthy. The coffee was for the rest of the day. Horace never told Chum much about himself, but they became friends through a few sentences of greeting each day. At first, Horace stood by the cash register while his "take out" order was being made. Then he took to sitting on one of the stools. But he always spoke to Chum in his nearby booth. Finally, he just walked over to Chum's booth and sat down. It was as natural as you please. And the conversations were easy, perhaps because neither of them wanted to engage weighty subjects, or neither wanted to divulge their personal demons. They talked mostly about the boats cruising down the waterway, although lately Chum had steered away from that subject.

"You know Chum," Horace said, "I once got in a little trouble on a boat over at Myrtle Beach. I lived on somebody's boat one winter while they were gone. I knew them. They just didn't know I was living there."

Horace said he didn't really think much about it at the time. He had helped paint the boat, and he knew the owner. He even stayed on the boat during the painting. And when the job was finished, he just stayed on. It was a 40-foot sailboat, with teak throughout, a full galley, and all the comforts. It just seemed natural to stay a few days longer. But when the winter was over, Horace was still there. And when the owner came for his boat, only to find Horace fixing dinner, he ordered the painter out immediately and threatened to call the police. So Horace moved on down the IC to New Smyrna.

When Chum heard this story, he recognized a kindred spirit, someone who moved with the tide, and flowed through life on the gentlest of breezes. They became friends, and began to satisfy the unquenchable thirst that most people have to confide in others.

* * * * *

Horace kept his egg sandwich wrapped in paper inside the brown bag, but sipped his coffee as he slid into the booth with Chum. Horace had a sharp mustache, rather unkempt, but nevertheless precise along the edges. Even in his twenties, it had a few flecks of gray that gave it maturity, and looked as if a few drops of paint might have splattered his face. But his eyes had a mischievous twinkle, as if he might be enjoying an innocent joke with his friend.

"Chum," he said, "I noticed your boat yesterday. Why don't you take it out and clean it up. I'll be glad to help."

"No," Chum said, "I'm waiting for instructions. I could be leaving in a month or two."

"Who's giving the instructions?"

"I can't tell you much about him," Chum said. "He hired me to take his friends out fishing. I did and it didn't work out. So now I'm waiting."

Horace saw intrigue in this answer, and a chance to show his friendship. He was cautious, but he wondered what had happened. "Was it a good fishing trip?" he asked.

"Not really," Chum said. "We had a man overboard."

"No shit!" Horace exclaimed. "What happened?"

Chum let the question sink in, wondering where it was leading and why. He looked at Horace again, from another perspective. What if Horace was a cop, or even just a nosey guy who liked to gossip? What if he told others about this new friend who won't clean up his boat?

"Nothing much," Chum said.

There was a silence when Chum realized he hadn't given much of an answer, and probably raised more questions from Horace; and Horace realized that Chum was either covering something up, or lying, or both. This unanswered question was bound to change the relationship, and they both had but a second or two to consider how.

"I realize this may be something you don't want to talk about," Horace said. "But did you get the guy back? Was he OK?"

"No," Chum said, "he didn't make it. We looked for him for

hours, but he never came up."

"Did you call the Coast Guard?" Horace asked.

"Wait a minute!" Chum exclaimed. "Why the questions? Shit happens."

"I know," Horace said. "Sorry."

"Let's talk about something else."

"How did you get into this business?" Horace volunteered. "You own your own boat. Must be doing pretty well."

Chum stared at his new friend, wondering about his motives, and the intensity of his questions. But Chum had spent most of his life in isolation, at least in those corners of life where people are not generally interested, where people don't inquire about your interests.

"People don't normally care," Chum said. "Why do you ask?"

"I'm just interested. Maybe I can learn something. I'm just a painter, but I'd like to own my own business," Horace said. "You know, last week I read that if I buy a van, and paint my name on the side, I can deduct the whole thing from taxes."

"That's true," Chum said. "In fact, you can deduct everything. I deduct the cost of bait, hooks, string, gas, scraping the bottom, paint, oil, maintenance, everything. Then I get paid in cash if I can, and never report that at all. When I was crab'n, everything was cash. Usually, I had a buyer waiting at the dock when I came in. He just dug out a roll of cash, put the crabs in his truck, and was gone. If he wasn't there, I took the crabs to the closest restaurant and they did the same thing. Hell, some years I had to make up income I didn't have, just to keep the IRS from coming after me."

"Of course," Horace said, "you guys didn't make much, did you?"

"Hell yes," Chum replied. "If you worked hard, you could make thousands of dollars a year. Deduct the mortgage on the boat, slip fees and a few other things and still have a hundred thousand left over."

"Wow. That's five times more than I make," Horace said.

"Well, you have to work hard though," Chum said. "Watermen all work hard and a lot of them don't make much at all. They don't trust banks either. Of course, now they're all getting wives who are smart enough to use the banks. The best crabbers have wives who keep the books and manage the money. But I'll tell you this; none of them will ever tell you how much money they really make. Poor as church mice, they tell you. And many of them are, of course. One year I only made about twenty thousand, but it was a bad year for crabs."

"How you do'n in the charter business?" Horace asked.

"Even better than crabb'n," Chum said. "Until this last trip. I got greedy and now look at me, sitting in this lazy little place doing nothing and scared to death."

"What are you scared of?" the waitress asked as she walked within hearing range. Marge carried a pot of coffee, filling empty cups as customers began filing out. Marge bought the IC in 2000 and looked at it as her golden goose, which she expected to lay its last eggs on her 65th birthday, still four years away. The way she figured, she worked every day and made about fifty thousand a year, after taxes, which paid for her car and a townhouse down on the waterway, a few new tee shirts and jeans every year, and a car trip to Maine every August.

"Nothin," Chum responded to her question, chagrined that he was overheard, but blaming only himself. "No more coffee Marge."

"Are you in danger?" Horace asked. "What the hell happened on that charter?"

"I gotta go," Chum said, shuffling in his seat. He saw that Horace was disappointed. Apparently he didn't have a job this morning. As he slid across the leather booth, and raised himself from the table, he said nonchalantly, "Want to go see the boat?"

"Sure," Horace responded. "We walking? I've got my truck."

"I walked down. I'll ride with you."

* * * * *

Chum and Horace walked down the boardwalk behind his town-house to a white fishing boat that looked like a patient in a military hospital. It was wounded. White canvas pieces were taped over the windows like bandages. A large blue tarpaulin of the kind purchased in K-Mart was draped over the fly bridge, and weighted down with plastic water bottles hanging on strings from the grommets. Rain had created small pools of water in the low spots on the canvas. There was no identity except that this was an injured boat.

"How do we get in?" Horace asked, not seeing any obvious bridge. Both boys stood on the dock and surveyed the boat, Chum wondering how his life could have deteriorated to this. It had been over two months since he pulled the *Scatback* into this slip. At that time, it seemed like a new adventure. He was in a new state, a new city, and a new home, however temporary. He had applied all the boat bandages in anticipation of moving into a new townhouse, and discovering his surroundings.

Now all those aspirations seemed ephemeral, vanishing in just a few days, with nothing left but empty days and no future. Chum walked to the side of the boat, grabbed the handrail, and stepped onto the deck where the tarp suggested a solid footing.

"C'mon Horace," Chum said, "I can't take it any more. Let's yank this canvas off and I'll show you the boat."

Horace stepped onto the boat, reached over the side and lifted one of the water bottles to empty it into the canal. Spiders ran in every direction. There had been enough rain to seep under the canvas cover and leave the dusty fingerprints of previous storms around the cleats and deck chairs.

"This is all day work," Chum said. "You want to help me clean up?"

"Sure," Horace replied. "Can we get her running?"

"If we have battery power," Chum said. "She hasn't moved in a long time. But oil and engine should be all right. Got gas. I'm tired of sittin around here."

Chum walked around the deck, rolling the tarp back, knowing he would have to take it off the boat, lay it out on the lawn, wash it down, let it dry, and then fold it up for storage in the hold.

"You know," Chum said, "I need to get back to work, fishing and making money. Hell, I don't even know what I'm hiding from. You know, there was a woman on that fishing trip. Cried some. Then walked off the boat, said to forget I ever saw her, and walked away. Then I got another call to come here, hide the boat and wait. Hell, Horace, I didn't do anything wrong. I never hurt nobody."

"Then why are you here?" Horace asked. "If you didn't break the law. You must have done something wrong."

"No. No I didn't. Except I didn't tell anybody about that woman."

"So what. A guy falls overboard fishing. That's not your fault. He was probably banging that chick and didn't want his wife to know. And the guy who called you was probably just his friend. Another waterman."

"You're right," Chum said. "I'm talking to a voice on the phone I don't even know. And I did nothing wrong. Hell with them. Let's go fishin."

They spent the rest of the day cleaning the boat. Working side by side scrubbing the hull was a bonding experience. Chum thought Horace was probably a little smarter than himself. At least he didn't think that Horace had committed any crime, although he wasn't posi-

tive about that. And it seemed that Horace shared his view of perma-
nence in the world, of a family without the stabilizing impact of regular meals, and church, and family outings. Nothing was permanent.

Chum's parents just never seemed to be around. His dad was an
electrician who signed on with different companies and building sites,
sometimes at distant locations. It was common for his father to be out
of town, in places like Detroit or Knoxville, where they were building
a big box retail outlet or shopping mall. Often, he could be gone for
two or three months before coming home for a weekend.

Chum's mom worked at the local hardware store, and she knew
every pipe and wrench and hammer in the store, even if she never used
them. She always volunteered for overtime to stock shelves or rearrange displays. Chum was left to fend for himself. Mostly the house
was empty. He would come home, fix a sandwich out of the refrigerator, and head for a friend's house down the road. Chum never had a
car until he could buy one himself, which was after he dropped out of
school and started working as a first mate on the charter boats. So he
walked. Everyone in the neighborhood knew him from the streets.
He wore low rider pants, hanging precariously on his butt, usually
with a tee shirt advertising some musical group. People would pass
him on the street, wondering if he was headed for trouble.

Chum wasn't particularly introspective, and didn't ponder his future for long periods. But he did wonder if his parents represented the
norm. He was lonely as a child. He wondered about other parents and
what they did at night. Did they sit and watch television, or read
books, or talk about their work? Chum thought that seemed reasonable but then, what would they read or talk about. His mind hit a wall
at that point, uncushioned by knowledge of issues or the presence of
books, he simply moved on to more comfortable surroundings. He
walked the streets and watched the animals, the birds and the squirrels.

He thought violently about them, wondering what it would be like to kill them, or capture them. But when he told his friends in the neighborhood, they shrank from him, or they laughed uneasily. And soon people generally thought he was killing animals, even though the closest he ever came was shooting a rabbit about seventeen times with a pellet gun. And when the rabbit didn't die, Chum just walked away.

Horace reminded Chum of the Captains he worked with on the fishing boats, before he bought his own. They were never warm and sympathetic, like parents were supposed to be. But they were a presence. Chum hadn't talked to anybody privately or personally since he came to Florida, and he liked Horace's company. Horace liked to talk.

Horace unfolded the white captain's chair and several small spiders scampered down the arm. It was wedged under the tarp where water had collected. But it looked like fine leather, although he knew it was imitation, probably naugahyde or some other plastic. As he eased into the chair, he could imagine fishing with the waves flashing behind the boat and a hot sun on his legs.

"Chum," Horace said, "let's take the boat south, maybe around Florida. We could pick up some charters in the Gulf of Mexico, maybe just keep moving from Fort Myers up to Tampa, maybe over to New Orleans and Texas. Hell, we could just follow the sun all the way to California."

Why not, Chum thought. "Let's get the *Scatback* cleaned up." He was warming to the idea, and beginning to see the possibilities.

Chapter Fifteen

The Nablani Center for Scull Based Surgery was located on the seventh floor of an all glass building, and the only identifying sign on Suite 62 was computer generated and scotch taped to the door, although lights were on somewhere and they glowed through the door's glass panel. Martha pushed the door open while I was still contemplating the location and newness of the office. You could smell the fresh paint. And I wondered why this wasn't in a hospital, or a medical center, or at least some building that indicated an association with medicine.

Inside, the waiting room was lined with wood trimmed chairs and warm leather seats, but no pictures. It looked like the moving van had arrived that morning, left the furniture, and departed, leaving only a well dressed receptionist behind the office counter.

"Good morning," she said. "You must be the Shannons."

"I am," Martha offered. "This is Ned Shannon, my husband's brother."

"Welcome," she replied. "Do you have your MRIs with you?" Martha was carrying them under her arm. She handed them to the receptionist, who wheeled around in her chair, and said, "I'll give these to Dr. Nablani. Please have a seat in the waiting room. He'll be with you in a few minutes."

We sat on a leather couch, and I remarked that the file cabinets behind the receptionist were almost empty. There was really nothing in the room to make us comfortable, or to instill confidence. Suddenly, the door opened and a young African American woman entered, with an older woman, presumably her mother. They took seats across from us, and the girl turned sideways. There was a horseshoe imprint on the side of her head, starting in front of her ear, rising to the top and back of her head and down the back of her neck. It was startling. My God, I thought to myself, it's so big; they've taken the whole side of her head off. Martha was as still as an anvil. I was sure she was imagining herself with such a scar. Clearly, the girl's head had been shaved before the operation, and now that some weeks had passed, the scar looked like a branding iron had left its terrible mark. I wondered how long it had taken for her hair to grow back, and would it ever cover the scar. Still, Martha was a stone. I was hoping that the girl would say something to her mother, or show some animation, but she seemed subdued. Her mother went to talk with the receptionist, and the girl remained in her seat, staring at the floor. My God, I thought, has she been traumatized, or paralyzed, or somehow turned into the stone figures I used to see on television of people with lobotomies? I never thought those old horror movies would come alive, and I vowed to never watch another movie or documentary on the subject. I looked at Martha and she was as pale as the ceiling. I put my arm around her shoulders and she accepted the gesture, softly muttering, "Thank you."

The receptionist soon appeared and invited us to follow her along a corridor of offices. It wasn't clear that anyone else was in the building. She showed us to a small conference room with a round table and six chairs, inviting us to take a seat and Dr. Nablani would soon arrive. Again, no pictures. But a light screen for viewing MRIs was on the wall, and a plastic human scull was on a credenza behind the table. It looked like a toy, perhaps for a young person to play with, to take apart like a puzzle with multicolored pieces. I assumed that it would be used to show us the operation.

Nablani walked in with a younger man, looking Egyptian, like Nablani, carrying Martha's MRIs. I recognized them from the scribbled notes on the back of the manila folder that I had made in the car, searching for the right address. Nablani was somehow older than I expected, at least 50, and his assistant was younger than I expected, probably 25. His complexion was dark, middle eastern, and a bit yellow around the eyes. But at least he smiled. I guess I was looking for a younger doctor, but it was nice to see a smile. He began immediately to ask Martha questions about her background, and the assistant took notes. He wanted to know about previous operations, none. Allergies, none. Any infections, none. Age, 35. Insurance, yes. And finally, who referred us?

Martha answered with a directness I had not often seen. In the few days since she first told me about the tumor, Martha had grown more controlled. She was all business, analyzing her condition, ready to ask questions and get answers she needed. She seemed newly aware of the gravity of the situation. It was her life. And she was a little impatient, wanting to ask Nablani about her condition.

The assistant kept writing, but spoke directly to Nablani. "She's a good candidate," he concluded. Then I realized the intent of the questions. Nablani didn't want someone who might die on the table, or couldn't survive a difficult recovery, or couldn't pay. Although I suspected survivability was even more important than money. I kept thinking of those percentages of hearing loss, or blindness, or death. This doctor wanted successes, patients who would give him every opportunity for a safe and complete operation. It was somehow reassuring that Nablani didn't care about bedside manner and nursing; he cared about solving the problem, getting that tumor out of her head, and having an assistant who would write it all down for his next book. In a way, that was our goal too.

"Let's look at the MRIs," he said, and placed the negatives on the wall screens. Martha and I had seen them so many times before; we had stopped searching for unseen changes or rays of hope. Our focus was on Nablani, to see if he recognized the complications every other doctor had described. He talked us through each negative, then he turned to face us directly and started to describe the operation.

"I will do a craniotomy," he said. "I will remove the side of the scull above and around the ear. Then I can examine the nerves that control various parts of the body, and see how they are impacted. Then I will remove the tumor from the top." He stopped, apparently to let all this sink in.

Martha leaned forward. "Does that mean you can do it?" she asked.

"I can do it," he said. "And I would like to do it Thursday."

We sat stunned, not expecting such a positive response, and not expecting to do it so quickly. It seemed like there should be more time for preparation, more time to adapt to the idea of the operation, more time to prepare. And then I started laughing, almost uncontrollably, aware that this was not a funny moment, and no one else shared my mirth. Martha just stared at me, and Nablani stared at her.

Finally, I spoke. "Forgive me sir, I admire your confidence. But how can you just say, 'I can do it,' when at least three other brain surgeons have said it's impossible. Two of them refused to operate at all, and the third said maybe in two operations. Now you say, 'I can do it.'"

Nablani fixed his gaze directly in my eyes. "Because I am the best," he said. "I am a surgeon's surgeon."

Silence. Martha still had not said a word. Finally, I said, "Can we have a few days to think about this?"

"Sure," he said, "but I need to know by Wednesday. We will do the operation Thursday, and I leave for Paris on Saturday. Are there other questions?"

Martha finally spoke, not surprisingly in a strong voice, "How long will the operation take and how long will the recovery be?"

"Eight to ten hours," he said. "And maybe two weeks in the hospital, and a couple more weeks as an outpatient. Let me show you the operation."

He reached for the plastic head on the credenza, brought it to the table, and showed us where the horseshoe incision would be. Then he started taking the brain apart, describing the multicolored pieces by their bodily function, and finally arriving at the core.

"This is where the tumor is," he said. "I think the top part is solid and I will lift it out the top. Then the bottom part can be taken out the side, or drained if it is liquid. Do you have any questions?"

It was just too much for me to absorb. Martha just stared at all the pieces laying on the table, I'm sure wondering how she could ever recover from that. How can you just take out pieces of the brain? How can you not disturb the nerves? It just seems impossible.

Nablani read her mind, and said again, "This is a very delicate operation, but I can do it."

Then he started putting the plastic pieces of the head back together. The first three or four pieces slid into place. But the next one didn't fit. He turned it in different directions, like turning a puzzle piece, trying to see the curves and angles that fit together. Then he placed it in position, but it didn't quite go all the way into place. Then he hit it with the palm of his hand.

Martha and I looked at each other, shocked and bewildered. Did we just see what we saw? It was the most incredible moment of irony and bewildering shock I'd ever known. Again, I started laughing. How could the surgeon's surgeon not even know where the pieces of the brain go, how they fit together, and most incredibly, how could he hit a piece to force it in. It was unfathomable.

Nablani stood and said, "Nice to meet you. Let me know by Wednesday about the operation." And he walked out of the room.

Martha and I stood up, both a little unstable. I took her by the arm for support.

"Come on, Marti, let's go back to Parkers," I said. "Philadelphia is only a few hours drive, and I think we should be home when we decide. Especially if we have to drive back in a few days."

Martha said very little on the drive home. She had gone inside herself, and I decided not to interrupt.

Chapter Sixteen

For perhaps the first time, I felt like I needed to be on the water, crabbing, to clear my mind. I couldn't seem to make sense of Martha's medical stuff. On the one hand, I have the divergent advice of three different doctors and hospitals who talk about the odds of living and paralysis as if it might be a day at the track, and on the other hand my sister-in-law fears her life could be snuffed out within two months because only one doctor thinks he can do the operation, and he's so looney he can't even put a plastic scull back together. How many removable parts does a brain have anyway? Maybe Vinnie can help me sort this out. So I called him.

"Vinnie," I said, "I need to be on the water tomorrow morning. I'll meet you at the boat at 7:00 a.m."

"You're on boss," Vinnie responded. "See you then."

I arrived at the Bayfront just before seven and could see Simy serving coffee at the bar to some of the other Captains. I decided to pass that encounter, just because I didn't want to talk to anybody, Simy or the guys. The *Martha Claire* was floating gently in her berth, a yellow light illuminating the cabin. Vinnie had obviously arrived earlier to get the boat ready. Empty crab baskets were stacked on deck, four bushels of alewives were waiting to be shoved into the empty pots after we had captured the crabs, and the diesel was running. I noticed the plywood floor was losing some of its grey paint. It's November and should be cold, and my car thermometer said 37 degrees, yet the weather forecast is "clear and 65."

Vinnie motioned me aboard with a cup of coffee.

"Should be a great day today boss," he said. "The crabs are running thin, but we have 300 pots out there and we should be able to get most of them out by noon."

"Everything ready?" I asked.

"The bow lines are off," Vinnie said in the process of moving around the boat, and slipping the lines off the cleats. "The stern lines are off. Let's go."

I took the helm and edged the boat out of its slip. This was the part I liked best, taking control of the boat in the early morning, when dew was still on the bow and it glistened in the morning sun. The big diesel was idling, and I edged it forward as we moved to the middle of the channel. I loved the deep roar of the engine, a low growl like a lion on the prowl. The speed limit is six knots, with an admonition not to leave a wake. Vinnie could feel the speed of the boat without ever looking at the gauges. I looked. The water was porcelain gray, like the flower vase on my desk, and smooth as silk, with water bugs skipping over the surface. I settled into the hum of the engine, thinking of Marti at home, taking care of Mindy and no doubt wondering if she would be alive for the little girl's future.

I knew the open water would drive these thoughts from my mind, and if not, working the crab pots would do it. Once you reach the first pot, your hands are flying from the wheel, to the throttle, to the clutch, to the wire cage that holds your catch. It's a synchronized process that captures your mind and body, driving out all extraneous thoughts. Even as you rev the engine to move from one pot to another, there is no time for daydreaming. You must be on buoy, and slowed to just the right speed to operate the hydraulic wench that raises the pot to the surface, and then you have to grab it, pull it into the boat, and turn it over to Vinnie. Three hundred pots and your mind is mush, not with big thoughts, but with the repetition of the work, and the knowledge that you must stay focused. Today I wanted all that consuming repetition more than ever and I'm kind of proud that I've mastered the process. I pulled on my Grundens foul weather waders with suspenders, and readied my rubber gloves for handling the crabs. The gloves only last about two weeks. Even on the first day you wear them, small holes appear from handling the pinchers and bony back of the crab.

I pulled the *Martha Claire* beside the first buoy, my left hand on the transmission lever, right hand on the throttle, which I release at idle as the boat slows to a stop. I grab the pot hook leaning beside me, reach into the water and scoop up the pot line just below the buoy. I thread the line over the roller just outside the cabin. The line immediately starts to reel in, bringing the pot up from the bottom. When it breaks the water, I lean over the gunnel and grab it with both hands and in one continuous motion, lift it to the small platform on the edge of the boat, turn it one way to empty any unused bait, turn it another way to release the crabs. In a handoff similar to the Olympic relays, I hand the wire pot to Vinnie who bangs it against a square metal basin and empties the crabs. He raises it back to the platform, grabs two handfuls of bait from the basket, refills the trap, and I begin to move the boat forward to the next buoy. Vinnie pushes the rebaited pot and buoy overboard. When I see them hit the water, I ram the throttle forward, then ease off again at the next buoy. Only 299 more pots to go, and let's hope each of them is full of crabs.

It's warming up now. Nearly every day in the fall starts out cold, but the pace of activity lets you ignore it. It's also the most beautiful time; usually a red and clear sky frame the boat like a Hudson River painting, and it's easy to be romantic about your life. Although few watermen would use that word. But I've heard the wives talk about their men and the water in almost romantic tones. They complain often that their husbands don't like going to parties, or don't want to attend church because of the congregation. The wives often say, "They only feel comfortable on the water." I think that's why so many of the watermen are uncomfortable with me; they don't understand how I could crab in the morning, and kiss ass, as they say, with clients in the afternoon.

But today, it's starting to warm up and the wind is picking up and raising waves across the water. The red has turned to yellow like maple leaves in October. And the boat moves around the sun's glow on the water, like a puppet on a string. As Vinnie pushes the pots over the side, the gulls gather in timeless fashion, as they have chased fishing boats for their waste since before Christ.

"It's a great morning," Vinnie said above the engine. "Not many crabs today though."

"They've gone deep," I said, "beginning to bury themselves in the mud for winter."

"The State is going to take away the females," Vinnie said. "Then we won't have any catch in the fall."

"Maybe we'll get a Federal bailout," I ventured.

"Are you kidding?" Vinnie said. "Never happen. They just give orders, not money. First, they'll say no female crabs after 11:00 a.m., or only two baskets a day. Then they'll say none at all. And most of them damn bureaucrats have never been on the water, let alone on a working crab boat."

"You're probably right," I allowed.

"Hell," Vinnie said, "if the politicians had any balls they would clean up the chickenshit on the eastern shore. That's what's killing the crabs. Chicken producers."

Vinnie liked to get philosophical about crabbing, especially after a couple hours on the water, when the roar of the engine blots out meaningful discourse, and becomes rhythmic background music for your thoughts. No response is wanted or expected. He just talks his way through 300 pots and expounds with ideas you would never hear on the dock.

"Watermen get no respect," he says. "But we do all right. I remember once we had a private plane take us to Atlantic City and a limo to pick us up. The Trump helo was nearby, no doubt having just delivered the owner of Trump's Taj Mahal. That's pretty good, don't you think."

After about three hours, I'm beginning to feel the pull of the water. I feel a part of the boat; its power and durability are my strength. I'm in control. My boat. My engine. God's crabs. Guaranteed income. Two miles from land and all the tentacles of society can't touch me. On the water, I am free.

The day was going well, at least in the sense that the engine was smooth, no storm warnings, and the winds were calm. Vinnie seemed in good spirits and I never had a moment to worry about Martha.

"Neddie," Vinnie said, "have you figured out what to do with your life yet?"

"No," I mumbled.

"You need a wife," Vinnie said. "Someone to provide a steady pattern to your life, a friend who will always have your back, someone to share things with, and a little extra income."

"Thanks, Vin," I said.

"Here's what's going to happen," he droned. Vinnie was in his groove now. Talking to the hum of the engine, not saying anything he would remember an hour later. But in full throat.

"Look at me," he said. "I started on the water with my dad, working as a deck hand and water boy on the skipjacks over on Tilghman Island, dredging for oysters. Boy, I thought that was the cat's meow until my arms started aching all night, and my legs would cramp up. I remember screaming in the dark with those leg cramps. Finally my dad came in and told me to get out of bed now. 'Now,' he screamed. 'Get out of bed and straighten those legs out. Kid, if you can't handle the work, get off the boat.'"

"I thought about that, and I figured maybe my dad was right. So I saw an ad in the paper for marine police and I applied for the job. They said I was young, but had the right experience, and they could teach me to be a cop. I ended up spending nearly three decades chasing watermen, from one end of this Bay to the other. I could tell you stories that would curl your hair."

"One time I came upon this Trumpy wooden yacht, with varnished teak all around, that looked stuck on a sand bar. I looked at the charts, and sure enough, the shallows were out there. So I moved my boat as close as I could get without running aground and yelled for the Captain. I could hear people talking. Course you know how the water carries voices. Then I see a face. And then this guy emerges and when the door opens I hear all kinds of hell. Some woman is screaming at him about being stupid and having a pecker for a brain, and bingo, she stumbles out behind him, as naked as a jaybird. She had big ole boobs hanging down and she didn't care if I saw them. She was going to finish her tirade. Then the Captain starts yelling for her to get back inside. She turns and goes back inside. But she was mad and she never tried to cover up nothing. I never told Velma about that episode.

"I remember back in the thirties. Oystering was the big thing on the Bay. In the beginning it was mostly hand tongers. A couple of guys in a small boat could row out from shore, find an oyster bed, stand up in their boat with a sixteen-foot hand tong, which is really just a couple of huge forks that grab up the oysters, and they could make a living. That's why so many black folks took to oysters. They left the tobacco plantations and went to the water.

"Then the big sailboats, the skipjacks, could dredge up huge quantities of oysters. At one time we had seven Oyster Houses around here to shuck the oysters and can them for sale. The old Leatherbury Oyster House is still here in Shady Side. And then the power boats came along with their hydraulic patent tongs, and replaced the skipjacks. Nearly cleaned out the oysters. Ironically, those old hand tongers were good conservationists because they were so inefficient.

"I arrested a lot of them power dredgers, and I was glad to do it. Those boats could make six hundred to a thousand dollars a day, and take all the oysters off a bed. Nothing left for the hand tongers.

"Another thing that happened is the State let some of those boys lease up to thirty acres of underground oyster beds. Then the watermen would lease open spots close to shore, dump the oysters from a good bed into the empty spot, and hold them till the prices went up. And the State sanctioned the whole business."

"Vinnie," I said, "you're a walking history book."

"No Neddie," he said, "I just been around a long time. And I still like being on the water."

"How many more pots do we have?" I asked.

"Getting tired?"

"A little."

"We probably have fifty pots to go," Vinnie said. "But we may run out of bait before we finish."

"Let's try to finish, anyway," I said.

Vinnie didn't mind. He just kept on working and talking.

"Now crabbing is on the way out, for the same reason as oysters," Vinnie said. "Back in the thirties, crabs weren't too popular. The main market was for soft crabs. So like always happens, the watermen got more efficient. They came up with seine nets, fifty or sixty feet long, and would drag them along the shore scooping up soft shells by the thousands. Man, it was like mowing your lawn. So they were outlawed, been forty or fifty years now.

"I remember once I got a call from a waterman who said he caught three guys from Mayo stealing oysters from his lease ground. I raced down there and the waterman had all three of them tied up, and he was holding a shotgun on em. I took em in to the jail, and the judge said he would hear the case that night. The judge started about eight o'clock in that little jail over by Gaylesville, not more than ten feet square, with a cell in the basement and the courtroom upstairs. All three wives showed up and asked to testify. All three of them said their husbands couldn't have done it because they were in bed making love during that time. The judge could hardly contain himself by this remarkable coincidence. He said he flat out didn't believe it and fined them each fifty dollars. Later, one of them Mayo boys told me it was the most expensive sex he ever had.

"These crab pots really started the decline of crabbin. We used to catch them one at a time. Now it's a half dozen per pot. I feel a little guilty every day we're out here. But I know the real villains are those chickenshiters over at Cambridge, and all these new houses around here with yards full of fertilizer. The runoff kills the sea grasses. No more crabs. Now we're accused of over crabbin.

"Now don't get too worked up Vin," I said, my voice straining over the engine. "We are always looking for better, faster, cheaper ways to catch more crabs. We're all guilty." After pulling 200 pots, my pants and shirt were soaked with sweat. Inside the rubber waders, the sweat starts pouring early in the morning. Now I'm itching everywhere, and as soon as we stop working I'll be cold. It's about now that the law books seem welcome, and I'm looking for reasons to go home.

I reached for the two-way radio hanging by its cord over my head, and punched in the special channel for private boats. "Let's see what the other boys are doing," I said.

Captain Bloom's voice crackled on the line. "I'm taken it in Neddie," he said. "Not enough crabs out here today."

I figured he was telling the truth because my catch wasn't very good either. Sometimes one crab per pot. Or a lot of pots with crabs too small to keep. State says they have to be a hand wide across the back. One of the good things about having a retired water policeman on board is he knows the law, and he's not always urging me to break it.

Captain Bloom is pretty straight. Some of the guys will always say they're going in for lack of crabs, but the real reason is they have their limit, and they want to beat everyone else to market. If we're all selling to the same restaurant, first boats off the water get the best prices.

I figure I'll ask the Captain if he has any excess bait. If he offers me some, and brings his boat over, I can see if he has empty bushel baskets. If he says he's empty and heads for home, I know he's probably full. Captain Bloom is a good ole boy, but he's competitive, just like the rest of us.

"I've known Bloomie for 20 years," Vinnie says. "Course I don't think that's his real name. Never heard that. 'Bloomie' has something to do with flowers he gave his girlfriend back in the seventies, but I don't remember the specifics."

Captain Bloom pulled his boat up close to the *Martha Claire*. "I love that old boat of yours," he yelled. "Made by Sam Hardin over at Easton. Used to have one myself."

"Got any bait?" I yelled.

"Sure," he said. "Here's a bushel."

"I'll pay you for it," I said.

178

"No. No. No," he said, stretching over the side of his boat. Both boats are at idle, and they rock with the waves. So I have to time my grab for the bucket. Missing a bucket, or knocking it in the water, is a serious matter. Captains don't mind giving away their remaining bait, but if it's lost carelessly, they'll be mad for days. We made the switch, and Bloomie waved, saying something about having a couple other little jobs to do, and turned for home.

Vinnie checked out the new bait as I headed the boat back to our buoys. "I think we can just about finish the line with this," Vinnie said.

I was ready to go home anyway. The crabs were getting smaller and fewer. Basically, we were just baiting pots. It was pretty slow, pretty slow. Then it dawned on me that the change was rather sudden. We were getting five or six crabs per pot, and now nothing.

"Vin," I said, "do you think somebody's stealing our crabs?"

"Could be, boss," he said. "Pretty common in this area. Lots of yellow jackets out here in pleasure boats. They pick up one pot for the fun of it, discover a half dozen crabs, and then pick up another five pots till they get a bushel for dinner."

"It's against the law to steal crabs," he continued. "When I was working the beat, we'd catch a lot of these pleasure boaters, give them a ticket and take away their crabs. They got nothing and I got a free dinner.

"The worst thing is when one waterman steals from another. It's pretty tempting if you're not catching anything, and you see somebody else's pots are full. In those cases, about all you can do is report it to the State police. But they won't do anything, and the bad guys will never be caught."

"What if I catch them?" I asked.

"That doesn't happen much. Most likely you'll find out days later when somebody gets drunk at the bar and starts bragging about what he did. That's when the bad guys discover that their boat is sinking, or a 'mysterious' fire consumes the boat. Funny how those bilge pumps will malfunction. The cost of raising and repairing your boat makes those stolen crabs pretty expensive."

"You mean like what happened to me?"

"Yeah, did you steal somebody's crabs?" Vinnie asked with a smile.

"No," I said. "Let's go home."

Chapter Seventeen

When Diane Sexton said she would be delighted to join me for drinks at the Willard, it cleared my mind quicker and more persistently than three hundred crab pots and the roar of a diesel. It reminded me that I had not been to the city in weeks, and anticipation was a new emotion. I used to drive to Parkers for the day, and regret my having to return to Washington with its traffic, and confusion, and urban threats. I clearly remember the fear of the city, having to turn on my street smarts to worry about muggers, and speeders, and drug use near my house. But now that I live in Parkers, suddenly those threats become exciting. I can't wait to pull my car up to the front door of the Willard, hand the keys to the valet, and stroll confidently through the golden doors and into the welcoming arms of marble columns and a Persian carpet.

Washington at night is a sparkling picture, like a cityscape painting with a light affixed to the frame that illuminates the streets. It's not bustling, like New York or London, but it's busy; enough people so you know the place is alive, that restaurants and clubs exist in enough quantity to draw people from their apartments, or workers from the suburbs. When I used to work at Simpson, Feldstein and James, leaving the office in the evening always meant a stop by the local bar, or dinner at one of many small restaurants in the heart of town. I've always enjoyed dinner alone in a restaurant, with other people nearby who didn't bother me, but gave me fodder for imagination. I wondered what they did, and listened carefully for snippets of conversa-

tion, and examined their clothing to judge their professions. I probably wasn't right, of course, in those moments of fantasy, but it doesn't
matter. The joy is in the dream, the fascination with others, and al-
leyways of thought that I was led into.

Those things don't happen so much in Parkers, and the homogenei-
ty doesn't provide so much excitement. We look pretty much alike, in
blue jeans and plaid shirts. But the tradeoff is in comfort, in the reassurance that we know each other, and we know the same places. The
city always scared me with the knowledge that diners at the next table
could be from another city, or axe murderers, or watermen dressing up
for a Saturday night.

The most rewarding parts of Washington are the monuments.
Driving to the Willard from Parkers takes you within arms reach of the
Nationals baseball stadium, the Capitol dome, down the mall with its
wide expanses of grass and inviting reflecting pools, around the Washington Monument, and right up to the back door of the White House.
In many ways, the White House and the Bayfront offer the same inspi-
ration. They are home; have been there all my life; and almost never
change. I can't go in the White House, of course, but still it's familiar,
in all my old school books, on the cover of local magazines, the center
of Washington social activities.

There weren't any cars waiting in the valet zone at the Willard.
Must be early. I stepped out of the car, left the front door open while I
reached in the backseat to get my sport coat. When I reached to slip it
over my shoulders, the valet was there, gave me a light assist, and took
my keys. I told him it would probably be a couple hours, not really
knowing what to expect.

It didn't seem likely that Diane and I would end up in the Jenny
Lind suite, a famous honeymoon room in the attic of the hotel. The
bed was in front of a large porthole of a window, with the Washington

Monument rising, and lit, in the middle of your sight. A wrought iron canopy supported rolls of lace cascading around the bed. I had never actually seen the two thousand dollar a night room, but my fellow lawyers said the view of the monument was like a national phallic symbol that invited achievement of extraordinary proportions. All of that seemed unlikely tonight. But we might stay for dinner, which could take a couple extra hours.

It seemed that every place in Washington invited comparisons with my new life, a result no doubt of my continuing judgmental review of my situation. When I emerged into the high ceiling expanse of the lobby, I noticed a half dozen people sitting on couches around the room. The huge yellow marble columns seemed like hiding places for settees and guests seeking some furtive spot. But the first thing I noticed was that everyone glanced up at me, took a second glance to confirm that I wasn't anybody important, and then looked away in disappointment. I used to do that too, wanting to confirm that I was in the presence of power or wealth. But I was out of the habit, and now it seemed slightly ostentatious to exhibit such a motive. I wondered if I stared at people entering a restaurant in Parkers. I don't think so. I wondered what it means to not have any expectation of being impressed, or surprised, or self important in these situations. I decided it was healthy, and headed for the door of the Round Robin bar.

I stepped around the corner and into the lounge, adjusted my eyes to the dimness until I spotted the breathtaking legs belonging to my former colleague at Simpson, Feldstein and James. Diane was sitting at the bar on the elevated walnut wood chairs, no doubt designed for showing off those personal assets. She turned and reminded me again of the sophisticated beauty that money can buy, and avarice can ruin. The Willard advertises this bar widely as the spot where Henry Clay introduced the Mint Julep to official Washington. They might do better by simply distributing a picture of Diane in dark suit and short skirt. But the historical reference does have its charm, although I can't remember a thing about Henry Clay and I don't think he was ever President. Maybe a Vice President or Senator. And I can't imagine drinking a mint julep anyplace outside of the Kentucky Derby. But history is important.

"Hi Ned," she said brightly. "It's great to see you. I can't wait to get caught up."

"Diane," I said, brushing my lips across her cheek, smelling the sweet fragrance of expensive perfume. "Thanks for coming. Do you want to move to a table, or stay at the bar?"

"Let's stay here. I'm already wedged in." I glanced at her chair to see exactly what that meant. The crowd was light, but several couples were situated at the wall tables, and several singles were on the opposite side of the bar. I recognized the bartender, even from the back, and figured I would say hello to him when he turned to take our drinks.

"Neddie," Diane said, "tell me about Parkers, and crabs, and the life of a lone lawyer."

"Well," I began, "the waterman side is doing pretty well. I enjoy being on the water. I'm making some money, at least enough to pay my deck hand, and I survived an attempt to put me out of business. But the lawyer business is about like you would expect in a small town."

"Like what?" she said. "I don't live in a small town."

"Well, I had a successful case last week and made four hundred dollars. I had a guy come in to say he wanted to hire me to deal with a neighbor lady. Seems he had a number of jousts with her over the years, primarily because of a fence between their properties. My client had a chain link fence erected about twenty years ago, before his neighbor moved in. But about a year ago, when we had the big hurri-cane come up the Bay, the fence was mangled and entire sections were washed away, most of which lay rusting in her yard. The neighbor lady came over one day and told my client to get them out of her yard right now. My client said he would, but it took a couple of weeks to find a trash hauler. Most of those guys with big trucks were pretty busy at that time.

"Anyway, my client hauled away the old fence, and proceeded to install a new one. But the neighbor lady didn't want a chain link. She said it was 1970s crap and she wanted a white picket, preferably plas-tic so it wouldn't deteriorate. My client agreed and brought in a sur-veyor to make sure it was installed in the right place. Naturally, the surveyor found the old fence was two inches inside her property. She started screaming about him stealing her property. My client said he was fine with moving the fence, but now he wanted a six foot stockade so he didn't have to ever talk to her again. And so it began.

"To make a long story short, my client bought a truckload of stockade fence and stacked it on the edge of the property. One night it caught fire, and my client and his neighbor started screaming at each other, so violently that the pile kept on burning before anybody called the fire department. The entire neighborhood had gathered, of course, mostly to watch the argument and then take sides as to who was at fault.

"So my client comes stomping into my office to say he had gone to a neighbor's cocktail party over the weekend, and the neighbor woman cornered him by the bar and screamed he was a 'no good sleaze ball son-of-a-bitch.' So now he wants retribution, or maybe a restraining order. The problem with a case like this in Parkers is: it's not good for business. Everybody in town takes sides and they don't take much stock in our law school principle that everybody deserves a hearing and a defense. A more limited view of the constitution prevails. So I wrote a letter threatening legal action and listing a dozen instances of trespassing, insult, public harassment, and slander. It seemed to work. My client hasn't heard from the woman since, and I charged him four hundred dollars. I didn't even have to open Mitchie's Annotated Code book to do it."

"Must have taken at least three hours to hear the story," Diane said. "I'd say you earned the money."

"I did," I replied. "So the client you got me, CRI, is still the best income I have. Although the resort boys aren't much fun at all."

"What's that mean? Clients aren't supposed to be friends or fun. You play, they pay, it's as simple as that."

"I tell you Diane," I said, "some of these cases are so weird I would take them just for the fun of it."

"That's another thing you don't do," Diane said. "Nothing is free. None of this *pro bono* stuff. Even if you only charge ten dollars, you have to let people know that you're in business to make money, not just to help your friends."

"I know all that. But last week I had a waterman come in from Virginia. He drove all the way to Parkers from the lower Bay because he heard I was a waterman lawyer and he wanted the best. I loved that."

"But what did he want?"

"He wanted tax advice. And I think he wanted the advice from a lawyer, cause he knew it wouldn't fly. And either way, he wanted to say his lawyer did it. And I don't think he wanted to deal with his hometown lawyer."

"Did he commit a crime?" she asked.

"Not really. He wanted to deduct his wife as a business expense, because she worked as first mate a few times a year. I think he was afraid to let his wife know how much he thought she was worth."

Diane's face broke into a knowing smile. She saw this coming.

"He wanted to deduct all her clothes, mostly blue jeans and work boots, and all of her hair cuts because one day on the water would ruin her frizz for weeks. He wanted to write off her old truck because she had written her name and phone number in spray paint on the side door. And he wanted to declare their kitchen as her office. The kicker for me was that he said all the other guys took these deductions. He just wanted to make sure they were legal."

"That's why they pay you the big money, Ned," she said. "Let's move to a table."

Talking to Diane about being a lawyer was natural and easy. Not so easy was talking about my brother Jimmy, who after all, worked for the same client she did.

We slid into a booth along the wall and the bartender brought our drinks to the table. It was the perfect opportunity to start a new conversation. I looked at Diane and her eyes sparkled, or perhaps it was the diamond necklace. In any case, there was an aloofness about her that sent a slight shiver down my spine. Maybe a small realization that I wasn't in her league anymore; I wasn't in her game; talking to multiple clients, reading several papers a day, planning lunch at a fine restaurant every day. I felt uneasy.

"Diane," I said, "let me ask you again about Jimmy and Chesapeake Resorts International. This whole thing has escalated beyond me. We now know my brother was murdered, for no obvious reason. The Captain of his boat has taken off for parts unknown. Somebody swamped my boat in the middle of the night. And my brother's body turns up wearing a woman's tennis shoe, polka dot no less. Now what the hell is this all about? I have to ask you about the Resort."

"Fine," Diane said with her usual certainty, "but I don't know anything about all this. I advised the Chesapeake Resorts International to cooperate in every way with this investigation."

"I know, but I keep getting an itch in the back of my neck that CRI is involved is all this. These boys are too slick, too high powered. As the watermen would say, there's too many tassels on their shoes."

"Ned," Diane said, "you've been over there in the land of pickup trucks too long. These Resort boys are businessmen. They come from Florida and other places where waterside hotels are common. And they make a lot of money, so they hire fast talkers from Ivy League colleges to do their business, but they're not killers. And besides, why would they want to get rid of Jimmy?"

I thought a while, and let the conversation drop. Why indeed? Ever since Watergate, the Washington pundits always say: follow the money. And in South County, Chesapeake Resorts International was the richest guy in town. They had the money, and wanted to make more.

"Listen, Diane," I said, "what could Jimmy know that would make him worth killing?"

"I have no idea," she said. But she did.

"Look, he was hanging with these guys at environmental rallies, and going to town meetings, and he was making their pitch. Maybe one of the good ole boys in Parkers saw Jimmy as the leader of CRI and thought, 'Take Jimmy out and they're gone.' You know that could happen."

"Not really," I said.

"Well, what about the money. You raised the issue," she said. "What are these permits worth? What if Jimmy decided he'd had enough and decided to sabotage some permits. Maybe he decided to quit and testify against the company. Maybe join the SARP environmental folks. Maybe go the State Attorney General and rat on the developers. There's a hundred ways Jimmy could make this company mad, and they decide to take him out."

"And me too?"

"Neddie, when you've killed one, you can kill two. You better watch your backside."

I didn't like the way Diane had brought the subject back to me, and she hadn't really given me any new information. No names of company officials. No suspects. No examples of malfeasance. I was beginning to wonder about her involvement, or at least about the fact that she knew all the players, and yet kept herself above the fray.

It would be a distracting drive home.

Chapter Eighteen

Chumbucket Roberts approached the ladder leading to the fly-bridge of the *Scatback*, climbed the five steps until his eyes cleared the salon, twisted his body off the ladder and looked up to see past the other slips and out to the Intra Coastal. It was a ribbon to freedom that stretched before him until it merged with the clouds and the fog and disappeared in a silver horizon. Then he took the wheel in both hands, and the chrome surface was warm from the morning sun. It felt like pulling on a pair of soft Italian leather gloves and feeling the confidence of control. His life was never more in sync than during those first moments at the helm, even before the powerful engines roared to life, and before any unexpected problem could send fault lines through his confidence, and while his dreams and aspirations were confined to the water before him.

He wouldn't give any orders to Horace. He organized his mind to the boat so that he thought of things in sequence, the stern lines before the bow lines, the prospect of a quick reverse at the end of the pier followed by a light touch on the throttle and a forward turn into the channel. He would wait for Horace to tell him he was ready, then make a visual check of the dock lines, then be gone. He wanted so badly to be away from the dock, unrestrained, moving; it was a feeling he had known since his first canoe, and the message was always the same.

Horace arrived at the boat early and brought a last thermos of coffee from the IC Diner, a duffle bag packed with all his belongings, and a large black comb stuck in his back pocket. He wanted to feel the boat and the morning mist in total silence; to say goodbye to this briefly adopted town. He thought of New Smyrna as a rest stop, rather like the fast food cafés on the turnpike that he would probably never visit again. But in later years he might want to remember this place and this moment. He wondered how many times in life do you just throw everything in a worn out bag and move on. Horace was ready. And when it came time to cast off the lines while his new partner sat high above him at the helm, he moved with some uncertainty around the boat. He slipped the bow and stern lines off the pylons, which Chum noticed out of the corner of his eye. The low growl of the engines signaled the boat's slow movement out of the slip, and they were gone. Horace unfolded the captain's chair and set it up in the middle of the deck. Then he relaxed, stretched his legs out before him, crossed his arms, and let the morning mist fill his nostrils. He thought how lucky he was to meet this new friend, although it might conflict with his instructions, which had never mentioned a sudden departure. Horace's uncle had just said, "Meet Dave "Chumbucket" Roberts, and let me know what he's doing."

On the bridge, Chum thought about where they might be going. He figured they could head down the coast of Florida, fill up gas at some obscure marina down near Stewart, Florida, where there were plenty of boats to hide their arrival. Stewart was a boat building area with plenty of vessels in various stages of repair, perfect for not drawing unwanted attention. As long as the weather was good, he shouldn't have to get on the radio. And if he could find a gas pump in the open harbor, the chances of getting in and out without drawing attention were pretty good.

But Chum couldn't resist thinking of the fish, of the long tranquil days he had spent with charter customers, just drawing huge circles in the ocean as they searched for fish. It was his world and he wanted it back. He turned around to see if Horace was still sleeping in his deck chair.

"Horace," he said, "how about getting out the charts. Let's see where we are."

Horace stirred himself, looked around at the open water, and climbed to the bridge. He noticed the chart drawers in the console near the helm station, pulled out the top drawer and read the title: Intracoastal Waterway. Chum glanced over and said, "Look further down. Maybe the bottom drawer."

Horace pushed his hair from his forehead, bent over and reached for the drawer.

"See if you can find Mexico," Chum said.

"Mexico!" Horace exclaimed. "I don't speak Spanish. Why Mexico?"

"Why not?" Chum said. "I'm tired of looking over my shoulder. Let's get out of here."

Horace found a chart for the Gulf of Mexico. Maybe it would go further south. He laid it out before Chum and began turning the pages.

"Does your GPS have Mexico in it?" Horace asked. "It has to have a computer map in it to pick up the signals, to know where we're going."

"I don't know, we'll know when we get there."

"Are you sure we don't need a little more planning before going to Mexico?" Horace asked.

"Why? We haven't planned anywhere else. If we can get gas, we can go. Plus there's bound to be marinas down there that have charts or memory discs for the GPS. We can't do everything at once."

Horace could see that it would not pay to argue Chum's decision. He figured to just let Chum think about it. He might choose a simpler course. Plus, he figured it would take at least three or four days to get to Mexico, and Chum might change his mind often by then. He climbed back down the ladder, moved his captain's chair to the back of boat, and propped his feet on the varnished aft railing.

Chum continued to study the charts, looking for a place to gas up. He calculated that he could get further south than Stewart, maybe even to the Keys, that string of islands stretching from Miami to Key West. And he had heard stories about some of the little harbors and marinas in the keys, so backwater that nobody lived there but druggies and vagrants looking for warm sand to sleep away the winter. In his mind, he pictured a small harbor, with a short dock in front of an unpainted and dilapidated clam shack that sold bait, tackle and gas. That's what he was looking for, all the way to Mexico.

The next afternoon, Chum started moving the *Scatback* closer to shore, closer to the island bridge that trailed down from Miami like a piece of string. In morning fog you could hardly see it. The bridge was a ribbon of concrete set on pylons that held it above the tide, and when the sun was at the exact right angle, it shimmered into the horizon so the bridge seemed to float like an exotic belly dancer swaying just above the water. Chum found it magnetic and moved closer until his depth finder registered less than six feet, and he could see into the harbors with their parking lots and palm trees and gift shops selling beach chairs and rubber rafts. It was easy to dream in the keys, but it was also lonely, perhaps because it's the end of America. Key West advertises the southern most tip of America, the last stop before Cuba. But Chum wasn't really looking to lose everything, to totally escape society and responsibility. He wanted to find a new place with new opportunities.

Then he saw an almost hidden inlet, marked with small jetties on either side of the channel leading into a beach. Beyond the entrance he could see a weather beaten building with the faded name, Ocho

Key, in block letters over the door. There looked to be several other small white frame buildings nearby, a park with three or four benches around the edge and small splashes of grass indicating that someone had attempted a lawn, but the sand had reclaimed most of it. There were two gas pumps in front of the Ocho, but no one was around.

Horace had come to the bridge to monitor the entrance.

"This looks good," he said. "I don't see anybody. Lots of empty slips and a nice park. Maybe we can spend the night and get a little land time."

"Let's do the gas first and see how it feels," Chum replied. "I'm going to ease up to the dock. You jump off and I'll throw you a bow line. Wrap it around that pylon by the pumps. We may have to wait a while to find someone to run these pumps."

Horace had lived on a boat, but he hadn't spent much time running one. He did remember, however, that the most dangerous moment for a neophyte was jumping on and off a boat, or somehow getting wedged between a boat and the dock. So he checked his footing carefully and made the leap.

"How about tying her down?" Chum shouted as he turned off the engine. "I'll go see if I can find someone." He jumped off the boat and headed for the little white shack at the end of the dock.

* * * * *

Johnny Simmons had long blonde hair that fluttered carelessly around his neck and a certain innocence in his tanned face that belied his years as a Deputy Sheriff who roamed the Keys. He heard the *Scatback* maneuver into the vacant slip at the Ocho bait shop, raised himself out of a torn corduroy recliner, and mentally ran through his options. The first was to do nothing and see if indeed the boat wanted fuel, or to wait and see who got off the boat, perhaps telegraphing their intentions, which could be nothing more than to find a hamburger and beer.

It could be a drug trafficker wanting to rendezvous with a later arriving boat. It could be a lost family that needed shelter before moving on to Key West. So he just watched.

Johnny was stationed up the coast at Key Largo and in his six years with the Sheriff's office had arrested very few boaters. His law enforcement record was bad. But his attitude was good. He liked the work and never asked for a raise, reasoning that he didn't do much real work, didn't want much responsibility, and he was developing an expertise. He could recognize and identify almost any boat made in the United States, and specialized in reciting the life story of any Captain or owner, just by looking at his boat, or at least by examining its upkeep and on deck appurtenances. He also read the internet alerts of boats traveling the East Coast with hidden purposes. The *Scatback* drew his attention because it wasn't shiny clean, like a charter boat, or cluttered with chairs and people like a family boat.

Johnny was Deputy Sheriff but today he was just watching the bait shop and gas pumps for his friend, Mia, who had gone to Miami for the day, so he turned on the gas pumps' switch and started for the dock. He didn't see Chum, who had apparently veered off to visit the outdoor restroom and shower facilities on the far side of the park. But he noticed Horace standing on the dock near the pumps.

Chum turned to look back and noticed Johnny heading for Horace, and he stopped in his tracks, edging slowly back behind a large palm tree. He saw Johnny ask Horace if he could help, but it was difficult to pick up the conversation. Horace was shaking his head and gesturing toward the south, perhaps pointing in the general direction of Mexico. Then Johnny held out his arm in a directing way, pointing to the bait shop, and the two started moving away from the dock and toward the building.

Chum spotted the Sheriff's car parked on the far side of the lot, and sure enough, it looked like Johnny and Horace were headed in that direction. It was getting dark and Chum wished he had waited a little longer before entering the harbor. He didn't move, not wanting to draw attention to himself or his boat. Then he saw the cruiser's door open, a front seat light came on and Chum could see that Horace was getting in the backseat, and the other fellow got behind the wheel and reached for his dash, probably the on board communications. It certainly looked like the cop was interviewing Horace and checking his computer for information on the boat. Not a good sign.

Horace was shaken by this sudden appearance by a cop with an attitude. He and Chum had never discussed what to say if they were stopped by police or Coast Guard, in fact, it never felt like they were running from the law. But he knew there was something terribly wrong or his uncle wouldn't be paying him to meet Chum and stay with him.

Horace hadn't told Johnny, the Deputy Sheriff, anything about the boat or himself, but he asked to call his home. Johnny agreed and Horace pulled his cell phone out of his blue jeans. He dialed the number for Parkers, Maryland. When the voice came on the line, Horace paused, then said, "Uncle Ray, I need your help." The Blenny Man pulled the phone away from his mouth and said, "Shit," before raising it again to ask the problem.

Chum was trying to think through his dilemma. He stayed behind the tree but figured he didn't have much time. Horace must not have mentioned him, or the Sheriff would be looking for him. He must not have mentioned the boat wasn't his, or the Sheriff would be searching it. But he knew that Horace would reveal all these facts soon, and once he started proclaiming his innocence, all kinds of calls would be made to try and identify the owner. Most significantly, there would be a call to the Coast Guard. And Chum knew that his new friend would not wait long to say they were headed for Mexico. That gave the Coast Guard quite a distance to find the *Scatback* and its "wanted" Captain.

Chum edged back to the dock, as darkness gave definition to the lights along the pier. He had decided to make a run for it, and now was the time for speed. He climbed over the gunnels of his boat, then rushed from one cleat to another, untying the dock lines and letting them quietly drop in the water. He went in the main salon, not want-ing to expose himself on the flybridge, and started the engine. He knew it would be heard, but he had no choice. He backed the boat away from the dock with no lights, and slowly headed out to the chan-nel. When he reached open water beyond the jetty, he slowly in-creased the speed, heading for deep water. He kept looking back, but seeing or hearing nothing. Maybe the Sheriff's Deputy was already calling the Coast Guard.

At about a mile out, Chum turned on his GPS to see his location. It lit up a six-inch screen with a map of the coast. He pushed the zoom button and the map backed away showing the entire coast. But he could still see the red line that the GPS had marked in the ocean as Chum had made his way from Cape Hatteras to New Smyrna to the Keys. It is perhaps the grandest feature of global positioning. No mat-ter where the boat goes, the Captain can always find his way home by simply following the red line back. Chum located the *Scatback* on the map. It was a black diamond at the end of the red line. Mexico was to the right, but Chum turned his boat to the left and put the diamond on the line.

"I'm going home," he muttered to himself. "Or as close to home as I can get."

Chapter Nineteen

Lillian Wildman wasted no time in organizing the community to help Martha. First, she went to Nails Hardware Store carrying a pickle jar with a computer generated label taped to the side that said: For Martha Claire Shannon. She assumed, no doubt correctly, that everyone in Parkers would know Martha and her condition, or they would know the minute they saw the pickle jar. The clerk at Nails, who had been counting out bolts and screws for 30 years, would tell them.

Lillian set the jar on the counter. "Margaret," she said, "I'm sure you know about Martha Shannon. Could we put a jar here for donations?"

"You sure can," Margaret said as she lowered her glasses to her chest. "How is she?"

"She goes in for her operation Thursday. Brain tumor. I don't know what her chances are, but it's bound to be costly."

"Is it cancer?" Margaret asked.

"Probably," Lillian replied, "but we won't know for sure until they operate. We don't know much about it, but they've gone all over America looking for a doctor."

"Who's helping her?" Margaret asked.

"Well, Jimmy's brother Ned is with her. That boy seems to take on all sorts of things, first the crab boat, then a law office, and now he's helping Martha. I don't know that he's much of a crabber, but he sure has taken care of Martha and Mindy."

"Well, we'll help any way we can," Margaret said.

"I know," Lillian said, as she moved away from the counter and toward the door. "I'm going over to the Moose hall now and see when we can get a fundraiser going. I'll let you know."

* * * * *

The Moose Lodge in Parkers is a red brick building in the middle of town with no shrubs to enhance the questionable beauty of un-adorned bricks. It was built for function and is maintained for the same purpose, mostly bingo nights, weddings and other gatherings of more than 50 people. I was last there for a family celebration to mark the return of a war veteran by nearly a hundred proud parents, rela-tives, friends and acquaintances. The Moose hall is a perfect venue for groups such as this because the rental cost is modest, there are no food preparation costs or minimums, and the renters can do almost all the work themselves. The veteran family, for example, brought all the food themselves in huge bowls of chicken salad, potato salad, and cut fruit with cakes and pies of every stripe. Afterward you can throw away the paper plates, serve wine or tea and the whole thing might not cost more than a few hundred dollars. And if you can prove the rental is for a good purpose, like a fundraiser for someone sick or dying, the special rate kicks in. Sometimes it's free. Further, if you want to have a silent auction, as Lillian thought about doing, you can probably clear two or three thousand dollars after paying the costs. Lillian has this down to a science, at least a couple times a year. The only question in her mind is the date that will allow the most people to attend. And she has a good mailing list for that too.

Incidentally, I've never met anybody who is actually a Moose Lodge member, although I do envision a group of guys saluting a moose, pledging a commitment to community service, and planning Fourth of July parties. I do know they make enough money to keep the place sparkling clean, the wood trim around the windows freshly painted, and the maple wood paneling in mint condition. The bar that runs the entire length of the building, and can be used for buffet purposes, is spartan but adaptable to many purposes.

"I want to fill this place up," Lillian told the executive secretary of the lodge. "And I want the first Saturday night next month. This is a fundraiser for Martha Claire Shannon. She's one of us, a waterman's wife, a local girl, and she has a brain tumor."

"You bet," he replied. "We all know the Shannons, and we'll help."

"Can I get the special rate?" Lillian asked.

"You bet," he said.

"How about a dance band," Lillian said. "We don't need to be glum just because it's for Martha. Let's have some fun. And dancing raises the most money anyway."

"I remember Martha Shannon and her husband Jimmy were here one night about five years ago," the secretary said. "They were having a hell of a time. Dancing and yelling. Jimmy stood up at one point and declared a toast to all the watermen. At hearing that, ole Patrick Moonsocket got up and chugged a whole pitcher of beer. It was running down his face and his shirt was soaked. His wife was screaming at him to stop. And hell, he wanted to drink another pitcher. But by then he was drunk and dizzy and could hardly sit down, let alone drink another one."

"Wasn't that the night we had a dance for Mabel Fergus when she got married again?" Lillian asked, knowing full well that the dance was one of Parkers' most notorious evenings. Mabel had run off with the owner of the Parkers Marine Railway, Sampson Brown. Sampson ran a crab boat out of his little marina and did a booming business with the Sampson Marine Railway. The railway ran from the water behind his house, up a gentle slope about thirty yards into a covered repair shop where Sampson performed boat maintenance of every kind.

A Scotsman named Thomas Morton invented the marine railway in1818 by extending rails well into the water, running a wooden boat cradle into the water at high tide, and floating a boat to be repaired onto the cradle. Then men or horses would pull the boat out of the water. He called it "slipping" a vessel.

Sampson Brown just called it hauling, and he used an electric winch to pull the boat to his shed. If the electricity was down, Sampson could use his pickup truck and pull the boat up the rails without much trouble. Sampson could pull a boat and power wash the barnacles off the bottom, or even repair an engine, in very little time. Between the railway and the crabbing, he became a relatively wealthy man and a reasonable target of affection for Mabel Fergus. Indeed, her marriage at age fifty to Sampson would just about lock up the waterman business in Parkers, a fact no one seemed to bemoan, and everyone wanted to celebrate. There was no better place to do it than the Moose Lodge, and the ensuing party had the parallel effect of making a folk hero out of Jimmy Shannon. Right up until his death by tuna, he was known as "that guy who joined ole Moonie in chugging beer at the Moose," and his wife Martha was given high marks for sticking by her man in his inebriated condition. These are the kind of incidents that create reputations for a lifetime in Parkers.

Lillian left the Moose Lodge knowing her fundraiser was off to a good start. The date was secured, and the Lodge, which is a community service organization with a special interest in health care issues, found this cause appealing. Plus, it would bring together the very fabric of the community. She was so excited by the prospect for a successful event, that she stepped out of the club into the sunlight, rummaged her purse for her cell phone, and slid behind the wheel of her car to complete the last segment of her mission.

Lillian hit her automatic redial and the phone started ringing in the Calico Cat, where Effie Humbolt started pushing around swatches of cloth to find her portable telephone, an instrument that never seemed to be in its cradle and often had batteries which needed charging. Effie's phone was a testament to her large circle of friends and relatives that received daily nurturing by telephone. Lillian knew she would be perfect to organize the food service, and childcare if need be, for Martha Claire.

"Effie," she said to the instantly recognizable voice, "this is Lillian Wildman and I'm calling about Martha Shannon."

"I know," Effie said. "Isn't it unbelievable? How could all these terrible things happen to her, in such a short time? I don't know what to do."

"Well, here's my thought," Lillian said. "I'm arranging a fundraiser at the Lodge to give her some quick cash. I don't know whether she needs it, but it's a way for everybody to help out. And in these times, it can't hurt."

"That's good," Effie said. "When is it?"

"No date yet, but we'll let everybody know," Lillian said, referring to the organization of women she was about to put together. "But I think we're going to have a more immediate need. I talked to Martha and she's going to have this operation within days. My God, it's a ten hour operation and they take a whole side of her head off. The doctors won't even project an outcome, except she has a five percent chance of dying and a fifteen percent chance of paralysis. My God, Effie, they're talking about all sorts of terrible things."

"How long has she had this thing?" Effie asked.

"Maybe 20 years," Lillian said, "and she isn't going to survive this with a couple of aspirin and a week in bed. We have to help with food, and rehabilitation, and that darling little girl of hers."

"What about Ned?" Effie asked, thinking of her office neighbor.

"I don't know," Lillian said. "But I know the watermen will take care of him. Vinnie is running his boat. I don't know anything about his law practice, but I think most of his clients are local and they'll understand. I'm not sure Neddie bargained for a family in this deal, but he's got one now, and I'm sure he can do it."

"Neddie's life in Washington may seem pretty good right now."

"Don't say that Effie," Lillian said. "That boy is home now and we're going to take care of him."

"What do you want me to do?" Effie asked.

"Can you do the food, for say two weeks, after she comes home?" Lillian requested. "Contact the wives, schedule them, figure out how many days a person can live on beef stew, and maybe make sure a few desserts are included. That should get us started and we'll figure out the long-term later. We just don't know what condition she's going to be in."

"I'll do it," Effie said. "What about transportation? Her rehabilitation could be over at Johns Hopkins or some place else. We may need a car schedule."

"I'll get someone else to think about that," Lillian said. "You know that book club that meets at the Bayfront. Those are young wives with a little free time, and they have good eyes for driving. I'll get them organized."

The town of Parkers was about to roar into action.

Chapter Twenty

Two incredible things happened to Martha during her "preparation" for the operation at Philadelphia's Good Conscience Hospital, getting admitted and the pinholes. Just getting in the place at 5:00 in the afternoon was traumatic. Tons of people were streaming out the double glass doors to the main lobby, apparently at quitting time or at least time for a shift change. I didn't know anything about hospitals except that it must require a huge staff to run the place day and night. And if Dr. Nablani wanted to prep Martha at 7:00 at night, there must be a large night crew that could operate the place at full steam.

We weren't quite prepared for such an old hospital. It looked to have had about three hundred additions since the end of World War II, and each one represented the advance of architecture. Jutting out of flat walls with small square windows would be a circular room with floor to ceiling glass made of the thick smoky cubes so popular in the 1950s. I could imagine it as a solarium for brain operation patients where things didn't go quite right; the patients were moved to the light where they could sleep all day waiting for a miracle to happen. Then there was a two story glass waiting room on the second floor signifying the invention of escalators, probably in the 1960s, and clear windows allowing maximum sun. And finally, another large wing wedged between the old building and a ten story parking garage.

But these were all superficial impressions, and in fact, most of my memory of that first night is a blur. Somehow we were whisked into the brain surgery wing, Martha was told to hang her clothes in a closet because she would be wearing them home in a couple of hours, and I was ushered down the hall to a small waiting room. One should never go to a hospital waiting room at the end of the day. Magazines were strewn everywhere. Newspapers were stacked on the corner table but all the sections were out of order and I knew there would be jelly or sugar residue on the inside sections. A family of Latinos was seated on the plastic covered couch, with one child asleep on her mother's lap and a teenager stretched out on a lounge chair, disheveled, tired and drinking from a Coke can. Their conversation indicated that a family member had been in surgery most of the day, and they had heard nothing. Mom and Dad were scared to death and the kids were just exhausted. I pictured myself at the end of tomorrow, after I had devoured several cans of soda pop, read every newspaper twice, and probably had lunch in the basement cafeteria with no windows and bland food. This was not a good start. I hoped at least for a cleaning crew. The doctor's plan was to do the 'prep' tonight, and we were to arrive at the hospital at 7:00 a.m. the next morning for the actual operation. So I didn't expect the 'prep' to take long.

But I soon realized my exhaustion, and fell asleep with the sounds of Spanish words forming a mental haze. The next words I heard, about an hour later, were, "Mr. Shannon, your sister-in-law is ready to go home." Those were actually very reassuring words. I awoke and managed a smile before falling in line behind the nurse on the way to Martha's room.

She was smiling. "I hope you're ready for this," Martha said. I went to her bed and took her hand, mostly to steady myself. I knew it was important to not say the wrong thing, not the words she might remember forever. So I said, "That looks pretty good."

Half her hair was gone. It looked like a Mohawk haircut, except the barber was called away before he could finish.

"Why didn't they just cut it all off?" I asked.

"The doctor said it was less shocking to patients and this is the way they do it now."

"What doctor? Nablani?" I asked.

"Well, I said doctor, but I don't know who it was. He said he was on Nablani's team. Looked young, probably a resident," Martha said.

I just stared. Finally I asked, "What else did they do?"

"They just made marks, and stuck some pins in my head," she said. "Didn't hurt."

I looked closely and could see the small blue marks that outlined the operation. Then I noticed the pin holes on her forehead, one on each side. I realized that in any situation where we have no real experience, we are victims of our private knowledge, right or wrong. All I could see was George Patton. I had seen an old black and white movie that portrayed Patton's shocking death at the end of World War II. It showed him in the back seat of a 1940 sedan, driven by his loyal young aide. But the driver came to a railroad track, had to brake fast, and threw the general forward with such ferocity that he broke his neck. The next scene was in an Army hospital and the great Patton with his pearl handled pistols was lying in bed, with a square wooden brace around his head, with pins in each corner that were stuck in his head and held it from any possible movement. And that's the way he died. My god, I could see those little pin holes in Martha's forehead and I realized the operation tomorrow would require just such a brace as the power saws tore into her head like a dental drill and the side of her head was removed. I shuddered and hoped Martha did not notice. We never said a word about it.

The next day we arrived at the hospital and the doctors put Martha on a gurney, said goodbye, and wheeled her down the hallway, presumably to the operating room. It was so fast I hardly realized it was happening. I stumbled to the little waiting room, trying to figure out the logistics. She would have to be anesthetized, which would take a couple of hours I supposed, the operation itself was supposed to take eight to ten hours, then recovery in the intensive care ward, assuming everything went all right. So it would be seven or eight o'clock at night before this was over. I started through the newspapers.

But there is loneliness like no other in a hospital waiting room. The faces are all strangers. Families of patients suffering all sorts of ailments, and one cannot avoid the speculation. Then you hear the conversations in piecemeal, of family heartaches, or friends who were at the movies only yesterday, and today they have a death sentence. How can that be? At what moment can it be when a single cell of cancer stands up in one's body and says, I'm here, the next several months of your life are destroyed in a haze of chemotherapy and radiation and weakness of mind and body. How does that happen? What does it mean for free will, and disease avoidance, and "taking care of yourself" in any way? It's so arbitrary and capricious that it destroys your confidence in the living. Then you are a victim of the disease as much as the patient. And finally, in that last painful moment of self pity and tearful fear of the world around you, you realize that no one shares these fears but your family. You realize that family is that small group of people who cloister around you in the remote corners of life and hold on to keep you warm, or take you to a bed, or find you a home, or give you food. It is a rescue so basic that you can never forget it, or live without it. And in Good Conscience Hospital, as the strangers moved through this little waiting room with me, the air passed out of my lungs until I was gasping. And only the two ladies on the couch beside me kept the decorum, kept me from yielding to my own shrinking and garbled thoughts until I screamed to an unholy god that had let me down.

I had no family but Martha and Mindy, who would never know her father, and might never know her mother. And I hoped she would never know what I felt at that moment: "I am so alone."

But then I looked down the hall, past the blood pressure machines and past the nurses' station with ghostly figures responding to red lights and bells, and two figures emerged from the elevators. They looked familiar. I squinted, closing one eye. And sure enough, it was a friend.

Pete and Lillian Wildman turned the corner and hurried toward the waiting room. I got up to tuck my shirt in my pants, arrange my hair, and otherwise look presentable. This was unexpected. Philadelphia is at least a three hour drive from Parkers, and would require a day's commitment to visit. Pete and Lil hadn't even called. They just took a chance. I had told everyone that the operation was today, and I probably named the hospital. But I never offered times, or a specific location, or an invitation. Yet my eyes were big as saucers and I felt like Mom and Dad had come down from heaven for a visit.

"Neddie," Lil shouted from the area of the nurses' station. "How are you?"

She was still about five steps from the waiting room, and one of the nurses shushed her as she walked by.

I gave her a big hug and it was good to feel her hands on my back. Nothing reserved. No peck on the cheek or social grasp. It was an honest to goodness family greeting that said "we care about you and Martha." I suddenly realized how long it had been since I had received one of these unrestrained hugs, without calculation or equivocation. I reached behind Lil's back and grabbed Pete's hand. His face was aglow. I couldn't tell whether he was excited to see me or just red burned from the sun and wind after a day on the water. I didn't care.

"Pete!" I exclaimed. "How are you buddy? They took Martha in about 8:00 o'clock this morning. I haven't heard a thing."

Lil backed away and searched my face for stress. When people hear brain tumor, they automatically think cancer, and ultimately death. And when I try to explain that this tumor isn't cancerous, but could still kill Martha in several different ways, it only introduces more confusion and greater fear. So I quit striving for clarity and accepted "reassurance."

"All we can do it wait," I said. "Come sit down. Or we can go get a cup of coffee."

"Neddie," Lil said, "I know you're not a big social animal. But you must know that you and Martha have many friends in Parkers. And some of them are coming. You don't have to do anything, just accept our friendship."

"Today?" I asked. "They're coming today? But we won't know anything till tonight."

"Doesn't matter," Lil said. "They'll stay all night if they have to. You've got us so get ready."

"Who's coming?" I asked.

"We better just wait and see. I don't want you to get agitated and then nobody shows up. But let's wait on getting coffee for a while just to see who comes."

"Fine," I said, and sat down on the couch facing the windows.

By the time Martha came out of the intensive care unit 12 hours later, seventeen people from Parkers, Maryland were waiting for her. The last couple to arrive was Judge Humboldt and Effie, the Calico Cat. I had never met the judge before, although I had often worried he might be a stuffed shirt. As a lawyer, I knew plenty of judges and I couldn't imagine taking a one of them out crabbing. I couldn't even imagine a one of them in blue jeans. But here came Judge Humboldt in jeans, docksider shoes and a blue button down shirt. He had a crew cut for hair, rare even in Parkers, and was unfailingly polite.

"It's great to meet you Judge," I said.

"What's Martha's status?" he asked, no doubt aware of his purpose in accompanying Effie to Philadelphia, and perhaps a little impatient to get the results. More like a judge, I thought. But he asked, "Have you talked to the doctor about swelling, or any side effects?"

"No, I haven't seen anybody," I said.

Effie grasped my arm to focus a question. "Ned, I want to help you with the insurance companies. Anything I can do. We've been through enough of this to know you can spend a year or more just directing bills to primary providers, and secondary providers, and then going back a third time with challenges."

"Thanks Effie," I said. "That's the kind of help I need."

Mansfield Burlington and Marilyn had been here since mid morning. It was great to have their support, mature and helpful. Most importantly, they entertained themselves, going to every cafeteria and snack bar in the hospital. They could give recommendations on best desserts, soggiest lettuce, freshest tuna salad, and strongest coffee.

Burl stepped up behind Effie. "That's the kind of help we all need. As we were leaving Parkers just this morning, there was a poster on the telephone pole that said, 'Need Health Insurance, Call Us Today.' You know health care is in trouble when you can buy it off a telephone pole."

"Actually, our area has a strong history of health care," Effie said. "Over in Deale, they used to have an organization called The African Americans United Sons and Daughters of Holland."

"Who was Holland?" I asked, wanting to stay in the conversation.

"I don't remember," Effie said, "but the organization was for poor black people who needed medical help. At the beginning of the 19th century, all blacks were poor, at least in South County, and so they incorporated in 1905 to help each other pay medical bills. It cost 25 cents a month till 1957 when they raised it to 50 cents. Sick members of the organization were given $2 a week for the first month of their illness and after that they passed the hat. These people took care of their own. And today in Parkers we still take care of our own. So we're staying until we know Martha is going to be all right."

"How long did the Holland organization last?" I asked.

"That's the most amazing thing," Effie said. "The Holland group lasted until 1983. Can you imagine that, until 1983. We had men on the moon for twenty years before that, and these people were still helping each other pay the bills. That's our history, Mr. Ned, and we have seventeen people here today to continue the tradition."

Just as I was ready to explore the traditions of South County, a doctor in blue operating pants and cap walked into the room. He had to excuse himself around Effie, then pulled his hat off and asked for Mr. Shannon. His black curly hair was glistening, presumably from perspiration. I hoped not from the operation. I hadn't seen him since our interview days before, and at one point had wondered if he was even here, but I pushed it from my mind.

"Mr. Shannon," Dr. Nablani said as the Parkerites put down their golf and entertainment magazines to listen. "Your wife is fine. She's in recovery. She had a craniotomy, so we have to keep her still for several hours. But she's alert, although groggy. You can probably see her in an hour or two, but she won't go to her room, so your friends probably can't see her till tomorrow. The nurses may let you in the intensive care unit two at a time."

"She lived." That's all I could think. I thought about telling Nablani that Mrs. Shannon isn't my wife, but who cares.

He nodded to Burl and the rest, then turned and left.

* * * * *

The next morning, after a round of coffee in the waiting room, the Parkerites started telling stories about their night in the Philly Arms, a small hotel near the hospital, selected mostly for its location so no one would get lost. It didn't have a restaurant, so the group convened at the chain seafood house across the street. I wondered why a bunch of watermen would not take this opportunity to have steaks, or something different from their normal fare. Burl said one of the watermen actually got angry because no oysters were on the menu. As Burl said, "Hell, ole Charlie probably eats 20 gallon of oysters a year and now he wants one more plate in Philadelphia." Effie said, "Now we're going to call you Oyster Charlie." Everyone was laughing, including Charlie, when the nurse popped in to say, "I'll take you in two at a time. Mr. Shannon first."

Martha was sleeping, which gave me a chance to examine her bandages without her awareness. Her head was totally wrapped from just above her eyebrows to the top of her head. Again I wondered why they left a half head of hair, when it was all covered with tape. Maybe they cut more of it off during the operation. Martha looked fine. I searched for the pin holes, but they must have been under the tape. I could see her breathing, and that was reassuring. And then, as silently as a floating leaf, her eyes opened. There was recognition, but no smile or movement of any kind. The nurse beside me said, "We don't think she can talk yet."

Over the next half hour, I gently prodded the nurse to explore Martha's condition, but to no avail. I sat in the corner of the waiting room and dozed. Dreaming, I could see into Martha's head, without the tumor. In my mind's eye, it was a large hole with dangling nerve ends that had slowly moved to the side of the brain by years and years of tumor growth, and now they found themselves dangling into an open cave like stalagmites of the brain, waiting to stretch their legs and resume the functions that had been suppressed. And it seemed natural that every function would now be jumbled, so that speech would be slurred, and vision blurred, and hearing lost, and words stifled. Please God, I prayed, just straighten them all out and let Martha be whole again. Finally the nurses decided to wheel Martha to her private room instead of bringing all her friends to the ICU. As she passed through the hallway, her eyes were open but there was no other sign of recognition. She was a lifeless form under a sea of bandages and I wondered how long it would take to resolve the mysteries of her mind. It was my first moment of hopelessness.

Her bed with the protective rails up and two nurses and myself in tow, moved away from intensive care to the room. We passed the waiting room with seventeen Parkerites lined against the wall, straining to see Martha's condition. Her eyes had closed and the group said nothing.

"Let us get her settled," I said. "And I'll come get you."

It was another hour before Martha opened her eyes and recognized me.

I asked how she felt, but there was no response. Then her lips moved, but no words emerged. My heart sank as I imagined all of her sensory abilities similarly impaired. I tried to think what to say, to guess what she would want to know.

"Mindy is fine Martha," I said. "I'll call her aunt as soon as we talk to the doctors. You can talk to Mindy..." and then I realized she couldn't.

Martha fidgeted, and opened her mouth. But she couldn't talk. Her tongue was swollen to the point that even breathing was difficult. I assumed that would go down, but no one had mentioned a tongue problem.

"Martha, you have all kinds of friends here. They came yesterday, stayed the night, and they want to see you. Some of them need to go home this afternoon. Can I just bring them in to see you're alive and well?"

I could see her eyes try to smile, although her mouth and face remained fixed. Her nurse advised waiting for the doctors, who she promised to find, and she left the room. I touched Martha's hand. Her fingers closed on mine and held tight. This moment must have been as frightening for her as for me. Things were happening or not happening and we had no idea why.

A young Egyptian doctor came in, shorter that Nablani, but smiling. I thought I had seen him with the group that took Martha into surgery, but with the masks, I couldn't be sure.

"I'm Dr. Nassif," he said. "I work with Dr. Nablani. He had to rush off to the airport. Going to Turkey for a lecture on meningioma. Back next week. In the meantime, I'll take good care of Mrs. Shannon."

"How is she, doctor?" I asked. It seemed strange to talk about Martha in front of her, especially when she couldn't talk. But I was determined to ask the questions for her."

"First," Nassif said, "she is in very good shape. All of our team feels she is capable of a full recovery, but it will take some time. There is swelling in her tongue, but it will go down, and she should be able to talk by tomorrow. Most importantly, there has been very little swelling in the brain, but she needs to stay very still."

Nassif moved to her side. "Mrs. Shannon," he said, "I need to ask you some questions. Can you just squeeze my hand, once for yes, and twice for no?" He took her hand and she squeezed it once. My God, I thought, I'm breathless over the first instruction. It was my first realization that paralysis could be a permanent situation. How would Martha take care of herself, of Mindy? What would be my responsibility? I told myself not to jump to conclusions, not to hurry things.

Then Nassif started the questions. "Can you see me?" Two squeezes from her hesitant fingers. He reached forward and put one hand over her left eye. "Better?" One squeeze.

"I think she has double vision, and probably blurry." Nassif never looked away from her face, studying every twitch and possible movement. I didn't see any, but maybe he could.

"Vision impairment is normal," he said. "It should steadily improve. I'll put some gauze over her glasses on one eye. That should help."

"Can you hear?" he asked. One squeeze. "She indicates she can hear, but I suspect there is some loss. Of course, she has bandages over her ears so that has an effect. Hearing loss to some degree is normal in this kind of operation."

"One last thing," he said. "Mrs. Shannon, think you can hold a pencil?" One squeeze. He put a piece of paper on the moveable server and pushed it under her arm. Then he took a pencil from his breast pocket and put it between her fingers. I was surprised that she seemed to grip it with firmness.

"Can you write your name?" he asked.

She started moving her hand, but it only left scratches on the pad. When she stopped moving the pencil, I reached over and turned the paper to see if I could read anything. Nothing. Nassif was cool. He said quietly, "That will improve."

"We need to get her up as soon as possible, maybe in a day or two, so she can start regaining her balance. She'll probably need a walker for a while. Once the brain starts to adjust, we should start seeing improvement. Remember, there is now a big hole in the middle of her head, and many nerve ends that have to adjust. But on the whole, her vital signs are good and she's alert. I think she's doing very well."

"When will you be back?" I asked.

"Every day," he said. "Here's my number to call anytime, day or night. And the nurses can always reach me, so don't hesitate."

"When will Nablani be back?" I asked.

"In a couple weeks," Nassif said. "But I'll take good care of her."

I stumbled back down to the waiting room to see our friends. Everyone hushed. Pete got up and gave me his seat on the couch. They waited.

"Well, I guess she's OK," I said. And I started through the tests Dr. Nassif had given her. But Lil started crying, and I almost did.

"Thanks to you all for coming," I said. "I don't know how to thank you. I don't quite know how we're going to work things out, but we should be home in a couple weeks."

Don't you worry," Lil said. "I know Vinnie's got that boat under control. And Effie's got the law firm covered. And Mindy is fine with your aunt. God bless you Neddie Shannon. And give Martha our love."

After that I only remember a cacophony of voices, and hand-shakes, and pats on the back. In a few minutes they were gone, vanished like apparitions in the night. I sat alone for a few minutes to pull myself together, then headed back to Martha's room.

Chapter Twenty-One

The Blenny Man stewed. He was starting his first cocktail of the evening, lounging in dark dress pants, terry cloth slippers of indeterminate style, and a Hawaiian shirt with a large blue palm tree on the back and beach on the front. He was not preparing for turmoil. But Horace's call reminded him of all the mistakes and anxiety of the last few months as he arranged for Jimmy Shannon's fishing trip, and Chum's trip to New Smyrna Beach, and his nephew's undercover assignment to form a friendship with Chum to keep track of his activities. Hell, he thought, this thing has been falling apart from the beginning.

He leaned back on the couch, pulled a small black comb from his pocket, stroked his hair and tried to figure out what to do. Then he ran his hands through his hair, as if it might stir a thought, then combed it again. His nerves were on edge and his clothes didn't fit right, pinching and pulling as he twisted. He stood to readjust, then sat again and reached for the phone on the end table. He started dialing the call he didn't want to make.

The phone stopped ringing so he knew it was answered, but no one spoke. Ray Herbst waited silently, then said in a low voice, "Mary Margaret, are you there?"

"Don't say my name," a woman's voice whispered in urgent tones. "Don't say my name."

"Mary Margaret," he said, "we have to talk."

"No we don't," she whispered, but this time in a spitting, angry tone. "They're listening. And you just said my name. Hang up." And her line went dead. No click or shuffling noise, just silence.

Blenny sat with the receiver in his hand, pondering the weirdness of this performance, by a woman he had known all his life. He had talked to her often in recent months and every conversation started in similar fashion. Sometimes the words were different, more urgent, more fearful, and more dramatic. But the message was always the same, she was threatened by unnamed detractors.

Blenny redialed the call. Again, the phone was answered but no voice came on the line. This time, Blenny concentrated on Mary Margaret's rules.

"Hello," he said, without receiving any return recognition. "We must talk. My friend in Florida has broken out. My nephew is with the police. What do we do?"

"Don't talk to me," the voice on the other end shouted. "They're listening. They're taping."

"If I can't talk," Blenny said, "how can I tell you what's wrong?"

"You know the rules," she said. "Bayfront at seven." The line went dead again.

Blenny knew the rules. He put down the receiver, replaced his slippers with black loafers, tucked his shirt into his pants, and walked through the house without turning out lights or locking the doors. He knew to drive to the parking lot behind the Bayfront, a large gravel lot of potholes and pickup trucks with the names of charter boats on their doors. Blenny liked "Stormy Petrel" best, a literary bent. It was evening and most of the fishing parties had long since departed. But a few of the watermen were cleaning up their boats in preparation for the next day's excursions. Blenny knew that in the middle of these trucks named Nip n' Tuck or some such thing, a faded beat-up pink 1971 Ford pickup truck would be parked and waiting. Inside, barely able to see over the dashboard and probably smoking a cigarette, would be Mary Margaret McCullough, known in the community as The Pipe Lady, and her two dogs. She was also Ray Herbst's mother, from her first husband, and possibly the richest woman in Maryland. Blenny had been putting up with her paranoia for years. She refused medication, or even medical attention. But as far as Blenny knew, no one was actually chasing her. Most avoided her, and her only steady mail came from Chesapeake Resorts International. And he thought it also likely that no one at CRI had ever met her. But they knew her as the anonymous person, acting under the name of Harbor Lights, Inc., who began buying their stock until she owned forty-nine percent of the CRI holding company. They sent her letters and all were returned, Address Unknown.

Yet remarkably, Harbor Lights had voted on every stock issue presented by the Board. The Board had considered sending an investigator to find the person behind Harbor Lights, but someone mentioned the name Howard Hughes and the Board decided to let the matter drop. If she wanted to be a silent stock holder, it was fine with them.

Blenny got out of his car, catching his shirt on the door latch and leaving a grease stain, so he got back in the car. He had parked as close to his mother's truck as possible, in case she wanted to talk through open windows. But her window stayed closed. He again got out of his car, closed the door quietly so it didn't latch, leaned toward her window and motioned her to roll the window down. He muttered, "This is ridiculous." And the window came down about four inches.

"That boy, Chum, knows nothing about us," she whispered.

"No but your grandson, Horace, does," Blenny said.

"He won't talk," she said. "Tell him to go home."

Before he could argue, the truck started, and began moving forward. Blenny leaned back to avoid the mirror, and watched as only the dogs stared back at him.

Blenny remembered when his stepfather, John McCullough, died nearly twenty years before and left millions to his mother. That's when it started. They lived in a large fashionable house on the edge of Parkers, set back from the road on about five acres of wooded property. Mary was never very active in society, but after the funeral she withdrew completely and took to walking the three or four miles for groceries from Flossie's store. Over the years, she added the Lab and the Mutt and took to smoking a corncob pipe. Her hair became gray and scraggy and no one had ever seen her without tennis shoes. Gradually the paint on her house began to peel and deteriorate into a combination of gray siding, green mold and heavy vines. Her lane to the main road was muddy and almost impassable most of the winter. Sometimes she would push her grocery cart as far as the rusty mail box, then leave it alongside the road and carry her packages to the house. This happened so gradually that people didn't realize how reclusive she had become. But anyone who noticed her and the dogs walking the highway, and took the time to discover where she lived and who she was, found a forlorn estate completely hidden in the woods, with only the tire tracks of a truck in the lane. And yet, her paperwork was perfect. Property taxes paid. Mail collected. Bills paid, such as they were. And not one plumber or electrician in Parkers had ever serviced her home. The assumption was, she did it herself.

As she pulled the truck away from the Bayfront, she began her conversation with the Lab and the Mutt. Many people had seen her along the road, smoking and talking to the dogs, or maybe talking to the gods, or to herself. No one seemed to get close enough to hear the exact words. But passing motorists reported her animation in the truck, gesturing with her hands on the steering wheel, pushing her hair from her eyes, and sliding her right hand across the Lab's head, which rested on her lap.

"Good boy," she muttered. "That damn son of mine has always been a coward. You don't care, do you boy? You only care about mama, don't you boy. We'll take care of this little matter as soon as we get home."

As her truck passed the new convenience store about a mile from home, she took the pipe from her lips, and holding the bowl, used the stem as a pointer. "See that little halfway store," she said. "That's what it's coming to. That's Parkers. Overpriced place, only sells bread, milk and day old hamburgers with powdered eggs. People are too lazy to go to Flossie's. Not us, boys."

She drove the truck to the back of the house, and stopped for a moment before entering. She said hello to the finches. Her one concession to public vanity was the bird feeder, hanging on a Bo Peep staff just off the porch. She spent hours sitting on the porch rocker, watching the bright yellow finches flutter out of the sky and onto the feeder poles. They were the most beautiful ornament in the yard, far outshining the red cardinals that beat on her windows to attract their mates, or the robins that looked for hiding places in every nook and cranny of the house to build their nests. The bigger birds would sit on top of the finch feeder, unable to get their beaks into the small finch holes, but angry and intimidating in their possessiveness. The finches simply waited in a nearby tree until the robins and cardinals left, then they glided down to the feeder like globs of yellow paint on the wings of an eagle. It was a marvelous display of patience that Mary admired, but seldom emulated.

She pushed open the screen door and walked straight to the phone, certain that the phone company was monitoring the call.

"I want the Governor," she told the voice that answered.

"Yes mam," the voice said politely. "Who may I say is calling?"

She hung up, waited a few seconds, and redialed the call.

This time a man's voice answered. "Is this our friend from Parkers?" the voice asked.

"Yes," Mary whispered.

"The Governor is busy, mam. Can I give him a message?"

She hung up again.

The Pipe Lady knew that her message had been sent. The voice would tell the Governor, and he would call her later, at another time and place. It had worked that way for years. She went outside to the little screened porch near the door, sat in the variety store folding chair picked up one afternoon near the Post Office, and lit her pipe.

The foliage was gleaming, as if a prom-goer had sprinkled silver glitter on the leaves and turned on the blue lights. The recent rain was still fresh, and it lit the yard as straws of light reflected through the trees, some reaching the ground. Mary Margaret loved the old Hickory trees because their limbs were crooked with age and character, but their blossoms were white and fine as lace and hung in the air from sparse branches, looking young and vigorous. Late in the summer, she knew the old limbs would break in the wind, the blossoms long since gone, and the osprey would perch on the high barren branches in the spring, searching for prey.

Mary Margaret thought God had made a terrible mistake with the gum trees that populate every corner of Parkers, and her yard. She wondered how they started. They grew tall and straight and strong, with every advantage that seemed to ignore the normal threats of root rot or drought or storm, and their leaves were as large as her hand and green as lettuce. But looking at the ground reminded her of the flaws in us all. Large gum balls covered the earth for forty yards from every tree, so hard and gummy in their core that they could not be broken, or even crushed. Worse, they were covered with sharp spikes that defied grasping, or stepping on, or human behavior of most kinds. Maybe it was God's defense mechanism, like snakes with camouflage colors or turtles with shells. Yet there was also the mystery of where they went every year, covering the ground in fall and winter, then slipping away in summer. The Pipe Lady meant to watch one summer and find their secret, but she always forgot. She imagined hollow trees in her yard, filled with gum balls, hidden by squirrels with tiny gloves.

She continued to puff the walnut flavored tobacco purchased in a plastic bag at Flossie's. The lab rose to his haunches when a pair of mallard ducks waddled across the yard. They came every year in early spring, presumably from Canada. Mary assumed they were married, or at least committed, because she had heard ducks mate for life. She didn't feed them anything but she knew they had plenty of bugs to eat, and they bathed daily in the pools of fresh water that dotted her swampy yard. Plus they could fly. So she welcomed their arrival in April and departure in June, a timetable she couldn't explain, but which was regular as clockwork. Ducks had their enemies too and Mary figured they beat the hunters out of Jenkins County well before the season opened.

She stroked the lab's head until he collapsed his mug between his toes and closed his eyes. "That's a good boy," she said. "I wish this Resort business would go away, and I could close my eyes again."

Then she started rambling. "Our stupid Governor had to be paid. He doesn't care about us. He just wants the money for his property. He's into those Resort boys for millions. And my son, my own flesh and blood, gave that crooked Governor the envelope with the Resort money. I knew the Governor's mother and I knew he was no good. He was a C student. Became an insurance man, and now Governor. Politics caught him by the throat and now we're all in trouble."

"I should never have given Ray the money to take care of that

Shannon boy," she muttered to no one. The Pipe Lady was shaking her head in disgust.

The lab never opened his eyes.

Chapter Twenty-Two

It was early morning on the Intracoastal Waterway and the sky burned red along the horizon, glowing like a computer screen about to flash the news of the day. Red sky at morning, sailors take warning. Chum had been moving at eight knots most of the night, tracing the red line on his GPS toward Cape Hatteras. The engine was running smooth and quiet, but it was enough to numb his mind during hour after hour of open water. His eyes fluttered as he fought off sleep. He hardly noticed the bow of the boat pulling along side, until he saw the orange stripe. Then he knew the game was over. Every muscle in his body relaxed as he realized that someone else was now guiding his life and he felt relieved of responsibility and burden. He waved to the Coast Guardsmen lining the deck of the cutter and pulled his throttle back to full stop. The bow of the *Scatback* dipped as if in salute to a higher authority, and Chum awaited his instructions.

* * * * *

The Bayfront was clanging with silverware and water glasses when I joined Vinnie at a family table for breakfast. The family table designation means those with more than four chairs to a table. At least by eight o'clock in the morning most watermen have come and gone, after pushing tables together and dragging chairs across the linoleum. The dishes are stacked, often by the diners, at the end of the table awaiting delivery to washers. It looked like breakfast was over, but several of the guys were sipping coffee, their caps pushed back and their legs stretched forward under the table. They were waiting for me.

"Morning Ned," Vinnie said, with a grin crawling across his face. "How's your night?" He knew what they all knew, that some development had occurred in the case of Jimmy Shannon, murdered at sea. And they were waiting for me.

"You know damn well, Vinnie," I said. "Not much sleep and I still don't know what the hell is going on."

Every table fell silent. Even Pete Wildman said nothing, but looked me square in the face, waiting for an explanation, the kind of response one old friend gives another. These boys were mates of Jimmy and friends of mine. Some had been to Philadelphia and their wives sent them to the Bayfront this morning for answers. The telephones were buzzing as one family after another checked on the Shannon family, and they agreed, Neddie will tell us at the Bayfront.

Nancy, the waitress who always looked at me with suspicion, which I assumed was a suspicion that I wasn't a real waterman in the way she was a real waitress. She had earned her stripes with 40 years of cleaning tables, and attending babies and deaths alike. She pushed several strands of artificially black hair from her forehead, and simultaneously wiped a few beads of sweat from her brow. Even at eight in the morning, the stains of life as a waitress had left their mark. She slid a heavy necked coffee cup in front of me, backed away from the table, crossed her arms over her apron and waited for an answer.

"Well," she said, "what the hell is going on? Did somebody kill Jimmy, or what?"

I glanced around and every person in the room recognized that old Nancy had hit the nail square again, and they waited.

"Here's what I know," I began. "The Sheriff down in Hatteras called me early this morning to say they picked up a guy named Chumbucket Roberts on the Intracoastal Waterway. He was in the boat that Jimmy was on. His nickname is Chumbucket; I guess they call him Chum. He was the Captain of the boat who reported Jimmy's death."

I hesitated a moment to make sure I had the right sequence of events in my mind.

"What'd he say?" Nancy said. She was matter of fact, not asking a question, but leading the discussion. How did that happen? How does a sixty-year-old waitress become the arbiter of conversation and seven Captains of the sea are ready to give her full rein? I turned my chair slightly to address her more directly.

"He said there was a woman on the boat."

"That little son of a bitch," Nancy said of Jimmy. "I knew he was up to no good. A new baby at home and that idiot goes fishing with a broad."

The boys groaned, shuffled their chairs, pushed their coffee around, and waited for the moral judgment to be pronounced. I never understood how they could sort through this kind of thing. Of the seven guys at the table, three were divorced and one had lived with about fifty women over the years, and two more could barely afford their trucks due to drinking and gambling. Yet their judgment about my brother was instant. Nancy didn't say it, but there was a tone of "the bastard deserved to die" that was hard to reconcile with her life experiences.

"I knew there was something fishy about that trip," she said, unfolding her arms, and heading for the kitchen. She had heard enough. In a flash, all present had a clear picture of events. The details weren't so important. The moral judgment had been rendered, the outline of a crime was drawn, and there was nothing left to do but move on. One of the guys got up and left. Nancy was gone, so I turned to Vinnie.

"Sheriff says the boy claims he never saw what happened," I said. "The woman was frantic. She just got off the boat and walked away."

"How can that be?" Vinnie asked.

"I don't know," I said. "Sheriff said he would call me back as soon as he knows more. Apparently this Chum has been living in Florida, and they've caught a friend who has been traveling with him, so maybe he'll tell us. I'm sorry boys, that's all I know."

"I'm sorry Ned," Pete said. "I hope they find who did it and they hang him high."

"Bring him here," Captain Neiman said. "We got a judge here that will draw and quarter whoever did it." He paused a moment to let his audience surmise. "Judge Humbolt. Did you see what he did to Captain Jerry? Charged him with poaching. You'd think he was stealing cattle, not fishing."

"What'd Jerry do?" Pete asked.

"You know Jerry's got those pound nets over near Clark's Point. Somebody turned him in. The State said he violated some regulation, lied about how many pounds of fish he caught last month. Judge says he wanted to make Jerry an example. Nobody can violate the State regulations. So he fines Jerry fifty thousand dollars and sentences him to two years in the slammer. Two years. Two years for catching a few extra fish. Christ. What are Mildred and those kids going to do for two years?"

"Sure," Pete said, "but those are regulations. And everybody on the State payroll protects each other, including this judge. Do you think he gives a damn about the people, the family? The State doesn't give a damn about fishermen."

"You're right," Vinnie said. "The guy who killed Jimmy will probably get two months probation."

"No he won't," Nancy said. "Not this time. The Judge will nail this dude to the wall. Effie Humbolt is a friend of Neddie and the Calico Cat won't let this guy off. Not if the judge wants to ever show his face around here again."

"Wait," I pleaded. "We don't even know what happened yet. You've got somebody guilty of murder and hanging from the Jenkins Creek Bridge. Let's wait and see." It was getting harder for me to represent the law and the arguments for equality of justice when I was the aggrieved party.

"I need to go home and wait for the Sheriff, Vinnie," I said. "Can you take the boat out? I don't really know what is happening. But I assume this Chum guy will have more to say, and his friend in Florida probably knows something. Prisoners always end up telling their cellmates about their crimes. I bet this kid does too."

"That's fine Neddie," Vinnie said. "I think Velma is going over to see Martha right now, just to be with her if she's needed."

"I called Martha right after I talked to the Sheriff this morning. Hell, she's probably talked to fifteen friends by now."

"At least that means she's got her voice back," Vinnie said.

"It's amazing how fast some of her senses are returning," I said. "Her speech was first to return, I guess when the swelling went down. But balance, vision and cognitive functions are the main problems now."

* * * * *

Martha was on the computer in the corner of her living room. When Velma knocked on the screen door it rattled and shook against the wood frame of the house, perfect for Velma's purpose of rousing Martha at eight in the morning. Not so good for keeping mosquitoes at bay. Martha came to the door with her walker, and wedged one of its legs to hold the screen open, always glad to have company.

"Come in Velma," she said. "You're off today?"

"No," Velma said, "just stopped by for a minute to see if you're OK. The shop doesn't open for another hour anyway. And believe me, there isn't a hairdo in all of Parkers that can't wait for a little while. I just wanted to see you honey."

"Come sit here by the flowers," Martha said. "Let me turn this computer off. I swear I never thought I'd get addicted to this machine, but the doctor says its good for my mind, and I can't get enough of it. Now I know how old people feel. I check my emails four times a day. Do you know that every ounce of knowledge ever known is some- where on this machine. I just have to be smart enough to ask for it. It's magic."

Velma looked around the room as Martha talked, looking for the telltale signs of neglect. But there weren't many. The morning paper was open on the couch, the metro section on top showing weather for the week in southern Maryland, but it was the only paper in sight. Martha's home was small and warm. She and Jimmy bought it when they were first married, and considered enlarging it, but decided in- stead to wait another year and build a new home. Jimmy may have had another motive, to buy a new boat with their cash, then mortgage a new house. In either case, Martha had been keeping the pressure on by constant reminders that a new house was coming. Now that was all on the back burner. First Jimmy's death, then the brain tumor. It was hard to keep looking forward.

Velma noticed the pictures, most of them new, of Jimmy with the baby.

"I haven't seen that one before," Velma said.

"It was taken in her fourth month," Martha said. "But I just got it back from the camera shop last week. I found the film when I was cleaning out Jimmy's drawers."

Martha was still wearing bandages around her head, not as large as when she first came home from the hospital. But they still covered the horseshoe scar, and prevented much styling of her hair.

"Martha," Velma said, "why don't you come by the shop this week and let me cut all your hair off. That half a Mohawk doesn't make sense."

"The doctor said most women wanted to keep as much hair as possible, so he quit shaving the whole head."

"I think he's wrong," Velma said. "At least if you cut it all, it wouldn't look like you just stepped out of a car wreck."

"Is that what I look like?" Martha asked, screwing up her face.

"I didn't mean that," Velma said hurriedly. "It's just that a total cut would look better. You could wear a hat, or a scarf, and then the whole thing would grow out evenly. I'll do it for free. Think about it."

"You're so kind," Martha said. "You know I sit here all day thinking about what happened, and I come to blank spots. Places where my thinking just stops, like potholes or dead end streets. Ideas form in my mind, or some part of my mind, and before I can express them, they just stop. It's not just names or places. I've never been too good with those. It's ideas. They just end and I can't get them back. I picture my head like a watermelon with a quarter section gone, with seeds hanging out the side like ideas severed by a cleaver."

"Oh, Martha honey," Velma said, "don't think that way. Besides, it's the wrong picture. None of your brain is missing. The doctor's didn't slice a piece out. They took out the tumor and left a big hole that has to fill up again. Think of your brain as being able to breathe again, to stretch out its nerves, to fill the gap and revive itself."

"I'll take it one day at a time. Did you hear what happened yesterday at rehabilitation?"

"Oh, how's that going? I knew the girls were driving you to the Center. What happened?"

"Well, it's mainly a place to learn to walk, to get my balance back, to think and to adjust my eyes. I just have to learn to do all these things again."

"Can you write?" Thelma asked.

"Not really," Martha said. "When I try to write, my hand just makes scratches."

"Does the doctor say that will come back?" Thelma asked.

"He says it will all come back. But he says it may take a month, or six months, or a year. I have to be patient."

"How's that working out?"

"Not so well. Yesterday Neddie came to pick me up after the session, and my nurse met him at the door. She was helping me with my walker. She thought Ned was my husband, I guess just because he is always with me. He's been so wonderful. So she tells him about the man I knocked down."

"You what?"

"She said, 'Sir, you're wife is a very aggressive woman.'"

Ned said he agreed with that.

"What did you do, anyway?" Velma asked.

"Well, we were playing duck-duck-goose. About eight of us in a circle. And there was a man standing next to me who had been in an auto crash. His head was all bandaged. But he didn't look any worse than the rest of us. So when the nurse said go, I took off around the circle with my walker and knocked the poor man down. And he hit his head on the floor. I think the nurse thought I had killed him. But he was all right."

"You are aggressive Martha, and you have to realize the situation."

"I know," Martha said. "The Center took us down to Flossie's to get us used to buying food, and paying for it. I pulled out my credit card. But the nurse said no, pay cash. Turns out she wanted to see if I could add up the money. And it turned out I couldn't. I stood there trying to add a nickel, two dimes and a quarter and I couldn't. My mind wouldn't add. I knew what I was supposed to do, but nothing came. So I cried. My God, Velma, what if all this doesn't come back? I sit at the computer, and peck out the letters one at a time, and wonder if this is all I can ever do. I wonder if Ned will take care of me."

"Martha, I have to ask this. Are you falling in love with Neddie? I'm not sure that's such a good thing."

Martha said nothing. She stared at Velma as if that question had never occurred to her. She clutched her hands on the velvet arm chair to lift herself in the seat, and Velma noticed her strength was adequate for the task. But Martha looked out the window and quietly said no.

"I have wondered about that," Martha said. "But it can't ever happen. We're too different. And I would always look at Neddie and see Jimmy. I don't even know what happened to Jimmy. It's funny though, affection toward Neddie has never occurred to me. Every day is a crisis here. Something new about the death, or about my head, or about Mindy, or just living. My God, Velma, I can't even fix dinner so don't ask me those kinds of questions."

"I'm sorry," Velma said. "But your strength will come back, a little bit at a time. And we'll take care of you. Ned will take care of you. And we'll take care of Mindy too. Parkers is your family now. You just have to be patient."

"I'll try Velma. Thank you."

"Is there anything else you want to tell me?" Velma asked, thinking about the morning phone call from the Sheriff, and her real reason for stopping by.

"I don't think so," Martha said. "Of course, I can't remember everything so maybe I'm just forgetting. But I'll think about that haircut, Velma."

Martha's phone started to ring and Velma got up from the couch. "I'll get out of your way," she said. She almost said "out of your hair." Velma opened the screen door, and turned to wave goodbye as Martha picked up the phone.

Chapter Twenty-Three

Burl and Marilyn Mansfield were bringing Martha to the Moose Lodge for the fundraising dance. I wanted to be fashionably late, whatever that means, so I went a half hour after the invitation time. I backed the Saab away from my little bungalow and edged into the street. It was easy to miss seeing street traffic because I never expected it. People just didn't come down my street without a reason, and I knew everybody on the block. Also, it was almost dark and no cars lights around, so I whipped it into reverse and backed into the street. My mind wandered. I thought about building the new house, the French chateau on stilts, but things were just too unsettled, especially now that we might have a break in my brother's murder. It was Saturday night in Parkers and by the time I pulled onto Main Street, traffic was heavy, probably people going to Annapolis. The parking lot at the Moose hall was about half full, a good sign.

I parked and walked through the gravel lot, tightening my tie and tugging the tail of my blue blazer, an all-purpose outfit that fit the words of most party invitations: business smart. I loved this jacket because it fulfilled the promise of being wrinkle proof, a promise never before fulfilled by any apparel. This one was tested. I had stuffed the jacket in overhead bins, trunks, car seats, and under folding chairs in the worst of bars. It never wrinkled. I even wore it to the Willard Hotel and felt proud as a peach when Diane Sexton said I looked splendid, especially with the white handkerchief peeking out the breast pocket. I exchanged that for a red silk pocket scarf on this occasion, adding a little dazzle to my charm.

I thought about combing my unruly black hair just before going through the door, but decided it was unnecessary. It seemed unlikely I would meet the love of my life here tonight, but Martha had a lot of girlfriends, and I hadn't met them all. So why not be optimistic? Also, I had written a few brief remarks, hoping to impress somebody with my quick wit. I thought the duck-duck-goose story was pretty funny and reflected well on Martha's condition. With a little flourish, I could paint a vibrant picture of Martha knocking down every patient in the rehab program.

It was dark inside, but the music was in full steam by the local band. The lead singer was my new friend, Chris, the bobcat driver, and on drums was our pile driver Turkey Dressing, who built most of the boat docks in Parkers. I'm not kidding about the name. No one could explain its origins, or what his original name was, or why he relished the name. Everyone called him Turkey, which I shied from until I heard about six other folks call him Turkey and he never seemed to mind. He had large solid shoulders and could really pound that drum. Not so much on finesse, but he could maintain a rock and roll beat that shook the rafters.

I looked toward the bar across the room, and spied Martha along the wall, surrounded by friends. Her walker was nearby. She was wearing a tan pantsuit, stylishly accented by two or three bracelets, and a gold necklace with a madras blue scarf that drifted over one shoulder. But most striking was the red scarf wrapped around her head and fastened in the back with a gold clasp. Her Mohawk hair was gone. And she looked beautiful. I could see the sharp features that must have attracted my brother, and a trim figure enhanced by weight loss that only hospital food can impose. She wore open toed shoes with bright red nail polish that said hello. It was her favorite saying about her dress and she lived up to the billing.

The girls around her felt my presence and edged aside.

"Hi Martha," I said. "You look gorgeous tonight. I love your hair."

She started to touch her head, then drew back.

"Oh Neddie," she said. "Aren't these people nice? I can't believe it. How kind everyone has been."

"Don't go tearjerker on me, Martha," I said. "We have a long night. You better save me a dance."

Burlington Mansfield appeared at my elbow and I backed away from Martha. Like a hole in the water, the space quickly filled.

"Ned," Burl said, "I understand there has been a new development in the case."

"I'm not sure, Burl," I said. "They found the Captain of the boat. Of course, we knew all along who that was, and the cops interviewed him several times. But he did go missing for a while there, which seems suspicious. And now they say he was hiding, or vacationing, or something in New Smyrna Beach, Florida. And today the Sheriff called to say they have another guy who was traveling with this Captain, and he doesn't seem to want to talk about anything. So I don't know what we have."

"Well, this all sounds good my boy. When the pigs start to squeal, the slop is on the way. I bet we know more soon."

"Ned," Marilyn said quietly, "thanks for all you've done for Martha. She looks great."

"You're welcome, Marilyn," I said. "It's wonderful to see you again. You take care of Burl. I haven't finished his will yet, but I'll have it soon."

"Oh Ned, don't you worry. Burl won't leave me anything but three old cameras and a buzz saw anyway." She was moving away as she spoke and soon disappeared into the crowd.

The knotty pine paneling at the Moose hall had absorbed about seventy years of loud music by every kind of band imaginable, and for at least fifty of those years the music floated on a cloud of smoke, so dense that the odor clung tenaciously to the bleach and ammonia that had been scrubbed into the floor and woodwork. Now it was all part of the concoction of fuels, including beer and wine, that drove the party forward. I had never liked these events, and the memories of the smells and the bodies reminded me of high school, the dances where I never had a date, standing in the corner, trying to stay invisible while I lusted for the homecoming queen who wouldn't give me a second thought. Her name was Sabrina, no doubt in honor of all the conceptions that occurred after seeing the movie by the same name, and she was incredibly beautiful as only freckles can be to a boy of sixteen. In later years, I thought there might be some justice in the fact that I became a lawyer while she married a waterman and still lived in a Bay-front cottage, except for the fact that I had returned to be a waterman and also lived in a Bay-front cottage. There's a morality lesson in that conundrum, but I chose not to sort it out on the dance floor. I wondered if Sabrina was coming tonight, but I doubted it since I had never seen her with Martha, indeed I hadn't thought of her in years. I made a mental note to check later in the week and see if she was still alive.

I danced with Lillian Wildman and thanked her for putting on this affair. She was in a dream world of achievement, generosity and sparkle that left her light as a feather. We pranced around the room. I'm sure she dreamed of being on a television dance show with a professional football player. But for tonight, her husband Pete and Martha were the stars of her show and Lil was appropriately enamored of both.

It struck me that once again I didn't have a date, but unlike high school, I now felt confident that I could change that at will. As I looked around the room, I could feel the eyes on the back of my neck, silently watching my moves. Simy Sims stood in the back of the room with the dark eyes of a sultress. I spotted her and winked, something I hadn't done in years, and I wondered if it actually happened, if the one eye closed and opened while the other stayed focused. A wink denotes a flirtatious gesture carrying invitations of mystery, but if it fails, you're a bungling idiot. And I hadn't felt myself wink in years. Amazing that I was moved to try.

Simy looked terrific, reminding me again that in Washington we see our friends in their professional costumes, while in Parkers we live in our private dress. I had never seen Diane Sexton in blue jeans and a sweatshirt, and I had never seen Simy in heals and a black sheath dress. From across the room, she looked smashing with a previously unnoticed figure, appropriate jewelry, and sling back heels that toned her calf muscles to accentuate her height. Her hair was black, although maybe the darkness of the room diminished the threads of white that appeared in the daytime, at least behind the bar. Her gold earrings were like framing a family photo, and I looked at her anew as she moved toward me.

"Hello Mr. Ned Shannon," she said as if introducing a stranger. "Martha looks wonderful tonight."

I agreed. "How are you Simy?" I asked.

"I'm great," she said. "Would you dance with me?"

"I'd love to." The music changed almost immediately to a slow tune, not one I recognized but one I interpreted as a good sign, an omen that Simy was meant to be. Of course, how many times had I misled myself on that score? One of my many failings in life involved going to a night club, spotting a beautiful women at a table near the band, and finding her willing to dance and converse with enthusiasm.

No matter how many times it happened, I always though it was for me. Is that ego, or what? I always thought the woman by the bar actually liked my looks, and by the end of the night when bourbon had blurred my vision and dulled my senses I learned that suddenly she was gone. The band had stopped and the drummer had led the lady out a side door for a smoke. It was always near this astounding moment that I realized I was just a place card for the evening, a substitute for her husband, or boyfriend, or lover. How could I have missed, or ignored, all the signals? How could I have wasted this entire evening of my life on the drummer's girlfriend? Great expectations down the drain. I finally quit going to bars, with the exception of the Willard, for this very reason, the humiliating and degrading evening in which I dreamed of sexual surrender. I wondered if Simy could be with the drummer.

We moved onto the dance floor and my arm slid easily around her waist, at just the right height so my wrist rested respectfully but suggestively around her waist. She moved into me with a smoothness of motion that surprised me, and I almost flinched, but didn't. I froze for an instant, telling myself to accept the offer of her body, but say nothing that might frighten her or alter the momentum of the moment. She put her hand around my neck and moved with me as if invisible. And I reminded myself it was Simy, the woman who had once made me a bar stool promise that still entranced my nights. But I moved on, afraid to stop and beginning to wonder how to get off the dance floor.

First, I had to get through the public ceremony, which involved my introduction of Martha and her thank you speech. She said she didn't need any help with the words, but I had no idea what she would say. As the band finished the next song, Lillian tapped me on the shoulder.

"I hate to interrupt this," she said, "but we're ready for the introduction, Ned. Can you tear yourself away?"

I said sure, and tried to hide my total absorption in Simy, although it must have been obvious that I was enthralled. Lillian made that clear. I backed away from Simy and she stood still, watching me move to the microphone. I took it as a signal that she didn't rush away, or return to her friends across the room. Indeed, the signal was that she was with me. Although I had misread so many signals from women, I couldn't be sure. And I really had no choice but to approach the microphone.

I told the duck-duck-goose story and everyone laughed. Martha must have taken great satisfaction in knowing that everyone in the room loved her, or at least cared enough to mourn her husband's death, and care for her during near death. Martha felt enormous appreciation for their support. I wondered about the magic of friendship, the bonds formed by people living together and depending on each other, just knowing about each other and all their problems. It was a warm sensation. When I first moved to Washington, it was the opposite. I was freed, unshackled from the small town bonds of responsibility for friends and neighbors. I wasn't responsible for anyone. Not the poor, because I didn't know any. They lived in another part of town. Not the sick, because I had few acquaintances, and none who weren't adequately covered by insurance and access to world class hospitals. Not neighbors, because I didn't know any. I remembered riding the city bus to work one morning, and falling into conversation with a middle aged woman who had once gone charter boat fishing from the Bayfront marina. When she got off, I realized I now knew more about her than anyone else in Washington, and I was fine with that. It was the freedom of anonymity, the exhilaration before the loneliness. Now I stood in a ballroom with hundreds of people who loved Martha, and through my family, me. I turned back to Martha's speech.

"I want to thank you all for your generosity and kindness," Martha said. "To Lillian for putting this all together. To each of you who has cooked food, or driven me to rehab, or picked up my groceries." And with these words she started to stutter. The tears eased down her cheeks. She started to change her course of thought.

"Many of you were Jimmy's friends. The watermen who knew his boat. Now we have his brother Ned on the *Martha Claire*. What a godsend he has been to me. And I thank you all for welcoming him back."

I thought about making a smart remark about myself, something to lighten the situation, but then I decided no. This was Martha's time and it wasn't a light situation. It was deadly serious on several levels. I just stood still and admired my sister-in-law. How could anybody survive a husband's death, and then have her own life in danger? Where's the hope in that? Where is the force of nature that pushes people to the future, that keeps them searching for solutions? Somehow Martha still had it. She was moving slowly, but moving forward.

"I just want you all to have a good time, and I'll be out and about again soon. Thank you."

She turned to rest a hand on her walker as the applause built in long and loud appreciation for her life.

I started to return to the dance floor when Simy touched my elbow. "I'm here," she said.

* * * * *

It was near midnight when we made the unspoken move toward the door. Martha left the party at least an hour earlier, to a full round of applause from her friends, and the crowd started dwindling after that. I thought it was time for me to go. I didn't want to become the center of attention, although that may already have occurred. Lust al-

242

ways drives one to a sense of invisibility, and sometimes worse. So when I asked Simy if she had a purse, she knew the plan immediately.

We drove separate cars to her house, with me following because I had never been there. Her small home was much like mine, one of the weekend cottages built in the 1940s, with window air conditioners and baseboard heating added in the 1970s. It was a block off the water, surrounded by a small yard and other cottages. No lights were on in the neighborhood, although a few outdoor porch lights cast overburdened candles into the dark.

Simy had the house key in her hand and looked up at me just before easing it into the lock. I gave her the last sign of approval by bending down to touch her lips. She was accepting but swiftly returned to the key, no doubt aware of neighbors who had seen this ritual before. We forged through the door and Simy reached for a light switch that awoke a small cloisonné lamp in the corner of the living room. I noted the calculation of a wall switch connected to a table lamp, and realized that my own door switch would activate three overhead flood lamps, more calculated to guide ships to shore than lovers to bed. I might have to change that.

Simy took my hand, then reached for my neck and placed a long kiss that spoke my thoughts. She pulled away slowly and led me through a door with hanging strands of beads that must have been plastic because they didn't jingle. There was a nightlight on someplace, perhaps a wall socket that gave a yellow glow to the room. It was the kind of atmosphere, when combined with enough bourbon, that seemed quite romantic. She reached for my belt with customary boldness, or at least I assumed it was customary, and we fell into bed.

When she finally closed her eyes with a hand on my chest and her head on my shoulder, we drifted into sleep with ease and warmth. I spent a few minutes wondering what had just happened, and what the morning might bring, but I decided to wait for the day and see what kind of dreams lay ahead.

I felt her grow restless on my shoulder, then turn toward the wall to seek the unobstructed breathing that brings restful sleep. I turned the opposite direction, thinking I would sleep till daybreak, which for a waterman, wasn't too far off. It was only a double bed, not much room for stretching, and my eyes took one last glimpse down the edge of the bed toward the bathroom and closets, when I felt Simy move again.

She edged out of bed, and I watched her body move around the room. She opened the closet door and a small overhead light came on automatically. She turned to see if I was awake, but apparently didn't notice that I was. She reached for her bathrobe, a Chinese kimono with paintings of geishas in almost life-sized portraits. I was struck by their beauty and opened my eyes for a better look when something caught my eye in the corner of her closet. It was only for a second as she closed the door and went in the bathroom. But it registered. I raised my head, at least enough to begin thinking, and to wonder what I had seen. Then it came to me. A blue polka dot tennis shoe.

It can't be, I thought. What are the odds? I tried to think of the tennis shoes the Sheriff had shown me in his plastic bag. Blue with yellow polka dots had stuck. It seemed so impossible that my brother could be wearing such feminine shoes. They were so bright. And not even matching. I tried to think of the other one. I hadn't focused very long that day in the Sheriff's office, but I seemed to remember plaid. Something totally incongruous with the blue and yellow polka dots.

Jesus. Why would Simy have the same shoes? Unless they were a matching pair. Then I remembered the summer fashion rage, several years ago, when women would buy two pairs of tennis shoes, and mix and match them. So there would always have to be two pairs the

244

same. Oh shit.

I heard the water still running in the sink, assumed Simy was brushing her teeth, so I slipped out of bed and edged to the closet. I pushed open the door just enough to activate the light. I saw the blue shoe in the corner, and I looked for the other shoe. I remembered that these mixed shoes were put together by buying two pair of shoes, and wearing one from each. So there had to be a second shoe. In a flash I saw it. Then the light clicked off in the bathroom. I jumped back a step and closed the closet door, meeting Simy as she emerged.

I mumbled. "You OK?"

"I'm fine," she said.

She moved back to the bed and I stepped into the bathroom, thinking, what the hell do I do now? Get out. Get out was all I could think of. My mind was racing toward frightening thoughts. What if she had been on the boat? What if she killed my brother? What if she wants to kill me? And I remembered how easy it was, how she had picked me up at the dance, and like a fool, I had once again fallen for her interest. No, that seemed impossible. But I had to leave.

I opened the bathroom door and left the light on.

"What's the matter, Neddie?" she asked.

"I have to leave," I said. "I have a client coming this morning and I have to get my act together." Simy knew more about crabbing and watermen than I did, so I didn't want to use fishing as an excuse for getting up. But she would know nothing of the law. I might have an early morning client.

I started searching for my clothes, and dressed as quickly as possible, although my hands were shaking and buckling my belt somehow seemed difficult.

Simy rolled in bed and looked at my shoes as I struggled with them. "Just leave the front door unlocked," she said.

I breathed easier, realizing she wasn't going to get up. I could avoid that long kiss at the door and promises to call or at least talk to-morrow. Still, I needed to get out quickly and I was getting scared. What if she wondered about the closet door and realized what I had seen? No, I had closed the door or the light would be on. I moved through the beads and watched my feet carefully in moving toward the front door. I didn't want to stumble. The door opened easily. I stepped outside, and hurried to my car. No lights were on in the neighborhood so it couldn't be more than four or five o'clock. I felt for my watch but it wasn't on my wrist. I thought I had stuck it in my pants pocket before getting into bed. But it wasn't there. Then I felt it in my rear pocket with my wallet. I pulled it out and noticed, 4:30 a.m. I started the car and backed into the street, turned the wheel and started for home.

Then I realized I couldn't go home, or anywhere that I might be found. What if Simy had called others to say I had seen the shoes? Or what if she was getting dressed right now and searching for a weapon? But I also knew the only safe place to go was a police station, so I headed for Annapolis, yet I knew no one there. Especially in the mid-dle of the night. How could I explain this story?

Instead I fumbled for my cell phone, trying to get my thumbs to land on the right numbers for the Sheriff of Hatteras, North Carolina. I figured to let him contact the local police, which he must have con-sulted on this case anyway. I turned at the next corner and headed back into Parkers and the one place I would feel safe, at least for a while. The *Martha Claire*. The safety of the open sea.

Chapter Twenty-Four

My hands were shaking when I started to ease the *Martha Claire* out of her slip at the Bayfront because in truth, I didn't know what to do. It seemed entirely possible that Simy was totally unaware of my discovery, which opened a related line of inquiry in my mind about why she seduced me just last night. If she had been on that boat with my brother, and if she was involved in his killing, why on earth would she want a relationship with me? Other than magnetic charm, of course.

I started to ease the throttle forward and realized I had forgotten to release the spring line from the side cleat. I yanked the throttle back to neutral, worked the line free, and returned to the throttle. The *Martha Claire* banged against the dock pylons, first one side and then the other, until I was finally free, and could turn into the main channel. I edged my speed up to six knots, "no wake" speed, and settled back in the captain's seat to collect my thoughts.

I had called the Sheriff from my car, got him out of bed, and told him the story of the shoes, how Barbara Bush in the late 1980s had virtually started this fad of buying two sets of highly decorated tennis shoes, then mixing them so they didn't match. And if my brother was wearing a pair when he went overboard, there must be another pair in somebody's closet, and there was. I found them. Although the Sheriff had a little trouble understanding why I was sleeping with the shoes, and how Simy was connected to Jimmy, and the watermen, and Parkers in general. He nevertheless said he would have local police pick her up for questioning, and confiscate the shoes, soon, presumably within hours. I had a feeling that would unravel the whole scheme.

As so often happens on the Bay, the sun rose in a startlingly clear sky, bright as a spoon reflecting quiet shimmers on the surface, but within an hour heavy grey clouds the color of aged boat docks were covering the sky. I headed the *Martha Claire* toward my field of crab pots near the shore. My mind wasn't really on it, of course, and I didn't even have bait to reset the pots. But I figured I could pull a few just to see if there was an overnight catch. The first two I pulled up were empty, so I gave up the task, and decided instead to head home. This entire trip was just to burn up energy, and divert me from the confrontations ahead. There was no real reason to stay on the water.

I called Vinnie on the cell to tell him I had the boat.

"Holy jumping geehosafat," he yelled when I came on the line. "What have you done?"

"What's happening?" I asked.

"Three screaming cop cars came barreling through town nearly two hours ago," Vinnie said. "Word is they blocked off the street in front of Simy Sims's house, got on the bull horn and ordered her out the front door. Neighbors are up, calling everybody in town. Word is you were putting the moves on her last night and took her home from the Moose Lodge. Fact is, everybody in Parkers knows it. Velma put two and two together, got scared, and went over to Martha's house. She's scared you died, or Simy died, or somebody killed you both. Where the hell are you?"

"I'm in the boat," I barked.

"Well, get your ass back here," Vinnie said. "Half the people in town think you killed Simy and the other half thinks Simy killed you. Which is it?"

"Neither, but I think Simy was involved in Jimmy's death," I said.

248

"Tell Martha I'll be over just as soon as I get back."

"When?"

"It's clouding up, but I should be back in a half hour. Meet you at the Bayfront."

"OK," Vinnie said. "Sun has turned to fog at my house. Hurry it up."

"I'm on my way."

I turned the *Martha Claire* to the west and started threading my way through the crab pot buoys. The fog was collecting just off the Holland Point oyster beds, forming a long wall of grey behind me. But I couldn't be more than a mile from the mouth of Jenkins Creek. I reached for the throttle and headed for the red channel markers.

Over my left shoulder I noted a speedboat, out early for a recreational boater, but bearing down on me from the open water. Must be trying to beat the fog home. His angle seemed wide and I calculated I would reach the channel ahead of him and he could fall in line behind me in heading for the marinas. It was near high tide and the water almost reached the lip of the jetty that protected the entrance to the harbor. I swung the *Martha Claire* a little wider to be sure I missed the rocks when I heard the first shot, like a firecracker, somewhere behind me.

I jerked my head around and the speedboat had changed course, heading directly for me. Two more shots and I reached for the binoculars to see who the hell was shooting. But the shooter was too close and I needed to escape. I let the glasses fall to the deck, grabbed the wheel with both hands, and swung the boat hard to starboard. Full throttle and the *Martha Claire* shuddered as her bow rose in the air. No way my old car engine could outrun a high powered speedboat. Actually, the *Martha Claire* probably couldn't hang together at a steady twenty knots, if I could even get her up to twenty knots.

The speedboat passed behind me and one shot rammed through the transom. A quick glance showed me a familiar face, black hair streaming over a light blue windbreaker. It was that bastard Blenny Man. It was still a quarter mile to the harbor. And this stupid guy might follow me all the way to dock. But at least I now knew the enemy. I figured a couple more shots and he might be out of bullets, assuming he brought the gun out just for this purpose. If he happened to store ammunition on the boat, I was out of luck, but that seemed unlikely.

I headed back out to the fog. I figured I couldn't really hide in the fog, or out run him, but at least he might have trouble aiming. The fog carried a slight mist and I figured that might work in my favor, so I started to circle into the wind. I hoped to put the wind and the mist in his eyes. I heard two more shots but there was no indication where they hit, if at all. I didn't hear any crash of the wood, or shattering glass, so I guessed he missed entirely. I had heard that sometimes in an adrenaline rush of this kind I might not even feel a bullet if it was a superficial hit, so I looked down at my legs and arms. Nothing. By my calculations, he had fired six times. Although I was a little uncertain about the first two or three shots.

I decided to take a chance and make a run out of the fog. I could hear the Blenny's engine revving behind me, so I looked at the compass and locked on the familiar heading that had taken me home so many times in the past, the one that should take me straight into the Jenkins. Blenny had moved off to my starboard side, maybe to cut me off when we cleared the fog. I figured that was good, probably meaning he was out of bullets.

I pushed the throttle down so hard I almost caught my finger on the dash. As I did, the fog thinned. I was almost at the edge. I strained my eyes, praying to miss the jetty and yet be close to the creek. Suddenly, I could see movement ahead, a line of white spots on the horizon, slowly taking shape in my vision. A line of work boats spread across my bow, like a row of swans, elegantly moving toward me like warships in the dawn.

"Yes!" I screamed. "Over here."

The *Loose Goose*, the *Uncle Duck*, the *Free Wheeler*, the *Stormy Petrel*, the *Sister Nancy* and the *Fish Forever* were lined up like the Sixth Fleet and racing toward me.

"Yes! Yes!" I screamed. I swung my arms wildly in the air, as if the boys of Parkers might miss me if I didn't.

I was saved. I felt the wind go out of my sails; my muscles relaxed as if a great storm had suddenly departed. But the pounding and gunning noise of the Blenny Man's boat was still in my ear. It had disappeared in the excitement of the six white apparitions ahead of me. When I saw them my head became dizzy and numb, crowding out all rational thought, eliminating any ability to assess my situation, and forcing my ears to hear only the six boats I willed to be at my side.

Now I looked up, and the Blenny's engine was louder than ever. He was coming for me and I screamed, "You bastard!" Then the bow of his boat raised up and over the side of the *Martha Claire*. I only saw it for an instant. There was a black stripe around the waterline of his boat that looked like a shark was rising to devour my boat. I thought I was in a movie, an unreal scene in which one boat tried to cut another in half. Then I was in water. Wood shattered and the cedar timbers, hidden for forty years by innumerable coats of paint, stuck up like a million toothpicks, as raw as the day they were cut from trees. It was as if someone grabbed my boat like an ear of corn and simply snapped it in two. The bow of the intruder stopped just short of my legs, but water was rushing in every corner, creating dozens of waterfalls over timbers and seats and debris. My last image was white-water and foam shooting in every direction. The boat sank straight down and away from my body. I could hear people yelling about life jackets and nets and Neddie. They were shouting for me, I thought, and the world went dark.

Chapter Twenty-Five

Simy began to toss and turn soon after Ned left, pulling the silk sheet over her shoulders and stretching her legs after a night of exercise, but she could not shake the reality of her dreams, that unquenchable moment when she approached Jimmy Shannon in the stern of the *Scatback,* swung the paddle from her shoulder, hitting him solid in the back of the head. He toppled into the water as easily and quickly as a toothpick off the shelf. The second his body hit the water, almost on top of the big tuna, she started screaming until she woke up. Thankfully. She stared at the ceiling, her mind frozen on the mental portrait of Jimmy struggling with the leader line and the gaff. She saw his feet clear the gunnels, and although this sequence had appeared in her mind many times, this was the first time she saw the shoes – her polka dot and plaid sneakers.

She raised her head and the memory flashed before her like a digital photo, of Ned looking in her closet, only for an instant, then he closed the door and the light extinguished. Oh no. What if he saw the shoes?

Simy rushed her feet to the floor, kicking aside the high heels so rapidly discarded hours ago, and she moved around the foot of the bed to the closet. She opened the door, hoping for a miracle, but it was not to be. The light clicked. There, in the back, were the shoes, and she knew her life was over. From that moment her morning flashed by in a rush of underwear, blue jeans, a tee shirt and sandals. She grabbed the phone, and dialed the number she could not forget, no matter the hour.

The Blenny Man answered on the second ring. He wasn't quite up this early in the morning, when the dark clouds still hid the stars and the moon peeked through the haze like a child in saw-grass. But he was always alert to trouble and a phone call in the dark was a clear signal.

"Hello," he groaned.

"Ray, this is Simy. Ned knows."

"Knows what?"

"Knows I was in the boat," she said.

"What happened?" Ray asked, trying to clear his thinking.

"I just told you. Ned was here and I think he saw the shoes."

"What do you mean?" Blenny demanded. "You said you trashed the shoes."

"I did," Simy said. "Jimmy's shoes. In the dipsy dumpster. But not my matching sneakers."

"What matching sneakers? What are you talking about?" Blenny asked.

"Listen to me, you goddamn idiot. No don't. I don't even care if you can't figure it out. It's over."

"Simy, what about the shoes?" Ray demanded.

Simy left the phone silent for a moment, enough to emphasize her impatience and disgust. Then she started.

"When Jimmy hooked into the tuna, he was pretty relaxed in the big chair with the rod holder. We had both kicked off our shoes and they were scattered about the deck. Jimmy grabbed the rod the second the tuna struck. He reeled in and let it out. Then he braced his feet on the rail of the boat and he fought the fish all over the damn ocean. But the rail hurt his feet so he stretched his legs to reach his shoes. He got mine instead. He never let go of the rod; he just drove his feet into my tennis shoes, and braced himself again."

"Jesus Christ," Blenny exclaimed.

"That's why I had his shoes when I left the boat. The problem is, I forgot I had another pair of those mix and match shoes at home."

Blenny understood at that point. "How could you be so damn dumb?" he yelled. "How could you forget about a polka dot shoe? And what's Ned Shannon doing in your house?"

"Go to hell, Ray!" she screamed.

"Shut up Simy!" he yelled with croaky morning voice. "I'll take care of Ned Shannon. You get out of town. Go and don't come back."

Blenny slammed his phone, and Simy slammed her phone. Then she slumped on the edge of her bed and cried tears of anger that she had ever accepted Blenny's blood money to commit a crime. How had she ever gotten involved with this murdering little bastard? How incredible. Now she was the murderer and calling Blenny names. She had told herself it was murder, over and over, but it didn't seem to stick. Yes, she hit Jimmy and knocked him overboard. She got the check for ten thousand dollars. And she missed Jimmy on Monday morning when his boat never left the Bayfront slip. But murder? It just wouldn't compute.

She thought she understood why she did this thing. She liked Jimmy, and hell, she liked Martha too, from their years together in Parkers School, in the Methodist Church, at the bar. This was just a case of her needing the money, and Blenny recognizing her position.

She wondered why she seduced Ned. Was there some dark and ugly demon that drove her to take risks, some love of danger that lurked in her personality? She had completely forgotten about the matching shoes, of course, but even without them how could she make love to the brother of the man she destroyed?

Simy raked the two shoes out of her closet and put them on the edge of her bed. They were like new. Barely worn. Perhaps never. She remembered putting them together just for the trip with Jimmy. She thought they would be unique, clever, for a man who owned his own boat and had a thriving business. Now they sat on her bed like headstones inscribed with the word, Murder, on each toe.

I don't deserve this, Simy thought. I don't deserve to go to jail, to be humiliated in front of my friends.

She knew that by mid morning, in just a few hours, everyone at the bar would be expressing their disbelief. She even thought about that idiot "Schooner," who sat at her bar every day and slobbered his vicious views right and left down the bar. He would be there soon, wearing a white tee shirt with Schooners Electric on the front and a two-masted ship on the back. She could hear him yelling, "Do you believe it, that bitch was serving me beer right here. For ten years. She could have killed me, and shoved me overboard. My God, who can you trust these days?" And all the boys would laugh, but they would be nervous, knowing that any one of them would have gone fishing with her, and more. And they would be more thoughtful than Schooner, at least until the beer flowed more freely later in the day, then they would grow belligerent and brag about knowing all along that the bitch was a man hater, their favorite term.

Why run? Simy thought. Where to? I have no family, no money for hotels, the cops will always find me.

Her mind lingered on every option, and they all seemed hopeless. Maybe she could get a day, but little more. And as each idea was rejected, the recurring dream of knocking Jimmy off the boat filled her head, the one that first surfaced when she returned from Hatteras.

She had hidden herself on the *Scatback* while the Coast Guard searched the sea for Jimmy's body. And when the *Scatback* berthed she had slipped off just before the Coast Guardsmen climbed aboard and started their search of the boat. She figured the Captain would tell on her. He was only a boy. But running was the only option, and she took it, through the marina parking lot to a nearby convenience store. She took off Jimmy's shoes that she had put on at the last moment, and threw them in the dumpster. She walked into the store barefoot, bought a pair of flip flops for less than three dollars, and headed for a bus stop, willing to go anywhere. It took her three days and four buses to get back to Maryland. And every time her eyes slipped shut, she dreamed of Jimmy and running, running so fast she fell, and then her legs would grow heavy and she couldn't move. Each step was as if chained to the ground. And then she would wake up. But at least then she had a goal, to get home, and she knew she could do it. Now, this morning, all certainty of anything was gone.

She just sat on the edge of her bed, as the first awareness of a barely audible siren floated to her ears. It was for her and she knew it. She breathed a sigh, pulling in the stale air from her bedroom. Escape seemed impossible. She knew it would be a local boy in the squad car. Probably Steve or Mort, both high school classmates wondering what on earth Simy had done now. When the Arrest-on-Sight warrant came in, they were both on the night shift. But it was like seeing a family name come across the ticker. They knew Simy all right, personally and well. They had both driven their cruiser past her house, not for an arrest, but for a glimpse that might lead to a conversation. Now they were screaming through the fog under orders to be alert for an armed and dangerous criminal.

When their car turned down Simy's street, she grabbed a ball cap off the sofa, and yanked the back door open, running for the back of her yard. She knew the fence from years of planting zinnias along the border. She knew it was chain link, with a steel pipe that framed the wire. Without stopping, she grabbed the pipe with both hands and vaulted over the fence. When the little neighborhood houses closed in around her, she felt protected from the view of policemen now entering her house. And she didn't have far to go.

Simy raced down the street, one block to the community pier where they had had July 4th picnics for years. There were no fences around the community right of way, maintained by volunteers with weekly lawn cutting, and she could see the lights come on in a couple houses. Her lungs were starting to strain, and her shins were aching. It had been a long time since she had run this hard, or this far. But she knew it was about over, and she could hear the bull horn, and then the sirens starting up again. The open area to the pier was only about 30 yards long, and when her feet hit the grass it was like a bedroom carpet, soft and welcoming.

When her feet first hit the dock, it felt good. She had made it. Maybe not the right course, but it was the only course. Her life had been difficult, and now it would be over. She hit the last plank with perfect timing and entered the water as if walking into a basement. Witnesses said she hardly made a splash, simply disappearing below the chop of the Chesapeake, and never coming up. She had hardly disturbed the morning.

Chapter Twenty-Six

I don't really know what to make of these events. I awoke later in the day in the hospital, with an IV in my arm, a bright sun casting venetian shadows across the bed, and Pete and Lil sitting in faded maroon chairs beside a blonde chest of drawers.

"Pete, what's happened? Lil, why are you here?" I asked.

"Well," Pete said, "we had to fish you out of the water so I figured we had better make sure you didn't hurt yourself in the hospital."

"How's the *Martha Claire*?" I asked. Years later Pete would say he knew at that instant I was a waterman.

"She's at the bottom of the Bay, in about six thousand pieces. Every time it storms, we'll be finding pieces of her at the Bayfront, probably for the next forty years," Pete said.

"Except for that Oldsmobile motor," Lil chimed in. "Oysters are laying eggs in that baby right now."

"I don't understand," I said. "What's going on?"

"First, the good news," Lil said. "Martha is on her way in. Should be here within the hour. Since it's clear you're not dying, I can call and tell her not to hurry."

"The bad news," Pete said, "Simy committed suicide this morning. Apparently she was on the boat with Jimmy, and somehow tied in with the Blenny Man, and when the cops came for her this morning, she ran down to the Pelican Bay community pier and jumped in."

"They're looking for her body now," Lil added. "And since the last time I saw her she was trying to rub the shine off your trousers, do

259

you have anything to add?"

"I have nothing to say," I said, thinking this is just too much to absorb. "What did she do in all this?" I was being a little disingenuous about this, especially since I did remember running from her house and calling the Sheriff. And I assumed she was involved with Jimmy's death, since he was wearing her shoes. But that's about all I knew.

"Nobody seems too sure of anything," Pete said. "Apparently, when Simy was running for the Bay, she dropped a piece of paper with Blenny's phone number. The cops called and apparently figured out he was on the water. And your boat was missing, so we put two and two together at the Bayfront, and launched the fleet. I must say we never figured to find Blenny and his boat on the deck of the *Martha Claire*."

"What was Blenny doing?" I asked. "I could feel his presence around me. Ever since I moved to Parkers. But I could never figure out what he was after."

"The resort," Pete said. "Apparently he was making land deals around the resort property. And by the way, that Sheriff arrived on the first plane this morning and stopped by to make sure you were alive. You were out of it. So he went over to the State's Attorney's Office to start putting a case together. All he said was, 'Tell Mr. Shannon that Chumbucket and the Blenny Man are talking like magpies.'"

* * * * *

Burl and Martha arrived later in the morning, happy to learn that I would be released in the afternoon. Burl was effusive about the events of the last 24 hours, and my role in them. He just rushed in the door and started talking. He was wearing his tweed jacket, with the pipe tobacco burns on the pockets, where he stuffed his pipe bowl as he went into buildings. Usually he emptied the pipe near the curb just outside his car, but invariably a spark or two of embers would survive all the way to his pocket and leave their telltale spot. In addition, Burl this morning was sporting a Scottish driving cap, brown tweed of course, but wrinkled to the point of demanding an explanation.

"Burl, where'd you get that hat?" I asked.

"Ned, I'm wearing this in your honor," Burl said. "I found it under some books in the attic, my volume on atom theory and some old books on auto mechanics."

"Were you going to Mars or the Good Times Auto Repair Service?" I asked. Burl looked a little sheepish and admitted he was really looking for his environmental law books, to bring to the hospital as a present. He hadn't used them in a long time, and felt he had memorized all the eco law he needed, so they might make a perfect gift for a lawyer about to lose his biggest client.

"Ned," Burl said, "I have some good and bad news, all in one fact."

"Don't tell me," I said, "you found a hundred dollar bill in the hat."

"No," he said, "but I've been getting calls about you all morning. And the best one came from the head of our Hijenks Committee. She says the Chesapeake Resorts International people have just locked their doors, circled the wagons, and apparently have something to do with the Blenny Man and your brother's death. You know I thought that all along. It's just like Watergate, we should have followed the money. That's what the Sheriff and the Maryland State's Attorney are huddled about right now. There's a rumor that even the Governor is involved, and you blew this case wide open. How about that?"

Martha had quietly entered the room with Burl, but moved behind

Burl to allow his excitement about CRI to flood the room. I noticed she didn't share his intensity. She looked at the floor, and glanced occasionally at Lil, who was on the far side of my bed, as if they shared a concern that was being ignored. My mind was flooded by Burl's new evidence, but even with all those questions, I was beginning to realize that Martha and Lil had another perspective that made me uncomfortable.

"I assume the bad news is that I no longer have a retainer from the greatest job-creating resort to ever hit the Chesapeake," I said.

"I'm afraid so," Burl said. "But those guys are crooks and you should be damn glad you're not involved with them. In fact, they may have been responsible for Jimmy's death, and maybe even your own threats. At least they had the kind of deep pockets that a blenny man can swim around in."

"I guess you're right Burl, but with my boat gone, my inheritance in question, and my biggest client in trouble, I'm having a little trouble enjoying the silver lining."

"And that may be the least of your trouble, my dear brother-in-law," Martha interrupted. The room went silent with her first words. The questions had to be spoken, and everyone in the room knew the moment had come. Certainly, no one left the room.

I noticed that Martha looked terrific. Her hair was completely gone, of course, and the sheik head scarf of the Moose dance was replaced by a baseball cap. Her jeans were snug and a light Irish sweater accentuated her figure. But her face was white, drawn and all the emotional facial lines were pointed down.

"Did you sleep with Simy Sims last night?" she asked. "The woman who killed my husband?"

Last night, I repeated in my mind. Was it only last night? Seems like a million years ago that I arrived at Simy's house. How could so much have happened?

There was no movement in my room. No one attempted to break the silence or change direction of the questions. I wasn't certain how to ever explain this, and especially not in this crowd.

"Martha," I said, "I am so sorry. I don't even know all the answers to these questions. Can't we talk about this later?"

"No," Martha said. "Now. Talk about it now. I want your friends to hear. And I want them to tell all our friends what you say."

"Well, I...."

Before I could say two words, Martha interrupted. "Wait. First, I want to say that I appreciate everything you have done for me and for Mindy. And I will see that the court approves your inheritance even without the *Martha Claire*. You deserve what Jimmy gave you. But our friendship may be over."

"Martha," I said, "I shouldn't have been with Simy, but I had no idea she was involved with Jimmy, certainly not that she may have killed him. It wasn't until I saw the matching sneakers at her house, the ones that matched the pair Jimmy was wearing, the ones that were on his body, that I knew she had some involvement. Please forgive me Martha."

"Forgive you? You've been sniffing around that woman for weeks. She killed my husband."

"Wait," I pleaded. "I didn't know that. I didn't know till I saw the shoes. Even then I couldn't believe it."

"Of course you didn't believe it!" Martha screamed. "You'd been banging her all night long."

"Wait!" I screamed, expecting a horde of nurses to run in at any minute. "She's the one who came on to me. She killed my brother, and she still came on to me. How outrageous is that? I wouldn't dream in a million years that she could do that."

263

Martha hesitated, trying to sort that out. Finally, she turned to pick up her jacket. "You men are so weak," she said. "Burl, take me home."

Martha turned and stomped out the door. Not until then did I notice that she wasn't using her walker. I was pleased by her continued physical improvement, but her abrupt and unyielding attitude about Simy was based on anger. Martha had a right to be angry. And so did I. At first, I thought maybe she wanted more explanation, or more pleading, or more tears of contrition. But I couldn't do it. I was having trouble putting it all together myself, especially Simy's role in all this. It would all just have to wait.

Burl waved his rumpled hat and followed Martha out the door. Lil walked around the bed and took my hand. "This will all work out," she said. "The authorities will sort it out. The explanations will come, and I know you'll be fine. Now Pete and I will go down to the cafeteria and get some coffee. You get your clothes together, and we'll take you home."

It took a couple hours to find the doctor, secure a release and leave the hospital. The doctor said I had received a concussion when Blenny's boat crashed into mine. He couldn't say how, of course, only that I had hit my head on something. But he thought I would be fine after a few days of rest. As the doctor left, calls were flooding into my room. I asked Pete to let Lil get the coffee, and empowered him to stay and answer my phone. I didn't want to take any calls. And if the police called, I wanted someone other than me to talk to them, or at least to find out what they wanted.

By the time I had dressed and prepared to leave, Pete had talked with the State's Attorney and the Sheriff. They had arrested Ray "The Blenny Man" Herbst on several charges including conspiracy to commit murder, racketeering, and several related charges. Jimmy had apparently been killed because he overheard, during a charter boat trip, that the Resorts group was paying off the Governor for his support. And supposedly my boat was sunk to get me to leave Parkers. Pete said he thought they would hold a press conference the next day to discuss the case.

I just wanted to sleep, and urged Pete and Lil to put me in the backseat where I could stretch out. This was my second hospital departure in the last several weeks and the experience was becoming less and less pleasant. This time I was in the traditional wheelchair out the door, riding, not pushing Martha. But in both cases there was a sense of extreme anxiety about leaving, about exiting the protective arms of nurses and doctors and finding myself totally responsible for my fate. Fortunately, the sun was warm against my face as Pete helped me into the backseat, and I felt better.

We drove back to Parkers trying to consider the many legal questions about to enter our lives. But it wasn't necessary, of course, to answer them. The central point, and new revelation that kept circulating in my mind, was that so many people in this little town of Parkers actually cared about me. Martha's anger about my night with Simy was a vivid memory. She expected more from me because she cared. Friendship implied a standard of behavior, a loyalty to certain standards. And I deeply regretted letting her down.

"Lil?" I asked. "Will Martha be all right?"

Lil knew exactly what I was asking. "Don't worry Ned, she'll get over it. Your friends understand. It's just that Martha cares a little more deeply for you than you may realize."

I decided to leave the conversation there, for another day, as my dad used to say.

"Pete," I asked, "how about driving over to Osprey Cove before we go home. I want to show you my property. Have I ever told you about my dream of a French chateau on pilings, with ten foot doors that open onto a deck overlooking the Bay?"

Lil's body went on full alert. She turned around in the front seat, with eyes as big as hubcaps, and asked, "What are you up to? Are you going to build a house?" Lil knew this would be a huge step, a commitment far greater than just running a crab boat or a law practice.

"Lil," I said carefully, "I have heard the oyster music."

"Hallelujah!" Lillian screamed. "Welcome to Parkers."

"Listen Ned," Pete said, "I want to talk to you about a new boat, a charter fishing boat. You could take the insurance money from the *Martha Claire*, make a down payment on a brand new fiberglass charter boat. It might cost two or three hundred thousand dollars, but you can handle it. What do you think?"

"Let's not go too fast, Pete," I said.

Pete slowed the car to make a final turn off Solomons Island Road and head for Osprey Cove. As we maneuvered around the corner, Lil pressed her face against the window and stared in silence. Walking along the road were the familiar figures of the Pipe Lady, the Lab and the Mutt. She was puffing confidently on her pipe, and small clouds of smoke rolled gently over the rim. Occasionally, she pulled the bowl from her mouth, and uttered several rambling phrases. The Lab never raised his head.

THE END

About the Author

Marlin Fitzwater is the author of several books including a memoir, a novel, and short stories. He received America's second highest civilian achievement award, the Presidential Citizens Medal, from President George H. W. Bush in 1992. He was Presidential Press Secretary to both Bush and President Ronald Reagan. He is from Abilene, Kansas and is actively involved with the Marlin Fitzwater Center for Communication at Franklin Pierce University. He is married and has two children.

CPSIA information can be obtained at www.ICGtesting.com
Printed in the USA
LVOW041615190712

290767LV00008B/51/P